PLAYING WITH FIRE

A SURPRISE BABY ROMANCE

PLAYING
BOOK 3

LAINEY DAVIS

CONTENT NOTE

This book includes an unplanned pregnancy. I wrote this story in a post-Roe America, where reproductive freedom has been stripped from millions. Tucker and Sloane have choices that many Americans no longer have access to—the ability to decide whether and how to continue a pregnancy, access to comprehensive prenatal care, and economic resources to support their decisions.

If I were writing this same scenario for characters without these privileges, this would be a fundamentally different story. The stakes, emotions, and journey would be drastically altered by the reality of restricted reproductive healthcare, abortion bans, and systemic barriers to care.

This book also includes:

- High-risk pregnancy complications, including preeclampsia and bed rest
- Medical emergency and hospitalization
- Discussions of systemic racism in prenatal healthcare
- Estrangement from family / absent parents

I recognize that reading an unplanned pregnancy romance in our current political climate may be difficult, painful, or even triggering. Please know that I am committed to fighting for reproductive justice for all people.

With solidarity, Lainey

ABOUT THE BOOK

One night. Two lines. Three lives changed forever.

I swore off hockey players after my ex-husband's betrayal. So, when I hooked up with a cocky stranger at a party, I had a few expectations: No strings. No repeats.

Because the guy I chose was Tucker Stag—Pittsburgh Fury enforcer and my ex's teammate.

Oh, and those condoms he endorses? They don't work.

Now I'm facing co-parenting with a man whose entire family smothers us, and I feel my hard-won independence slipping further away with every casserole and helpful suggestion.

Tucker fights hard on the ice and plays harder off it. He says he'll change and be a real father. He says he's nothing like my ex. He says a lot of things when his hands are on my body and his mouth is making promises against my skin.

But when my past collides with our present and threatens everything we're building, I have to decide: Can I trust the bad boy who's trying to be good? Or will I lose myself to another hockey player who puts the game above all else?

Playing with Fire is a hockey romance with a forbidden relationship, a surprise pregnancy, and a love story that will leave you breathless.

CHAPTER 1
SLOANE

I came to this pool party ready to start a new chapter. Or, as I just told my roommate, to cleanse my chakras.

"Test drive a new joystick. Snake my pipes?"

My roommate, Mel Ortega, sends me a sly grin. "Grease the wheels?" She adjusts her ponytail as she maneuvers her wheelchair away from the window of our shared first-floor guest room. "Find a locksmith who makes house calls?"

We've been roommates for three months—ever since I left my ex-husband. I've been hibernating that whole time, so today she forced me to drive her to a law school graduation party in some posh vacation house owned by one of her classmates.

We decided it's time for me to get back on the proverbial horse and then get right back off so I can focus on school again.

"So, which of these guys do you recommend?" I adjust my bikini top and peek out the window at the party outside. "Nobody whose firm might have represented Josh." I try to keep the bitterness from my voice. I never did get used to life in the spotlight as a hockey wife, and since I chose to be classy and keep our issues private, the press has decided I am a frigid witch.

Mel wheels over beside the bed where I'm sitting. She and I met during undergrad at Michigan in a program for students of color. We lost touch when I moved to Pittsburgh, but I'm so grateful she looked me up when she moved to the city for law school.

"Nobody here knows about that stuff," she says, squeezing my shoulder. "They're all too wrapped up in their own post-graduation anxiety."

"At least they have something to be anxious about," I reply. "They have plans, careers, futures. Meanwhile, I'm twenty-five with an unfinished degree, a divorce settlement I never wanted, and a dried-up vagina."

"And a killer booty," Mel adds, trying to lighten the mood. "Don't forget your curves, chica."

I roll my eyes but smile. My body is the one thing I've maintained control over during this whole mess. In the months since I split from my marriage, I thickened up a bit, and it's good to hear Mel's reminder that my butt is banging.

I try not to focus on the idea that the real way I'd love to gain weight—a pregnancy—is never going to happen for me.

"Come on," Mel says, spinning her chair toward the door. "There's a gorgeous infinity pool with a lift and enough expensive alcohol to lube our spokes."

"Do spokes get lubed?" I frown at her wheelchair, suddenly very curious about her maintenance needs. Mel laughs and rolls down the hall without responding.

———

Two hours later, I'm floating in the pool, the water cool against my sun-warmed skin. Mel abandoned me to talk to some federal prosecutor, and I'm perfectly content to be alone with my thoughts and the spectacular mountain view. She gave me strict instructions to get my oil changed, but so far, I haven't found the right mechanic. My third glass of rosé sits on the pool deck within arm's reach.

The buzz of conversation washes over me, all these brilliant legal minds discussing the upcoming bar exam, firms, and cases. I close my eyes against the setting sun, wondering where exactly my life took its detour. Was it when I met Josh? When I dropped out of Michigan to follow his hockey career? Or was it earlier, when my grandmother died my freshman year, leaving me unmoored from the only real family I'd known?

The low rumble of a luxury engine catches my attention as someone arrives up the long drive adjacent to the pool and patio. I hear our host's exasperated voice greeting the newcomer, but I don't bother opening my eyes.

"Tucker, I begged you not to make a scene." Our host—his name is Stellan Stag, a guy from Mel's class—is clearly not happy with the newcomer.

I crack open one eye to see a blond himbo drape an arm around the stern, newly minted attorney. "Chill, cuz," he drawls. Mirrored aviator sunglasses flash above a blinding white grin. "I will save all these hot men for you and only schmooze with your lady guests. Deal?"

Stellan shoves the muscled arm from around his shoulders. "I hope everyone here sues you," he mutters, stalking away as Mr. Good Times approaches the pool fence. I am fully alert now, keyed into the one person here who seems ready for a no-strings cardio workout.

Tucker. Something about him is familiar, but I can't place it. When he disappears inside, I find myself watching the door for his return.

"That guy's a hothead," says a voice beside me. I turn to find Druj, one of Mel's classmates, sitting at the edge of the pool with his feet in the water. "According to Stellan, he's trouble."

"Trouble how?" I ask, my interest piqued. I wait for Druj to tell me about all the ladies this guy has deflowered.

"Drives too fast, parties too hard, that whole rich playboy thing." Druj adjusts his glasses. I laugh at Druj's assessment. And then it hits me. Tucker isn't just some random rich boy. He plays hockey with my ex.

My insides swirl. I came here for just one thing, but casual sex with Tucker could bring me a very satisfying spite-gasm.

When Druj wanders off to refill his drink, I find myself watching for my mark. Sure enough, he emerges a few minutes later in board shorts and a fitted black T-shirt that clings to his muscled chest. He removes the cotton garment like he's on stage in a club, and I drink my fill of the show. He slides into the pool some distance away, but I feel his presence like a current in the water.

In my previous life—my married life—I would have avoided him completely. I lived with a deeply disciplined man who believed perseverance and routine would deliver all we need in this world. And look where that got me. Something shifts inside me as I watch this beautiful stranger sip his beer and casually survey the party. Before I can talk myself out of it, I push off from the wall and glide through the water toward him.

"You're not a lawyer," I say, surprising myself with my directness. I can totally play this part.

His easy smile reveals charmingly misaligned teeth. "That obvious?"

"I'm Tucker," he says, eventually.

"Sloane," I reply, offering nothing more. The anonymity is freeing—he doesn't know who I am, about the divorce, about my messy, unfinished life.

I notice his eyes drop to the water lapping at my collarbone, then quickly return to my face. The appreciation in his gaze ignites something low in my belly. When was the last time I felt desired? When was the last time I allowed myself to want?

"And what do you do, Tucker-with-the-aviators, when you're not crashing law school parties?"

He grins and lifts his sunglasses, revealing startlingly blue eyes. "I sell socks and condoms," he deadpans.

The unexpected answer makes me laugh, a genuine burst of amusement I haven't felt in too long. "All right then."

My eyes drift to his chest, where black ink peeks above the water line. A tattoo of a leaping stag, the lines clean and bold against his tanned skin. It's hot. He's hot. And he plays hockey with my ex.

Stuck in a mire of emotions, I reach out and trace the outline of his ink with my finger. His skin is warm despite the cool water, and his firm muscles tense beneath my touch.

I want him.

I want filthy, unhinged sex with this man specifically, because he seems like a good time, and because I spent too long being cautious. If I bump uglies with this beautiful white guy, it could be the ultimate fuck-you to my ex, and I'm in the mood for some mischief.

I let my finger continue its path along his collarbone, enjoying the subtle shift in his breathing. Our eyes lock, and I see the surprise in his. He's used to being the pursuer, not the pursued, I think. Good. I need this—the power, the control, the simple pleasure of wanting and taking.

I spent five years making choices to support a man who deceived me and robbed me of the future I imagined. Surely that earns me an afternoon of debauchery? Of the pleasure I know Tucker Stag can dish out?

He doesn't know who I am, or else he's more aloof than he seems. The hunger in his gaze gives me the final push I need. I back up to the wall and lift myself out of the pool, deliberately taking my time, feeling his eyes on me as water sluices off my body. I grab a towel, dab myself casually, and throw a glance over my shoulder before walking into the house.

My heart pounds as I make my way to the kitchen. Have I lost my mind? Am I really going to hook up with this stranger? Am I so petty that I'd fuck my ex's colleague?

Yes. Yes, I am.

———

The kitchen is mercifully empty. Stellan hasn't set out any snacks, so I open the refrigerator, suddenly aware I haven't eaten since lunch. Bending to examine the contents, I hear the sliding door open and close, followed by footsteps approaching the kitchen.

"Looking for something specific?" Tucker's voice is closer than I expected.

I straighten and turn, finding him leaning against the doorframe, a study in casual confidence. "I realized I'm starving."

"Liquid diet not cutting it?" He pushes off the frame and moves closer, opening a cabinet above my head. The proximity brings the clean scent of chlorine and something distinctly male. "Stellan's mom is a chef. She'd be horrified that he's not feeding us."

Tucker reaches past me, his arm brushing mine, and pulls down a tin of expensive crackers and a jar of something that looks homemade.

"Fig spread," he explains, setting the snacks on the counter. He clearly spends time here, or else he just has good luck sniffing out food. "But watch out for the seeds. They'll get stuck in your teeth and you'll need help to fish them out."

"I take it you don't volunteer?" I ask as he locates a bowl and a knife.

"I could be convinced." He winks, dumps some of the crackers into the bowl, and twists open the jar of jam.

"Hm, I'll have to see what persuades you." I hop onto the counter, letting my legs dangle.

He spreads jam and some cheese onto a cracker, and I watch his hands move, admiring the tendons in his forearms and the veins on the backs of his hands. He glances up at me and offers a jam-covered cracker, one brow arched. "Try this."

I take a bite, the sweetness of the fig pairs perfectly with the tang of the goat cheese he's pulled from the fridge. "That's amazing," I say after swallowing. "And my teeth are just fine."

"Told you." He finishes preparing the morsel and pops it into his mouth. "So, what about you? What legal dynasty do you hail from?"

I laugh, the sound hollow even to my own ears. "No dynasty. Just me."

"Your parents don't own a firm?"

"Mom's not in the picture. Took off in a grief spiral after my dad died in a car crash," I have no idea why I'm sharing this with him. The whole goal here was anonymous seduction. I grab another cracker to give my hands something to do. "My grandmother raised me, but she passed away a few years ago, too."

Tucker's expression softens, and I brace for the pity I've come to expect. Instead, he says, "Then we should make a toast to her," and pulls a fancy bourbon from a collection of bottles on the counter. He pours two fingers into tumblers and hands one to me.

"To your grandmother," he says, clinking his glass to mine.

"To Grandma Essie," I echo, taking a sip. The liquor burns pleasantly down my throat.

Tucker leans against the counter across from me, close enough that my knees nearly brush his hips. "What was she like?"

"Tough. Kind. Worked two jobs most of her life to raise me." I smile at the memory. This connection is unexpected. He's flirting, sure, but he's attentive. And I just keep sharing truths like he's my therapist or something. "She loved the Tigers—baseball was her thing. Took me to games whenever she could afford it."

"Tigers fan, huh? Dangerous revelation with a Pittsburgh guy."

"I think I like danger," I reply, meeting his gaze directly.

His eyes darken, and he puts his glass down. "Is that why you led me in here? Looking for danger?"

I take another sip of bourbon, letting the warmth spread through me. "Maybe I'm just tired of playing it safe."

Tucker moves closer, positioning himself between my knees, his hands resting lightly on the counter on either side of me. Not touching, but surrounding. "What's the safest thing you've ever done, Sloane?"

The question catches me off guard. "Stayed in a relationship that wasn't working," I answer honestly. "Because it was easier than starting over."

Something flickers in his eyes—recognition, maybe. Understanding. "And the most dangerous?"

I set my glass aside and place my hands on his chest, feeling his heart hammer beneath my palms. "Probably this."

His gaze drops to my lips. "Eating crackers? This isn't dangerous." He lifts a hand to tuck a stray curl behind my ear. "But it could be."

"Show me," I whisper.

Tucker's smile is slow and promising. He takes my hand and tugs me gently off the counter. "Remember those socks and condoms I mentioned? Want to see a prototype?"

I laugh, the sound bright and unfamiliar. "Is that what the kids are calling it these days?"

"I've been told my marketing needs work." He twines his fingers with mine, pale pink among tawny digits. "They're in my bag."

I should hesitate. I should consider the consequences. I should remember every lesson I learned from my failed marriage.

Instead, I squeeze his hand and say, "Lead the way."

CHAPTER 2
TUCKER

THIS PARTY IS SO MUCH BETTER THAN I HOPED. WHEN I CRASHED MY cousin's shindig, I was just trying to take my mind off being stuck in Pittsburgh for the entire off-season. My teammates are all on yachts in Monaco fucking scantily clad European women.

I've been on my couch with an ice pack on my mangled mouth, alternating terrifying sessions with the team dentist and boring preparations for my brother's upcoming wedding. An unfortunate side effect of the best job on earth.

But I've got my temporary crown and nobody's getting hitched this week, so I thought I'd come out to the family ski house, rag on Stellan and his nerd friends, play video games, and pass out.

Instead, I'm leading a gorgeous woman by the hand, her golden-brown fingers interlaced with mine, her bare feet padding silently behind me.

When I tug her along, a conspiratorial smile plays at the corners of her mouth. That smile has been driving me crazy since I first spotted her in the pool—natural, uninhibited, entirely unlike the calculated expressions I've grown accustomed to from women who recognize me.

The puck bunnies want me for my fame, so they can say they bagged a hockey player. Sloane seems like she just wants to do something wild.

Stellan stuck me in the basement bunk room–a barracks-style

space with four twin double-deckers. It'll do just fine for what I have in mind. I push open the door and flick on the lamp, bathing the room in a warm glow. It's rustic but comfortable, with exposed beams and knotty pine walls.

"So, this is where you're planning to seduce me?" Sloane asks, eyebrows raised as she takes in the bunk beds. "Bold choice."

"Just living out a summer camp fantasy," I say with a grin. "Though I promise I've graduated from the awkward teenage fumbling."

She laughs, the sound sending a pleasant warmth through my chest. "Good to know."

I walk to my duffel bag, unzipping the side pocket. "Anyway, I wasn't kidding about the condoms." I pull out a small box with 'THIN ICE PROTOTYPE - NOT FOR RETAIL' stamped across it. "They sent me samples to 'test' and give feedback. These are the new ultra-thin ones."

Sloane steps closer, taking the box from my hands. "So, you really do sell condoms."

"And socks. Though I don't have those with me." I watch her examine the box, struck by how utterly normal this interaction feels. She's not swooning over my stats or asking how much I'm being paid. She's just... interested. In me.

"Do you always carry prototype condoms with you?" she asks, setting the box on the nearest nightstand. Her hair is a mass of big, bouncy blonde curls—a soft, voluminous mass of natural springs. She is stunningly gorgeous.

"Professional responsibility," I say with mock seriousness. "I take my market research very seriously."

"I'm sure you do." She steps closer, until we're nearly touching. Barefoot, the top of her head barely reaches my chin, and I have to resist the urge to lift her to my level.

Instead, I reach out, running a finger over her collarbone like she did to me earlier. "You're gorgeous," I tell her, the words coming out more reverent than I intended. "And not at all what I expected to find at my cousin's stuffy law party."

"What did you expect?"

"Not you," I say simply.

Her eyes darken, and she places her hands on my chest.

She sighs. "I … know who you are."

Damn. Not so anonymous after all. Oh well. I shrug. "That happens a lot."

She shakes her head. "No. I … my last name is Grentley."

"Grentley?" I clench my stomach, like I'm waiting for our surly goalie to punch me or something. I take a step back and really look at Sloane. "You're Grentley's wife?"

She shakes her head, curls bouncing. "Ex-wife. We are divorced. Everything's final. My name change is just taking a minute, that's all."

I am in the basement with the ex of a guy who hates my guts.

Josh Grentley, who was a dick to my brother Gunnar and has all sorts of things to say about how I spend my time off the ice. Holier-than-a-priest Grentley, whose wife never came to games. Grentley, whom I'm supposed to protect, even though he acts like I'm beneath him.

Sloane takes a step toward me, closing the space I made, nudging my duffel bag with her polished toe. "I'm not trying to start anything lasting. The exact opposite, actually."

My mouth drops open of its own accord as I search for something to say. I'm not used to being the one requiring encouragement to be bad. Sloane puts a warm hand back on my shoulder, the heat of her skin soaking through the damp T-shirt that's annoyingly in between our bodies. "Do you want to be irresponsible with me, Tucker?" Her lips curl into that smile again as she slides her hands up to loop around my neck.

And that's just it. I do. I want to do everything with her. From the moment I saw her, sunlight gleaming off bronze skin, her bold approach in the water … I feel drawn to her. The sunburst pendant around her neck pulls me like a tow line.

Grentley has never done me any favors or been nice to anyone in my family. He's a jerk, and he doesn't like me anyway.

Fuck it.

I lean down, capturing her mouth with mine. The first touch of her lips is electric, soft, warm, and faintly tasting of bourbon and fig. I meant to start slow, to savor this, but the moment she responds—pressing herself against me, opening to me—all restraint evaporates. This is worth whatever Grentley comes up with for payback.

My hands find her waist, then slide lower to cup her ass, lifting her against me. She makes a small sound of surprise when she feels my hard-on, then wraps her legs around my hips, deepening the kiss. The weight of her in my arms, the press of her core against my thickening cock—it's intoxicating.

I walk us to the nearest bed, lowering her onto it without breaking the kiss. Her hands are everywhere—tugging at my shirt, tracing the muscles of my back, threading through my hair. When we finally part for air, her chest is heaving, her lips swollen.

"Too fast?" I ask, bracing myself above her.

She answers by pulling my shirt over my head and tossing it aside. Her eyes roam over my chest, lingering on the tattoo again before she traces it with her fingertips. "Not fast enough," she says.

I catch her wrist, bringing her hand to my lips. "How do you want this to go, Sloane?" My voice drops lower. "Dirty? Gentle? A little rough?"

Her eyes darken with interest. "How rough?"

Oh shit. "I can talk dirty to you, baby. Pull your hair." I maintain eye contact, watching for any hesitation. "But with your hair, I want to ask first. I know curls are a little different."

A small smile plays at her lips. "You definitely cannot pull it," she says.

The permission sends heat straight to my groin. "And the rest?"

"I'd like that," she says, her voice steady despite the flush spreading across her chest.

I nip at her neck. "If I do something you don't like, say so and everything stops, no questions asked." I lower my mouth back to her neck, no longer holding back as I suck hard enough to leave a mark. "Now turn over for me."

Her eyes widen slightly, but she complies, rolling onto her stomach. I help position her on her hands and knees, running my palms down her back to her perfect ass.

"God, you're beautiful," I say, giving her backside a squeeze, my fingers lingering between her cheeks. The small gasp she releases tells me I've done good. "Such a dirty girl, hooking up with a stranger at a party."

I trail biting kisses down her spine as I remove her bikini while my free hand comes down in a light smack against her ass cheek. She jumps slightly, then pushes back against me.

"You like that?" I ask, my voice rough with need.

"Yes," she breathes, the word barely audible.

I deliver another light smack to her other cheek, reveling in her moans and the way all that golden skin jiggles at my touch. "Good girl. Now spread your legs wider for me."

She complies immediately, and I reward her with a gentle stroke between her thighs, finding her already wet and ready. "Look how wet you are," I growl, circling her entrance with my fingers. "All this for me?"

"Yes," she moans, dropping to her elbows, changing the angle of her hips.

Her skin is still warm from the sun, smelling of chlorine and that sunscreen. But she also smells like she wants me. Bad.

She's totally bare, and I stare at that beautiful mound, exploring her body with my hand, learning what makes her gasp and what makes her moan. With each response, I feel a growing need to please her, to make this more than just another hookup. This woman mesmerizes me. I want Sloane to remember this, and that realization doesn't scare me.

She looks at me over one shoulder. Her eyes are heavy-lidded, her curls a wild halo around her face. "You're staring," she says, a hint of vulnerability in her voice.

"Can't help it." I run my hands up her thighs, spreading them gently. "I've got this beautiful body aimed right at my face."

Her laugh turns into a gasp as I lower my head between her legs, trailing kisses up her inner thigh. All thoughts of anyone else in our lives vanish. There is just us and crackling desire. At the first touch of my tongue against her center, she bucks against me, a surprised moan escaping her lips.

"Oh god," she breathes, her fingers kneading the sheets. "It's been—fuck—years since anyone did that."

I lift my head, genuinely surprised. "Years? That's criminal neglect."

She laughs breathlessly. "I don't want to talk about it. I just want more."

I'm more than happy to oblige, kneeling between her thighs on the cramped bed, ignoring my discomfort and dedicating myself to her pleasure.

I flip her onto her back so I can do this more comfortably, lapping at her while she drops her hands into my hair. Her responses guide me—the tightening of her fingers in my hair, the way her breathing changes, the small sounds she tries to muffle. When I add my fingers to the mix, curling them inside her, her back arches off the bed.

"Tucker," she gasps, the sound of my name on her lips sending a jolt straight to my cock. "Please, I need—"

I know what she needs. I intensify my efforts, focusing on the spot that makes her thighs tremble. Within moments, she's coming apart, her body tensing and releasing as she bites her lip to stay quiet.

I kiss my way back up her body, enjoying the aftershocks that ripple through her at each touch. When I reach her mouth, she kisses me hungrily, tasting herself on my tongue, her hands fumbling with the waistband of my board shorts.

My cock springs free, and she sucks in a breath. I palm my length and grin at her. "You hungry for this, Sloane?" She lets out a whimper, and I shuck my shorts the rest of the way, grabbing the condoms and rolling one on.

Positioning myself between her legs again, I tease her entrance with the tip of my cock. "Tell me what you want, Sloane. I want to hear you say it."

She stares at me, eyes heavy with desire. "I want you to fuck me, Tucker. Hard."

The crude language on her lips sends a jolt through me. I enter her with one powerful thrust, earning a cry that she muffles with her fist. I palm her tits with one hand, tweaking her brown nipples as I set a punishing rhythm.

"Such a perfect dirty girl," I praise, watching where our

bodies join. "Taking my cock so well. You like it rough, don't you?"

"God, yes," she gasps, meeting each thrust.

I reach between us to find her clit, circling it with my fingers. "Touch your tits," I command. "Show me how you like it."

She does, one hand moving to cup her breast, pinching her nipple. The sight nearly undoes me.

"That's it," I encourage, my voice strained. " fucking sexy."

I can feel her body beginning to tighten around me, her movements becoming more erratic. I increase the pressure of my fingers, matching the rhythm of my thrusts.

"You going to come for me?" I demand, feeling my own release building. "Come all over my cock like the dirty girl you are?"

"Yes," she cries, her body tensing. "Tucker, I'm—"

"Do it." I tighten my grip on her hip. "Come for me now, greedy girl."

She breaks with a cry that she barely muffles against the pillow, her inner muscles clenching around me in waves. The sensation pushes me over the edge, and I follow her into release, burying myself deep inside her as pleasure crashes through me.

My body tingles, nerve endings on fire as my blood thrums through my veins.

I carefully withdraw, yanking off the condom before pulling her against my chest. We're both breathing hard, skin slick with sweat.

"You okay?" I ask, suddenly conscious of how aggressive I'd been.

She nods against my chest. "More than okay."

"Your hair alright? I didn't pull too hard?"

Her laugh is soft and satisfied. "You handled it perfectly."

I brush my lips against her forehead, surprised by the tenderness I feel. "Good. I like knowing what you like."

She melts into me, her curls tickling my chin, her hand resting over my heart. The silence between us is comfortable, not awkward.

"Well," she says finally, a smile in her voice. "I can see why they hired you to endorse those."

I laugh, the tension in my chest dissolving. "Wait till you try the socks."

She props herself up on one elbow, looking down at me with those incredible green eyes. Something about her gaze makes me feel exposed in a way that has nothing to do with our nakedness.

"What are you thinking?" I ask, tugging on a curl and watching it spring back into shape.

"That I wasn't expecting this," she admits.

"The mind-blowing sex, or the Thin Ice condoms?"

She swats my chest lightly. "Both, I guess. But mostly... you."

I understand exactly what she means. In my world, people see what they expect to see—the hockey player, the enforcer, the Stag family troublemaker. But Sloane's looking at me like she sees something else entirely.

"I know what you mean," I tell her, tracing patterns on her bare shoulder. "This feels... different."

She doesn't ask how or why, just nods like she understands. Then she stretches, her body moving sinuously against mine, reigniting the hunger I thought was temporarily sated.

"So," she says, trailing her fingers down my chest. "Those prototypes. How many do you have to test?"

I grin, rolling her beneath me again.

CHAPTER 3
SLOANE

Tucker's mouth is everywhere at once, it seems. His lips trail fire across my collarbone, down my sternum, between my breasts. I arch into his touch, my body responding with an eagerness that surprises me. We've been at this for hours, yet I want more. Need more.

"On your knees," he commands against my ear, his voice a deep growl that sends shivers down my spine.

I immediately comply, rolling onto my stomach and pushing up onto all fours. His hands slide up my sides, then back down to my hips, gripping me hard enough that I know I'll have fingerprint bruises tomorrow. The thought thrills me rather than worries me. The position is vulnerable, exposed, and utterly intoxicating. Josh never wanted me like this—always missionary, always predictable, always...safe.

Tucker is anything but safe.

He presses more bites into my skin, each one leaving a sting that fades into pleasure. The first nip of his teeth makes me gasp, but I push back against him, silently begging for more.

It should be ridiculous, this giant man fucking me in a bunk bed, but the confined space seems to urge him on as he hunches over me and uses his hands to flick and pinch and stroke.

"You like that?" he asks, his voice rough with desire.

"Yes," I breathe, my face heating at the admission.

He rewards me with a harder bite, sucking the sensitive skin between his teeth, marking me. The pain-pleasure has me moaning into the pillow, my body trembling.

"God, I love how responsive you are," he groans, soothing the bite with his tongue before moving behind me to my leg and repeating the process. "Going to have my teeth marks all over these gorgeous thighs."

I glance over my shoulder to find him reaching for another condom from the Thin Ice box. The sight of his muscular body, glistening with sweat in the dim light of the bunk room, sends another wave of desire through me. He catches me looking, and his expression turns predatory, with that cocky smile that somehow manages to be both dominating and devastatingly sexy.

"Can't get enough, can you?" he asks, tearing open the wrapper.

"No," I admit, the word slipping out without hesitation.

His expression darkens with lust. He rolls on the condom and positions himself behind me, one hand fisted in my hair again, the other digging into my hip. He somehow manages to be incredibly considerate and dirty as hell. His first thrust makes us both gasp.

"Fuck, Sloane," he breathes, his grip tightening. "So tight, so perfect for me."

From this angle, he feels impossibly deep, hitting places inside me that I didn't know could feel this good. I drop to my elbows, changing the angle further, and he rewards me with a growl of appreciation.

"That's it," he encourages, setting a hard pace that has me clutching the sheets. "Take what I give you. Take what you need."

I do, pushing back against him, chasing the building pleasure. The bunk bed knocks against the wall, and Tucker reaches out to brace against it, steadying us both without breaking his rhythm.

"Get up," I pant, suddenly wanting more. "I want to feel all of you."

He withdraws, hauling me to my feet at the edge of the lower bunk with surprising strength. I bend over the bed, my hands on the mattress and my ass in the air, and look back at him expectantly. His eyes devour me as he takes in the view, one hand running down my spine, the other still gripping my hip hard enough to leave marks.

"Like this?" he asks, voice strained as he positions himself behind me again.

"Yes," I hiss as he enters me with one powerful slide.

The new position has him even deeper, and I bite into the sheet to stifle the sounds threatening to escape. His thrusts become more forceful, more demanding, and he leans over me to sink his teeth into the junction where my neck meets my shoulder. The sharp sting, combined with the fullness inside me, has me seeing stars.

"You're mine tonight," he growls against my ear, the possessive words sending an unexpected thrill through me. "Fucking mine."

Behind me, I hear a dull thud followed by a muttered curse.

Tucker laughs darkly, ducking his head. "Hit the upper bunk," he explains, barely slowing his pace. "These beds weren't made for this kind of fucking."

I can't help but giggle, glancing back at him. "Maybe we should lie on the floor."

"Next time," he promises, punctuating the words with a particularly deep thrust that makes me gasp. His fingers find my clit, circling with just the right pressure.

The dual sensation has me spiraling toward release again. Tucker's breathing becomes more ragged, his rhythm faltering as he nears his own climax. Suddenly, I'm overwhelmed by a completely irrational desire.

"Pull out," I gasp. "I want to feel you finish... on me."

He stills for a fraction of a second, then groans. "Fuck, Sloane. You want me to mark you? Want me to come all over this perfect ass?"

"Yes," I plead, not entirely understanding my own request but desperate for it, nonetheless. "Please. I want to feel it."

He withdraws quickly, and I watch over my shoulder as he removes the condom with one hand while the other keeps working between my legs. I come again with a muffled cry against the pillow, my body shuddering with release. Moments later, I feel the hot splash of his orgasm across my lower back, his hand still gripping my hip with that deep intensity.

I come again to the idea of it, the white, sticky, potent mess of it, so obscene, so perfect, exactly what I asked for. I'm whimpering into the mattress as Tucker repeats my name on ragged exhalations.

For several heartbeats, we stay frozen in that position, both catching our breath. Then he leans down, pressing a kiss between my shoulder blades, just above where his jizz cools on my skin.

"God, you're incredible," he murmurs, his voice rough.

He steps away briefly, returning with what feels like a T-shirt to gently clean my back. The tender gesture makes my throat tighten unexpectedly. When he's done, his fingers drift to my inner thigh, carefully tracing the edge of what must already be a darkening bruise from his teeth.

"Too much?" he asks, his voice soft as he gently massages the marked skin.

I shake my head, surprised by how much I like the idea of carrying this evidence of him on my body tomorrow. "No. I like it."

His eyes meet mine, understanding passing between us before he guides me back onto the bed, pulling me against his chest as we lay on our sides.

His fingers trace lazy patterns on my hip as our breathing slows. The silence is comfortable, intimate in a way that transcends the physical connection we just shared.

"That was..." I trail off, unsure how to articulate what just happened.

"Yeah," he agrees, seeming to understand.

I feel a strange melancholy settling over me as my mind drifts to my request. Why had I been so fixated on feeling his semen on my skin? The thought makes my cheeks burn with embarrassment and something more profound, more painful.

Tucker seems to sense my mood shift. "What's going on in that head of yours?" he asks, his breath warm against my ear.

I consider deflecting, offering something light and meaningless. But in the darkness, with this man I'll never see again, honesty feels safer.

"My marriage," I say quietly. "It ended badly."

His hand stills on my hip, then resumes its gentle movement. "I'm sorry."

"Don't be. It needed to end." I turn in his arms to face him, searching his expression in the dim light. His eyes are serious, all traces of the playboy momentarily gone.

"This is just a one-night thing," I reiterate, needing to establish boundaries before I lose myself entirely in whatever this is.

His thumb brushes my cheekbone. "Doesn't have to be just one night. We're both in Pittsburgh, right?"

The thought is tempting—continuing this, having more nights like this. But reality intrudes. I'm putting my life back together, still figuring out who I am without Josh. And Tucker... Tucker is exactly the kind of man I should be avoiding.

"Let's not complicate it," I say, offering a smile to soften the rejection. "Tonight was perfect."

Something flickers in his eyes—disappointment, maybe—before he nods. "Whatever you want, Sloane."

The conversation drifts to lighter topics. He tells me about growing up in a house full of brothers, about summers spent learning to kayak, about his love of fast cars. I share stories about my grandmother, about college classes I enjoyed before dropping out. I don't tell him I've always dreamed of my own house full of kids.

Growing up as an only child of an only child, I didn't have cousins. I never had what Tucker describes, but I've always wanted it more than anything. A huge family to yell, tease, and celebrate. A baby on my hip, slung on my back, asleep at my breast.

At some point, I drift off in his arms, more comfortable than I should be after fucking my ex-husband's co-worker.

I wake to the sound of his even breathing, the room now completely dark except for the faint moonlight filtering through a small window. The clock on the nightstand reads 3:17 AM. Carefully, I extricate myself from his embrace, gathering my discarded bikini pieces.

He stirs slightly, mumbling something in his sleep before settling again. I watch him for a moment, memorizing the lines of his face, the curve of his lips, the tousled blond hair. This beautiful stranger, who, for a few hours, made me forget everything else. I probably shouldn't have sought this out with this specific man, who knows my ex. But boy, did Tucker Stag deliver what I was looking for.

I dress silently, resisting the urge to leave a note or wake him for a proper goodbye. Better this way—clean, simple. A perfect memory unmarred by reality.

At the door, I pause for one last look. "Thank you," I whisper, though I know he can't hear me.

Then I slip out into the hallway, closing the door quietly behind me.

As I tiptoe up the stairs, I can't help comparing tonight to what sex had been like with Josh. My ex-husband approached sex like everything else in his life—with discipline and restraint. It was satisfying in a basic way, but never passionate, never spontaneous.

Never like tonight.

Tucker had been attentive, playful, intensely focused on my pleasure. He'd asked what I wanted and then delivered with enthusiasm. The freedom to express my desires, to be as loud or quiet as I wanted, to change positions on a whim—it was intoxicating.

I creep back into the room I'm sharing with Mel and quickly shower before sliding beneath the covers of the giant bed. My body aches pleasantly, bearing the memory of Tucker's touch. Tomorrow, I'll return to Pittsburgh, to my uncertain future, to the process of rebuilding. But tonight, for a few precious hours, I'd been just Sloane—desired, fulfilled, and completely free.

As sleep reclaims me, I wonder briefly what might have happened if we'd met at a different time, in different circumstances. Then I push the thought away.

CHAPTER 4
TUCKER

I WAKE TO SUNLIGHT STREAMING THROUGH THE SMALL BASEMENT window, my arm stretched across empty sheets. For a moment, I'm disoriented—where the hell am I? Then it all rushes back: the law school party, the pool, and Sloane.

Grentley's ex.

I bolt upright, scanning the bunk room. Her bikini isn't on the floor where I'd tossed it last night. The space beside me is cool to the touch. She's been gone for a while.

"Fuck," I mutter, running a hand through my hair.

I grab my phone from the nightstand, checking for any messages or missed calls. Nothing but social media notifications —mostly my teammates, Howie, Spinner, and Mayhem, posting stories from Monaco. Pristine turquoise water, women in tiny bikinis, bottles of champagne. I should be there with them instead of waking up alone in my cousin's basement.

But then I wouldn't have met Sloane.

Or boned my goalie's ex-wife. Am I that much of a fuckup?

Something catches my eye as I swing my legs over the side of the bed. A glint of gold between the wooden bunk frame and the mattress. I reach down and fish out a delicate gold necklace with a small sun pendant—the one Sloane was wearing last night. My fingers close around it, the metal still warm somehow, like it holds her essence.

For a brief instant, I'm elated that I'll get to see her again to return it. Then I realize that I will have to see my teammate's ex-wife again, knowing what she looks like with me splattered all over her skin, and somehow act professional. Im-fucking-possible. The Fury defense is already held together with non-stick athletic tape. I can't imagine how the team would react if they knew I was intentionally acting on these caveman urges.

———

I shower quickly and head upstairs, hoping against reason that she might still be around. The kitchen is alive with activity, law students in various stages of breakfast preparation. They all look annoyingly alert and put-together, having apparently spent the evening studying for the bar exam rather than partying.

Stellan stands at the stove, expertly flipping pancakes in our massive cast-iron skillet. He raises an eyebrow when he spots me.

"The dead do rise," he says, sliding a hot pancake onto a plate. "There's still coffee."

I grunt in response, making a beeline for the pot. As I pour, I survey the room, looking for honey-colored curls and green eyes. Nothing.

"Looking for someone?" Stellan asks, too perceptive for his own good.

I shrug, aiming for casual disinterest. "Just seeing who's around."

"Uh-huh." He turns back to his pancakes. "Most people headed back to the city already."

I take my coffee to the counter, adding enough sugar to make my dentist weep. But I don't want to think about my teeth right now. "So, who was that woman? The one with the curly hair? In the pool?"

"Subtle," Stellan murmurs. Then louder, "Mel's roommate. They drove up together."

"Mel?"

"Mel Ortega. My study partner from law school." He slides me a plate of pancakes. "She was the one in the wheelchair."

I vaguely remember seeing a woman in a wheelchair chatting with a group of Stellan's friends last night, but I'd been too focused on Sloane to pay much attention.

"So you know Mel and her friend?" I try to sound only mildly interested, like I'm making conversation. "Have they lived together long?"

Stellan gives me a knowing look. "Why don't you ask her yourself?"

"Would if I could," I mutter. "Where is she?"

"She and Mel left around six, apparently. Mel has a bar exam prep class today." He studies me curiously. "This isn't like you, Tucker. Aren't you usually the one sneaking out before dawn?"

I don't have a response to that because he's right. I've perfected the art of the unattached hookup, the clean exit, the no-strings policy. So why am I standing here like a lovesick teenager, trying to extract information about a woman I spent one night with?

Given who this specific woman is, it's really better if I just let last night be what it was: absolutely perfect.

And utterly forbidden.

———

After breakfast, I pack up my stuff, carefully wrapping Sloane's necklace in a clean sock and tucking it into the side pocket of my duffel. I check under the bed, half-hoping to find some other forgotten item, another excuse to see her again.

"You coming back for the Fourth of July?" Stellan asks as I load my bag into the McLaren.

"Probably. Dad usually insists everyone shows up for the fireworks."

"Good luck with that." He claps me on the shoulder. "Drive safe. And Tucker—"

"Yeah?"

"If you're that interested, I could get her number from Mel."

I consider it for a moment, then shake my head. "Nah, I'm good. Just curious."

The lie tastes stale on my tongue, but my pride won't let me admit I'm genuinely disappointed she ditched me. Stellan nods and heads back inside.

———

The drive back to Pittsburgh gives me too much time to think. I find myself replaying moments from last night—the way Sloane laughed, how she traced my tattoo, the sounds she made when I was inside her.

I no longer care that she's entangled with Grentley. I just want more of her. Which sucks, because obviously I can't have her. Grentley would put his fist in my jaw, for starters.

My phone rings through the car's speakers, Alder's name flashing on the display.

"What's up, mirror image?" I answer, forcing cheerfulness into my voice.

"Where the hell are you?" he asks without preamble.

"Dramatic much?"

"I literally held your hand while you cried as Lena worked on your mouth the other day."

"Ah," I merge onto the turnpike. "So she's Lena now." My brother is so obviously smitten with the new team dentist. Which is great, because he just got out of a truly terrible relationship and needs something good in his life.

My twin sighs. "She's my roommate, Tuck. I can call her by her first name."

"Sure," I mutter, trailing off as I remember Sloane breathing my name into my ear. My mind is still very much back at the ski house.

"Are you even listening? I thought we were working out today."

"Sorry, just driving. Got distracted by..." I trail off, not wanting to explain.

Alder is quiet for a moment. "I guess I'm working out without you."

I drag a hand along my unshaven jaw. I hate disappointing my twin. All my brothers. "You can't get Gunny to sweat with you? Or Odin? We have all these siblings, Alder…"

He growls into the phone. "Something's up with you, Fucker. Where even are you?"

I sigh and stare at my darkened phone on the magnetic holder. "Hung out with Stellan and his friends. Nothing big."

I consider telling him about Sloane, but something stops me. I don't want to hear Alder's take on it, don't want him to reduce it to just another conquest story.

"Bullshit. Stellan's in some cave doing bar exam prep."

"Look, can we talk about our family whereabouts later? I'm trying not to die on these mountain roads."

Alder sighs. "Fine. But I'm coming over tomorrow with kettlebells."

"Whatever you need, bro."

We hang up, and I crank the music, trying to drown out my thoughts.

———

Back in Pittsburgh, I pull into the private garage beneath my building and take the elevator up to my loft. The doors open directly into my living room, all floor-to-ceiling windows and sleek modern furniture that my decorator picked out. I toss my keys onto the floating glass console by the door and drop my bag on the leather sofa.

The place feels emptier than usual. Sterile. I wander to the kitchen and open the refrigerator, staring at the sparse contents—protein shakes, sports drinks, and takeout containers from restaurants I don't remember ordering from.

Without really thinking about it, I find myself searching for Sloane online. There are paparazzi photos of her and Josh doing regular shit like walking into buildings. He never has his arm around her. She never smiles in any of the photos.

Some sports blogs mention the divorce, and, of course, they make it all sound like her fault, but none of them list any specifics. Sloane is way too classy to talk to the press about whatever went down with her and Josh. I only knew her for a few hours, but I could tell that much.

Frustrated, I toss my phone onto the counter and unzip my duffel. I pull out Sloane's necklace again, the gold sun catching the afternoon light streaming through my windows. It's simple but elegant, probably not expensive but clearly meaningful to her. I should find a way to return it.

It's the chivalrous thing to do.

I walk into my bedroom and open my underwear drawer, carefully placing the necklace inside. Not because I'm some creep who collects trophies, but because I don't want it to get lost. Because I need to know it's safe until I can find a way to get it back to her.

Because it's all I have left of a night that felt like something more than what it probably was.

I close the drawer and sit heavily on the edge of my bed. My phone buzzes from the kitchen—probably Howie or Spinner sending more yacht photos, rubbing it in that I'm missing the trip of a lifetime.

But I'm not sure I would trade last night for anything, not even Monaco with the boys. And that thought scares the shit out of me.

CHAPTER 5
SLOANE

THERE IS A WAR INSIDE ME. ON ONE TEAM, THE PLEASANT SORENESS in muscles I had forgotten about, thighs deliciously sore and visibly bruised with tiny bite marks.

On the other hand, a dread-soaked ache, the absence of my grandmother's necklace. Unimaginable loss compounded with guilt.

Mel throws a piece of cereal at me. "You ready to talk yet?" She sits at our rigged-up kitchen counter, getting breakfast together. When I moved in and saw how she couldn't reach anything, I rearranged the furniture and sawed a few inches off the legs of a rolling island so she'd have a workspace to prepare her own food.

"I lost my necklace," I manage, still pawing at my empty throat.

"Oh, babe. I'm sorry. Want me to call Stellan?"

Mel knows that the necklace is the only physical thing I really care about. My grandmother, who always worked two jobs to feed and house us, bought me the gold pendant when I started college. She was so proud that her grandchild was going to a university.

The small sun charm was her way of reminding me to "find light even on dark days."

And now it's gone. Probably lost somewhere in that basement

bunk room, between sheets that smelled of chlorine and bourbon and sex.

Maybe it's fitting. A sacrifice to the gods of One Night Stands. A physical reminder that I'm letting go of the past, starting fresh. My grandmother would understand. She always said material things were just things—it was the memories that mattered.

I just need time to accept that it's gone. I grab mugs from the cabinet—Mel's favorite Wonder Woman one and my chipped Carnegie Museum cup—and fill them with coffee as Mel maneuvers her chair to the small table by the window.

Her question unanswered, Mel hums at me until I stare at her. She taps her fingers on the laminate surface. "You gonna at least spill about the pool boy?"

"There's not much to tell," I lie, bringing both mugs to the table.

Mel gives me a look that could wither plants. "You disappeared with Hot Playboy and didn't return until four AM with sex hair. Then you passed out without wrapping said hair. There's plenty to tell."

I can't help the smile that spreads across my face. "Fine. His name is Tucker, and yes, we hooked up."

"And?"

"And it was good. Really good." I sip my coffee to hide my expression, but Mel's not having it.

"Sloane Elizabeth Whatever-Your-Middle-Name-Is, I did not drag my ass to the middle of nowhere and entertain boring law students so you could give me 'it was good' as your only review."

I laugh. "What do you want to know? Size, stamina, technique?"

"Yes, all of that. In graphic detail."

"He was..." I search for words that won't sound like oversharing. "Attentive. In charge but not controlling. And very, very skilled with his mouth."

Mel fans herself dramatically. "Hallelujah. After Ice Man Grentley, you deserved someone who knows what oral sex is."

I nearly spit out my coffee. "Mel!"

"Am I wrong?"

She's not. Josh approached sex like he approached everything—efficiently, perfunctory, and with minimal mess. It wasn't bad, exactly. Just... underwhelming. Tucker had been anything but.

"Anyway," I say, changing the subject. Sort of. "There is a small problem in addition to the necklace." She arches a brow, blowing her coffee. "He is a hockey player. On Josh's team."

Mel actually spits coffee across the room. A full blast of shocked explosion. I reach for napkins as she begins to laugh hysterically. "I'm sorry." She wipes her eyes. "It's too much."

She's right about that at least. I drink my coffee and stare out the window, wishing I had more friends to talk this through with me. "I guess go ahead and ask Stellan if he found the necklace. But absolutely no other details, and I'm not talking to Tucker again. It was a one-time thing."

My roommate nods, pulling out her phone, still chortling. "Orgasm therapy," she mutters, clicking the phone back to locked when she's done. "You're crushing your checklist."

Mel is referring to a plan we jokingly named the "Season of Sloane": sex, then school, and finally serenity. I smile, actually excited to go to campus today and meet with the registrar. I left my public health degree just shy of graduating. Of course, I was going to finish school when Josh and I got settled here in Pittsburgh, but then the team went to the playoffs that year, and my degree kept getting pushed down our priority list.

I absolutely nailed my first task—now I just need to focus on the others.

I find the admissions office on campus and wait nervously to speak with someone about late registration for summer classes.

A middle-aged white woman with kind eyes calls me over. Her nameplate reads "Susan Mitchell, Admissions Advisor."

"How can I help you today?" she asks.

"I'm hoping to transfer here," I tell her. "I was a student at the University of Michigan a few years ago, but I didn't finish my degree."

"Do you have your transcripts?"

I slide her the paperwork with just a few classes remaining for my bachelor's in public health.

Susan hums. "Let me see what classes still have openings for the summer term."

As she types, I think about my mother, who flitted in and out of my life depending on her grief and sobriety, and my father, who died before I even met him. My grandmother had been my rock, the one consistent presence until she died during my freshman year of college. After that, it had been easy to lose myself in Josh's world, to believe his certainty was stability.

Now, I know stability can't come from just one person. I want to be part of systems and structures that support people. I want to help weave the safety net for the people currently falling through holes in the webbing.

"You're in luck," Susan says, pulling me from my thoughts. "We have spots in Sociology, which is a really popular course. And you'll need Statistics for Health Sciences—it's being offered this summer as well."

Statistics. Math. My least favorite subject. But I need it, and maybe it's better to face it head-on.

"I'll take both," I say, surprising myself with my conviction.

Susan smiles. "Perfect. Second session classes start next week. Let's get you registered." She says I should be able to finish my degree in the fall semester if I can handle six classes and a service learning project. Then she recommends I join the Alliance for Students of Color, which has action plans to address racial disparities.

I have nothing to stop me. Nothing is standing in my way this time. Nobody is begging me to be by their side, to move me to a new home, or to be their emotional rock.

"Let's do this," I say, and sign all the forms necessary to finish something I started finally.

An hour later, I'm officially a part-time student with a new university ID and a growing sense of purpose. I wander around campus, mapping the locations of my classes, finding the library where I'll undoubtedly spend hours studying.

I exhaust myself marching up the hill and pass the athletic complex, a state-of-the-art facility with Pittsburgh University's wildcat logo emblazoned on the doors. A memory surfaces: sitting in the stands at a Michigan hockey game, watching Josh play, believing that supporting his dream was enough of a dream for me, too.

My phone buzzes with a news alert. Before I can stop myself, I open it.

FURY GOALTENDER GRENTLEY CONTINUES RECLU-SIVE BEHAVIOR DESPITE TEAM PR EFFORTS

The article is brief, noting that Josh has declined all interview requests regarding the team's playoff loss. There's a reference to our divorce—"following his split from his wife earlier this year"—but no details. Not even my name, which fits because only the athlete matters in relationships with pro hockey players. I learned that the hard way. The reporter speculates about whether Josh's "monastic approach" will benefit or harm his focus.

Most of the post-season furor had been about a love triangle involving one of the defenders and his boyfriend, but it was only a matter of time before that cooled down, and the public turned back to hating on the goalie.

I never learned the finer points of hockey, but even I know the fans are always quick to blame the goalie for a loss. That always bothered Josh.

But I don't need to worry about his hurt feelings. Never again.

My phone buzzes again—this time, a text from Mel.

> How's registration going? Did you sign up for basket weaving and nap time?

I smile, typing a response as I walk toward the bus stop.

> Sociology and STATISTICS. I hate myself already.

I'm chopping vegetables for stir-fry when Mel rolls into our apartment, tossing her bag onto the sofa with a dramatic sigh.

"If I have to memorize one more Supreme Court precedent, I may actually die," she announces, wheeling into the kitchen. "Something smells amazing."

"Just the basics," I say, scraping bell peppers into a bowl. "How was your day?"

"Brutal." She pulls a bottle of white wine from the refrigerator. "But I got some good news. Stag Law called—I have an interview next week."

I pause. Mel is the sort of overachiever doing two degrees at once, so she's just now being wooed by significant firms as she finishes a master's in policy while studying for the bar. "Stag Law? I thought we agreed to avoid Stags."

She pours a glass of wine. "I'm not stopping communication with Stellan just because you boned his cousin." She waggles her eyebrows. "His dad's law firm is my dream job. They do equal pay cases and recently started working with the Paralympics." She winces. "It's a long shot, but even getting the interview is huge."

"That's amazing, Mel!" I accept the glass she offers. "You'll crush it." I find myself envious of her certainty in her path. I love what she's studying and the work she aims to do.

"I'd better. The competition is fierce." She takes a long sip. "Enough about me. How was your first day as a co-ed?"

I tell her about my day, skipping my response to the article about Josh. I try not to think about Mel going to work with Tucker's family.

"I'm terrified about statistics," I admit, adding chicken to the wok. "I barely passed algebra in high school. And I managed to avoid math the first time I tried this college thing…"

"You'll be fine," Mel says confidently. "You know how to work hard, Sloane. That's half the battle."

"I'm not sure hard work is enough for statistics."

"Trust me, it is. I've seen you tackle things you thought were impossible." She wheels closer, stealing a piece of bell pepper. "Hello? You made me a food prep station I can reach."

I shake my head. "That was basic."

"No, it wasn't. You're persistent. You don't give up." Her voice softens. "That's why I know you're going to be okay, post-divorce. You're already rebuilding."

Her faith in me brings a lump to my throat. This is what I'd been missing in my marriage—someone who saw me, who believed in me as an individual, not just as an extension of their life.

It reminds me, unexpectedly, of how Tucker looked at me. How he asked what I wanted, as if my desires mattered. How he focused on my pleasure as much as his own. For all his playboy swagger, there had been moments of genuine connection there, moments where I felt seen in a way I hadn't in years.

"Earth to Sloane," Mel says, waving a brown hand in front of my face. "You just glazed over. Thinking about statistics again?"

I shake my head, feeling my cheeks warm. "Just... processing everything. It's been a lot of change lately."

"Good change, though, right?"

I nod, turning back to the stir-fry, happy for the first time in years to be making my own choices based on my wants. "Yeah. Good change." If only I felt as confident as my words.

CHAPTER 6
TUCKER

MY HEAD THROBS IN TIME WITH EACH REP OF THE KETTLEBELL SWING, and not because of my knocked-out tooth. I grunt, pushing through the pain of my self-inflicted hangover as sweat drips onto the training mat I've rolled out in my living room.

"Your form is shit," Alder says from where he's doing perfect Russian twists: my twin brother, ever the technician, ever the perfectionist. Even our workouts are a study in contrasts—his movements precise and controlled, mine powerful but erratic.

"Your face is shit," I mutter, regretting the bottle of bourbon I nursed alone last night while scrolling through social media, scouring the internet for traces of Sloane Campbell Grentley.

"Real mature." Alder switches to mountain climbers without missing a beat. "Seriously, Fucker, you're going to wreck your back if you keep swinging like that."

I drop the kettlebell with a thud that reverberates through my skull along with the entire building. "Happy now?"

"Ecstatic." He pauses, studying me. "You look like hell, by the way."

"Thanks for noticing."

"Late night?"

I grab a towel and wipe the sweat from my face. "Maybe I'm just road weary. Some of us had to drive back from the mountains yesterday."

"Right. Stellan's thing." Alder takes a long pull from his water bottle. "You seemed distracted on the phone. Meet someone?"

The question is casual, but my brother knows me too well. I consider lying, but what's the point? "Maybe."

His eyebrows shoot up. "Maybe? Since when is Tucker Stag uncertain about his conquests?"

"She's not a conquest," I snap, with more heat than intended.

Alder sets down his water bottle, suddenly interested. "Well, shit. Tell me."

I shake my head, regretting having said anything. "Nothing to tell. Met a woman, had a good time, she left before I woke up. End of story."

"Except it's not, or you wouldn't be moping around your apartment getting drunk alone and looking like someone stole your favorite Bauers."

"I'm not moping. Maybe I'm depressed about my tooth." I pick up the kettlebell again, channeling my frustration into another set of swings. "Speaking of… How's Lena?"

Alder's expression shifts, his ears reddening slightly. "She's fine."

"Just fine? Not spectacular, amazing, life-changing?" I force a grin, grateful to turn the tables. "Still just roommates sharing longing glances across the breakfast table?"

"Fuck off."

"That's not a denial."

He throws a towel at my head. "We're colleagues. Roommates. Friends."

"Sure. And I'm Mother Teresa."

"You know it's complicated. She's the team dentist, I'm a player. There are rules."

I snort. "Since when do you care about rules?"

"Since I actually like my job and want to keep it," he says, but there's something in his expression—a softness when he mentions Lena that I've never seen before.

"You want more with her," I say, and it's not a question.

Alder stares at the ceiling, suddenly fascinated by the recessed lighting. "Maybe. I don't know. It's… different with her."

I understand more than he realizes. Something was different

with Sloane, too—something I can't articulate without sounding like a lovesick teenager.

My phone buzzes on the coffee table, saving me from having to respond. It's a group text from the guys.

> **HOWIE**
>
> Tiki boat. Today. 1 pm. It's a paddle boat, so that's exercise.

They don't even pause for jet lag, I guess. They just got back stateside. However, it's not like we aren't used to constant travel. Immediately, the replies start flooding in.

> **SPINNER**
>
> Already packed the cooler.

> **ROOKIE**
>
> I'm bringing the smoke show I met at Diesel last night.

> **MAYHEM**
>
> No, you're not. Bros only. I'm not listening to you try to impress some rando all afternoon.

I glance at the time: 11:23 AM. Usually, I'd be the first to respond, the instigator of such plans rather than a recipient. Today, though, I hesitate.

"The children are summoning you?" Alder asks, nodding toward my phone.

"One of those tiki booze pedal boats."

"Sounds exactly like the healthy decision your liver needs right now." He stands, gathering his things. "I've got plans with Lena. We're sending manure to our cheating exes."

"Wholesome," I tease, but there's no bite to it. Part of me envies the simplicity of his day ahead.

"Better than playing 'who can get alcohol poisoning first.'" He heads for the door, then pauses. "You good, Tuck? For real?"

I force a smile. "Never better. Go play with poop."

After he leaves, I stare at my phone, debating. The last thing I need is more alcohol, but the alternative is sitting here alone with my thoughts, which feels even less appealing.

I'm in. But someone else has to pedal. My thighs are wrecked.

———

The Pittsburgh Party Pedaler is precisely what it sounds like—a floating tiki bar powered by bicycle pedals, drifting down the Allegheny River on a perfect June afternoon. Howie, a self-appointed captain, wears a plastic pirate hat as he steers us around a small motorboat.

"Hard to starboard!" he shouts, clearly having no idea what the terms mean.

"That's right, dumbass," Spinner corrects from his pedaling station, already three beers in. "We're going left."

"Whatever. Just go faster. We're professional fucking athletes." Howie adjusts his sunglasses, scanning the shoreline for women to heckle. So far, we've received three middle fingers and one phone number written on a napkin, thrown from another boat.

I'm stationed between Rookie and Mayhem, pedaling half-heartedly while nursing my second beer. The hangover has mellowed into a dull throb, but I'm not eager to replace it with a fresh one.

"T-Stag, you're slacking," Mayhem says, his massive quads powering his cranks with twice the effort of anyone else. Despite his intimidating appearance—six-foot-five with tattoos crawling up his neck—Mayhem is the most thoughtful guy on the team. He reads philosophy books on road trips and sends his mother flowers every Sunday.

"Just pacing myself," I reply, taking another sip of beer that's growing warm in the afternoon sun.

"Since when?" Rookie laughs. "You're usually halfway to blackout by now."

"Maybe I'm evolving."

Spinner snorts. "Yeah, and I'm joining a monastery."

"You have been pretty quiet," Howie observes, leaning closer. "Still bummed about missing Monaco? Because I've got to say, those yacht models were something else."

I shake my head. "Nah, just tired. Didn't sleep great."

The conversation shifts to Rookie's alleged conquest from the flight home, a tale that grows more implausible with each adjustment. I let my mind wander as we drift past Point State Park, where the rivers converge at the heart of downtown Pittsburgh.

That's when I see her.

Sloane is jogging along the riverside trail, her honey-colored curls pulled back in a pouf, her athletic figure showcased in running shorts and a fitted tank top. She's even more beautiful in daylight, her skin glowing with exertion.

Before I can think, I'm on my feet, nearly capsizing our floating bar.

"Sloane!" I call out, waving my arms like an idiot. "Hey! Sloane!"

She turns her head in our direction, shading her eyes against the sun. For a moment, I think she sees me—her pace falters slightly. Then she adjusts her earbuds and continues running, disappearing around a bend in the trail.

"Did she just ignore you?" Howie asks, incredulous.

I sink back onto my seat, deflated. "Guess so."

"Who the hell is Sloane?" Spinner demands.

"No one," I mutter, but it's too late.

"Holy shit," Rookie crows. "Did T-Stag just get rejected? In public?"

"She probably couldn't hear me," I say, but the excuse sounds weak even to me. I don't know what I was thinking anyway, calling our goalie's ex-wife, surrounded by Fury players. That's low even for me.

"The great Tucker Stag, shot down like a duck in hunting season." Howie clutches his chest dramatically. "I never thought I'd see the day."

"Maybe you're losing your touch," Spinner suggests. "When's the last time you even hooked up with someone?"

The irony isn't lost on me. "Two nights ago, actually."

"Wait." Rookie's eyes widen. "Is that her? The one who just curved you?"

I take a long swallow of beer instead of answering, which is answer enough.

"Oh man," Howie cackles. "This is too good. The enforcer lost his rizz."

"She didn't *curve* me," I insist, worrying this is low behavior, even for me. "She probably just didn't recognize me from that distance."

"Sure, buddy." Rookie pats my shoulder condescendingly. "That's definitely it."

"You know what you need to do," Spinner says, already mixing another round of drinks at the boat's small bar. "Next time, you need to really make an impression. Show up at her place with a boombox over your head. Women love that John Cusack shit."

"Yeah, because stalking is super attractive," Mayhem interjects, giving me a look that says he sees more than I'm letting on. "Maybe just let it go, man."

"Agreed," Howie adds, "you move on. Best way to get over someone is to get under someone else, right?"

I force a laugh and accept the drink Spinner hands me. "You guys are reading way too much into this. It was just a hookup."

But as the afternoon wears on and the drinks keep flowing, I find myself checking the riverside trail every time we pass it, hoping for another glimpse of her. By the time we dock at sunset, I'm significantly more drunk than I'd intended to be and no closer to forgetting Sloane.

————

Back at my apartment, I pull out my phone and navigate to my texts with Stellan before I can overthink it. I drop the damn thing a few times but eventually manage to tell Stelly what I need.

> Needfavor. Your frind Mel. The one in the
> wheelchair. You sed you'd get roommate's info.

The response comes nearly an hour later, by which time I'm sprawled on the couch, staring at the ceiling, Sloane's necklace dangling from my fingers.

STELLAN

Why? You planning to stalk her?

I scowl at the phone.

No. She lft something at the house. Trying to rtrn it.

STELLAN

You're drunk. Go to sleep, Tucker.

I toss the phone aside, frustrated. The room spins slightly as I close my eyes, the necklace still clutched in my hand. The last thought I have before passing out is of Sloane, running away from me, always just out of reach.

The Fury team conference room is way too bright, loud, and definitely way too early the next morning. I slouch in my chair at the back, slurping my second coffee and wearing sunglasses indoors like the cliché I am. Coach Thompson stands at the front, going through his pre-season expectations with all the enthusiasm of a drill sergeant.

"Conditioning begins sooner than you think, gentlemen. I expect everyone to be at fighting weight by then." He glares around the room, his gaze lingering on me. "Some of you have further to go than others."

A few chuckles ripple through the room. I resist the urge to flip everyone off.

"This season is crucial," Thompson continues. "After last year's playoff disappointment, management expects results. We've made minimal roster changes, which means each of you needs to step up."

I tune out as he drones on about systems and strategy. My attention drifts to the other side of the room, where Josh Grentley sits alone, with a full empty chair on each side of him. He's always been a loner, but there's something different about him now— a hardness to his features, a deliberate distance from everyone else. And I doubt it's still lingering frustration over sharing a starting rotation with my brother, Gunnar.

"And T-Stag," Coach's voice snaps my attention back. "We're going to need your particular skills more than ever this season. The Eastern Division's getting nastier. Lot of teams targeting our skill players."

I straighten slightly, recognizing my cue. As the team's enforcer, my job is as much about deterrence as it is about actual fighting. Most games, my presence alone keeps opponents from taking liberties with our stars. When that fails, I make examples of people.

"I want you setting the tone early," Thompson continues. "Let them know there's a price to pay for touching our guys. But—" he raises a finger, "—I need you smart about it. No stupid penalties when we're up by one in the third. No getting ejected in the first period of playoff games. Controlled aggression. You understand?"

I nod, resisting the urge to remind him that I've been doing this job since I was fourteen. "Yes, Coach."

"Good." His gaze flickers briefly toward Grentley, then to my brother Alder and a few others who were involved in the mess that played out in the media at the end of last season. Coach mutters something about character and admirable behavior off the ice.

The meeting wraps up, and I'm one of the first out the door, eager to get home and back to bed. I'm nearly to the parking garage when a voice stops me.

"Stag."

I turn to find Grentley following me, his expression unreadable. I paste on an exaggerated grin. "What's up, G?"

"I saw your little boat party yesterday," he says, no preamble. "All over social media."

I bristle instantly. "And?"

"And we just sat through a meeting about character and training. About representing the team with dignity."

"It was a tiki boat, not a coke bender," I retort. "Since when are you the fun police?"

His jaw tightens. "Some of us take this job seriously. Some of us understand what it means to be a professional."

The condescension in his tone sparks something hot and defensive in my chest. Fuck this guy. "Some of us also understand that it's the off-season, and what I do with my free time is none of your fucking business." *And you don't even know the half of it, asshole.*

"It is when your drunken antics reflect on all of us," he says coldly. "Some of us are trying to maintain a certain standard."

Before I can respond, Howie appears at my side. "Everything cool here?" he asks, glancing between us.

Grentley steps back. "Just a friendly reminder about priorities. Nothing to worry about."

"Great chat," I say through gritted teeth, hating his self-righteous attitude, trying not to blurt something shitty about driving his wife away. "Let's do it again, never."

He walks off without another word, his posture rigid, shoulders set in a straight line.

"What was that about?" Howie asks.

"Hell if I know. Guy's got a stick up his ass the size of a ketchup bottle." I push through the door to the parking garage. "Always has."

But as I slide into my car, I can't shake the feeling of being judged, of falling short. It's a familiar sensation, one I've carried since I was the wild child among my more focused brothers, the enforcer on a team of skilled players, the Stag who seems perpetually out of step with the family legacy. Man, if Grentley only knew the whole truth.

And what's worse is I can't stop thinking about her. I am obsessed, and not because I'm bad or trying to get back at him. We connected, me and Sloane. There was a spark between us. A sizzle that had nothing to do with revenge or drama or anything other than two people, maybe meant to find one another.

I start the engine; the decision crystallizes. I'm going to find Sloane again. I'm going to show her—show everyone—that there's more to me than they think. That I'm worth a second look, a second chance.

My phone buzzes with a text from my agent about upcoming

endorsement meetings, but I ignore it. That's the Tucker Stag everyone expects—the party boy, the entertaining loose cannon, the guy who sells socks and condoms with a wink and a smile.

But there's more to me than that. There has to be. And somehow, I'm going to prove it.

CHAPTER 7
SLOANE

I'M LOST. COMPLETELY, TOTALLY LOST.

The professor's voice washes over me like white noise as incomprehensible symbols fill the whiteboard. Statistical Analysis for Public Health seemed like a straightforward class to take, but fifteen minutes in, I'm already drowning. I glance around the lecture hall at my fellow students—most look fresh out of high school, furiously typing notes.

I stare down at my nearly blank notebook page. I've managed to write the date and "Statistical Analysis" at the top, followed by a single formula that might as well be written in Sanskrit.

"When we talk about standard deviation, we're discussing the dispersion of a dataset relative to its mean," the professor, Dr. Khan, explains. She clicks to the next slide in her presentation—a bell curve covered in Greek letters that makes my head spin.

I lean back in my seat and close my eyes briefly. What was I thinking? That I could just waltz back into academia after five years away and pick up where I left off?

I can't imagine what I was thinking, leaving so close to finishing and then never actually doing so. I started college early and earned credits from my advanced government classes in high school. I was hot shit, academically. But then Josh had been drafted to play for Pittsburgh, and I'd been so sure that being with him was more important than my degree. I remember packing up my dorm room, giddy with excitement about starting our new life together. The glamour of being with a professional athlete, traveling to different cities, living in luxury—it had all seemed so romantic.

My roommate had thought I was crazy. "You can finish your degree in Pittsburgh," she'd said, helping me fold my clothes into suitcases. "They have college there. You don't have to drop out."

But Josh had wanted me with him immediately. There were apartments to tour, social events to attend. "You can go back anytime," he'd promised, kissing my forehead. "We're young. We have our whole lives ahead of us."

Five years and one divorce later, here I am, starting over, surrounded by kids who probably still get an allowance from their parents. Not that I'm any better, with my alimony lump sum that doesn't change anything about my crushed dreams to start a family.

But I've also got to wrestle with drunk party hookups hollering to me from a booze cruise, surrounded by my ex's teammates. I can't escape it.

What did Tucker think would happen, calling to me like that with half the Fury around him? If he'd shown up at my apartment, alone, in the dark, I probably would have opened the door. But in public? I can't even let myself imagine it.

"For tomorrow, please read chapters one through three and complete problem sets A through C," Dr. Khan says, jolting me back to the present. People around me start packing up, and I realize with horror that I've missed most of the lecture.

I shove my notebook into my bag and escape into the hallway, gulping air like I've been underwater. This was a mistake. All of it—coming back to school, thinking I could just pick up where I left off, believing I could build a new life after wasting so many years.

My phone buzzes with a text from Mel.

How's the first day of school? Made any friends
to sit with at lunch?

Despite my panic, I smile.

Currently having an existential crisis. Want to meet for coffee in an hour? I need to vent.

Her response comes immediately.

MEL

Let's grab lunch at Green Bowl in 45.

I slip my phone back into my pocket, feeling marginally better. At least I'm not entirely alone in this city.

Green Bowl is a trendy café near campus, with exposed brick and reclaimed wood, mismatched vintage furniture, and local art on the walls. Mel has already claimed our favorite corner table, the one with extra space for her wheelchair and power outlets for our laptops.

"That bad, huh?" she asks as I collapse into the chair across from her. Her law books are spread across half the table, color-coded tabs sticking out from every direction.

"Worse," I groan, dropping my head into my hands. "I understood maybe ten percent of what the professor said."

"First day jitters," Mel says, pushing a mug toward me. She's already ordered my usual—bush tea with honey. "You're smart, Sloane. You just need to get back into student mode."

"I don't think I remember how to be a student," I admit, wrapping my hands around the warm mug. "Everyone else seemed so... together. Taking notes on their laptops, asking intelligent questions. Meanwhile, I was having flashbacks to the day I dropped out."

Mel's expression softens. "Having regrets?"

I stare into my drink. "Not exactly. I mean, yes, I regret not finishing school back then. But at the time..." I trail off, remembering the excitement, the certainty that I was making the right choice. "At the time, it felt like an adventure."

"You were in love," Mel says simply. "People make decisions in love they wouldn't make otherwise."

"And look how that turned out." I take a sip of my tea, savoring the bitterness beneath the sweetness.

"First of all," Mel says, tapping her pen against her legal pad, "I know you feel a certain way about your settlement." She was the one who recommended my lawyer and then held my hand and told me to say yes to the money. "Half his shit is legally yours, and holding onto that guilt isn't helping anyone, especially not you. Second, you're twenty-five, not ninety-five. You have plenty of time to build the life you want."

I know she's right, but the panic from the classroom still lingers. "I just don't know if I can do this. Statistics? What was I thinking?"

"That public health is important to you, and statistics is part of the package," Mel says pragmatically. "You'll get it. We'll study together. School and serenity, right?"

I pull out my textbook and flip it open. The symbols swim before my eyes, and I feel that wave of panic rising again.

"I don't know," I murmur. "Maybe I should—"

The bell above the café door jingles, and I glance up reflexively.

The world stops.

Tucker Stag stands in the doorway, sunglasses pushed up into his tousled blond hair, wearing a Pittsburgh Fury t-shirt that stretches across his broad, muscled shoulders. He looks tired, irritated, and unfairly gorgeous.

Our eyes meet, and his entire demeanor changes. The scowl vanishes, replaced by genuine surprise that quickly transforms into a smile that could power the whole city.

Oh no.

"Isn't that..." Mel starts, following my gaze.

"Shh," I hiss, ducking my head as if that could somehow make me invisible.

Too late. He's already weaving through the tables toward us, his face lit with a kind of boyish excitement that makes my stomach flip.

"Sloane," he says, stopping at our table. "Hey."

I manage a smile that I hope doesn't betray the riot happening in my chest. "Hi, Tucker."

He turns to Mel, extending his hand. "We met at Stelly's party."

"I remember," Mel says, shaking his hand with an amused expression I know all too well. "I'm Mel."

"Right, Mel. Tucker." He nods, then turns back to me, his eyes so intensely blue I have to look away. "Whatcha doing here, Sloane?"

"Just studying," I say, gesturing lamely at the open textbook. "First day of class."

"You're in school?" He sounds genuinely interested, which is... unexpected.

"Just started. Public health." I'm painfully aware of how awkward I sound, like I've forgotten how to form complete sentences.

"That's awesome," he says, and he seems to mean it. He shifts his weight, looking like he wants to say more but is holding back. "Actually, I've been trying to find a way to contact you. You left something at the house."

My hand flies instinctively to my throat. "My necklace? You found it?"

His smile broadens. "Yeah. It was wedged between the bed and the wall. I've got it at my place."

"Oh my God, thank you." The relief in my voice must be palpable. "It was a gift."

"I figured it was important." He glances at the counter where a barista is calling out an order number, then back to me. "I should let you get back to studying, but..."

He pulls his phone from his pocket and slides it across the table to me. "Will you type your number? So we can figure out how to get your necklace back to you."

"Thanks," I say, taking the device. Our fingers brush, and I try to ignore the small jolt that runs through me as I quickly add my number to his contacts.

He grins and texts me a smiley face, smiling even bigger when my phone vibrates with the incoming message. "I'm grabbing a green smoothie," he gestures toward the counter. "Gotta ramp up my nutrition...anyway, I'll let you get back to it," he says, backing away, clearly reluctant to leave. My heart pounds, probably because he found my treasured gift. "But text me, okay? About the necklace."

"I will," I promise, and he flashes that smile again before turning toward the counter.

The moment he's out of earshot, Mel leans forward. "Holy shit," she whispers. "He is, like, fully in love with you."

I feel my face heat up. "Keep your voice down!"

"He's gorgeous," she continues, unabashed. People actually approach him in line, and he snaps selfies. Because he's a famous hockey player who works with my ex-husband. "And he was looking at you like you hung the moon."

"It was one night," I mutter, trying to ignore the warmth spreading through my chest. "It doesn't mean anything."

"That man did not look like someone who thinks it meant nothing," Mel says, gesturing with her pen toward Tucker, who's now waiting for his order, sneaking glances in our direction. "And he found your necklace. That's basically the plot of a rom-com."

"I would have had the necklace days ago if you actually texted your friend, the host, about it." I roll my eyes, but my heart isn't in it.

She squints and taps her lip with her pencil. "I'm trying to decide how bad it is that he works with Josh."

I resist the urge to pull Mel's hair or pour soup on her lap. "Can we please focus on statistics? I'm having an academic crisis here."

Mel gives me a look that says she's not fooled, but mercifully turns her attention back to my textbook. "Okay, so standard deviation. It's actually not that complicated..."

I try to concentrate on what she's saying, but I'm acutely aware of Tucker at the counter, of his number burning a hole in my pocket. When he finally leaves with a small wave in our direction, I feel both relieved and disappointed.

"You should text him," Mel says once he's gone, not even pretending to talk about statistics anymore.

"I will. About the necklace."

"That's not what I mean, and you know it." She leans forward. "Sloane, when was the last time you saw a guy look at you like that? And don't say Josh, because he never looked at you like *that*."

The comment stings, partly because it's true. Josh had always looked at me with approval, like I was a sensible purchase he'd made. Tucker looks at me like I'm something extraordinary.

"It doesn't matter," I say, flipping a page in my textbook without reading it. "I'm trying to put my life back together, not complicate it with... whatever that would be."

"Fun?" Mel suggests. "Happiness? Mind-blowing sex with a hottie who clearly knows how to use all of that." She makes lewd hand gestures.

I glare at her, but she just shrugs, unrepentant. Things were simpler when Mel and I were undergrads. Now, I'm well aware that amazing sex doesn't cancel out all the other risks that come along with Tucker Stag.

"I'm just saying, you don't have to marry the guy. But maybe getting your necklace back isn't the only reason to call him."

I stare down at my statistics book, the formulas blurring before my eyes. Part of me—a bigger part than I want to admit—wants to pull out my phone right now, to text Tucker and see him again. To feel that rush, that electricity that I'd forgotten could exist between two people. Because even though I was embarrassed and frustrated when he waved at me the other day, I still went home and remembered every ... single ... detail of what we did together at that ski house.

But the part of me that spent five years becoming someone she barely recognized in service to a man's career and ego is terrified. I remember how it started with Josh, too. The excitement, the butterflies, the feeling of being swept away.

I'd put my entire life on hold once for a man. I'd disappeared into his world, his needs, his dreams. I never even got to enjoy the perks of being an athlete's wife since Josh was so superstitious and reclusive. We didn't party. Paparazzi didn't mob us. I hardly even went to his games—he said it messed with his focus, and after a while, I stopped asking. I'd emerged with nothing to show for it but a pile of money I'm too ashamed to spend and a hole where my self-worth should be.

I can't do that again. I won't.

I push my phone deeper into my pocket and force myself to focus on the formulas in front of me, trying to ignore the lingering warmth of Tucker's smile and the quiet voice in my head, wondering what would happen if, just this once, I let myself follow that feeling again.

CHAPTER 8
TUCKER

I GLANCE AT MY WATCH FOR THE FIFTH TIME IN AS MANY MINUTES. She said she'd be here at eight. It's 7:53. I'm not usually the guy who waits around for women—and now that I've tasted my own medicine, I see that it's sour. I'm pacing my apartment like a teenager before his first date.

This is ridiculous. I'm Tucker Stag, professional hockey player, Thin Ice condom brand rep, and certified man-about-town. I don't get nervous about women coming over.

Except, apparently, when that woman is Sloane.

Who, I remind myself, was married to my teammate.

I survey my penthouse with fresh eyes, trying to see it as she might. Not that I need to care what she thinks. But the massive flat-screen dominating the living room wall suddenly seems ostentatious. The leather sectional feels impersonal. Because it is. God, I didn't even pick out my own furniture. The glass-and-chrome coffee table is littered with hockey magazines and a few endorsement contracts my agent, Brian, dropped off yesterday.

I hastily gather the papers and shove them into a drawer. I don't know how to spruce this place up to look less like a pretentious bachelor pad in … I check my watch. I've got three minutes.

I quickly stash empty protein shake bottles in the recycling and fluff the decorative pillows I've never once used. I grab the half-empty whiskey bottle from the bar cart and hide it in a cabinet.

Am I seriously trying to impress her? I never expected her to suggest coming by tonight to get her necklace.

The necklace. I hurry to retrieve it from my underwear drawer, where I've kept it safe. The small gold sun catches the light, spinning slowly as I hold it up. Such a simple thing to have occupied so much of my thoughts.

The doorbell chimes, and my heart rate kicks up. I shove the necklace into my pocket and take a deep breath. It's just a woman coming to retrieve her property. Nothing more. Even if I haven't been able to stop thinking about her.

The elevator door opens to reveal Sloane looking somehow even more beautiful than I remembered. Her curls are loose around her gorgeous face, and she's wearing a simple sundress that shows off her athletic figure. She looks slightly nervous, which makes me feel marginally better about my own inexplicable anxiety.

"Hey," I say, stepping back to let her in.

"Hey, yourself." She enters, her eyes widening slightly as she takes in the floor-to-ceiling windows with their panoramic view of the Pittsburgh skyline. "Wow. Nice place."

"Thanks. It's, uh, a bit much, I know." I close the door, suddenly self-conscious about the obvious display of wealth.

"No, it's..." She pauses, a hint of amusement in her eyes. "Very you."

"I'm not sure if that's a compliment."

"Neither am I." But she smiles, taking the sting out of her words.

I lead her further into the living room, uncomfortably aware of her eyes on me. "Can I get you a drink? Wine? Beer? Water?"

"Wine would be nice," she says, wandering to the windows. "The view is incredible."

I head to the kitchen, grateful for something to do with my hands. I open a bottle of red that my brother Gunnar suggested I buy, some expensive vintage I know nothing about except that it costs about the same as my fancy whiskey.

When I return with two glasses, Sloane has moved to my shelves, examining the few personal items I have displayed—

mostly team photos and family pictures from various Stag gatherings.

"Your family?" she asks, nodding toward a photo from last Christmas.

"Yeah. My brothers and cousins." I hand her a glass, careful not to brush her fingers with mine. Even so, I feel that same electric awareness that's been haunting me since the ski house. "Big family."

"I can see that." She sips the wine, her eyes still on the photo. "You all look alike."

"Dad says the Stag genes are strong," I say without thinking. "My dad and his brothers could be quadruplets."

She turns to face me, and for a moment we just stand there, too close, neither of us moving away. I can smell her perfume— that light and floral scent that dances in my dreams and makes me want to bury my face in her neck.

"I have your necklace," I say, my voice rougher than intended. I pull it from my pocket and hold it out to her.

Her eyes light up, genuine delight spreading across her face. "I can't believe you found it. I was sure it was gone forever."

I watch as she takes it from my palm, her fingers brushing mine. "I figured it was important."

"It was from my grandmother." She fumbles with the clasp. "The one who died."

"Essie. Right." Without thinking, I step behind her. "Here, let me."

She hands me the necklace and lifts her hair, exposing the nape of her neck. I move closer, acutely aware of her warmth, the subtle curve where her neck meets her shoulder. My fingers feel too large, too clumsy for the delicate clasp, but I manage to secure it.

Instead of stepping away, I stay there, breathing her in. "There," I say softly. I trail a finger along the chain, feeling her smooth, soft skin beneath my calloused hand.

She turns, still close enough that I feel the warmth of her body. Her hand moves to the pendant at her throat. "Thank you."

We're so close I can see the flecks of gold in her green eyes, the slight unevenness of her breathing. Neither of us moves, caught in a moment of shared awareness that feels both familiar and entirely new.

"We should sit," I say finally, breaking the spell. We should not sit. I shouldn't fucking *sit* with Grentley's ex. "The wine's done breathing. Or whatever it does."

She smiles and nods, following me to the sectional. I sit at a respectable distance, but the space between us feels charged, alive with possibility.

"So," I start, searching for safe conversation. "Public health. That's your major?"

"Yeah." She tucks one leg beneath her, getting comfortable. "I'm just starting back. It's... intimidating, going back to school after so long."

"Why public health?" I'm genuinely curious, I realize. I want to know more about her, everything about her.

A shadow crosses her face. "Family history. My dad was killed in a car accident while my mom was pregnant with me. Mom treated her grief with substance abuse. I'd like to work in prevention programs someday."

I hadn't expected such honesty. "That's... really admirable. You know, my mom grew up in foster care..."

"I didn't know."

I tip my glass toward her, ceding her point. "Yeah. She works in family law now. She said the same thing, about wanting to make a difference for families like hers."

Sloane adjusts her posture, looking slightly embarrassed. "It's definitely something I care about. Family. Helping families. What about you? Is hockey your passion?"

Her question takes me by surprise. I thought my answer would be an immediate yes, but so much of what I love about hockey is wrapped up in my family being on the ice with me. I blurt, "Hockey is all I've ever known," which I know isn't the same thing, and Sloane's face reveals she hears the difference. "But family is really important to me."

Her expression darkens, and I try to work out where I messed up, remembering she mentioned her grandmother. I decide to lighten the mood, lean in to what she and I have already established as talking points. "Plus, you know, I've got that sock money."

Sloane wiggles her bare toes on the couch, and we both laugh.

I shift slightly closer to her. "What else should I know about *you*?"

Our eyes meet for a moment, a brief, silent recognition of the main thing we know about one another: our shared connections to Josh Grentley. And then it's like he's gone from the conversation, from our thoughts, from our consciousness.

"Not much to tell." She glances around the apartment again. "I'm a lot less interesting than all this suggests you are."

"I doubt that." I study her, the way her fingers trace the stem of her wineglass, the slight tensing of her shoulders when she feels my gaze. "You're the most interesting woman I've met in a long time."

She laughs, but there's a nervousness to it. "You don't even know me."

"I'd like to." The words come out more sincere than I intended, closer to the truth than I'm comfortable with.

Her eyes meet mine, and something shifts in the air between us. The pretense of casual conversation falls away, leaving only the raw awareness that's been simmering since she walked through my door. Since the ski house, if I'm honest.

She sets down her wineglass with deliberate care. "Tucker."

"Yeah?"

"You and I cannot be a thing."

My heart rate doubles. "No?"

She shakes her head, then moves toward me with sudden purpose, closing the distance between us. "What happened was a one-time thing. Just sex."

I swallow, worried the wine will solidify in my throat. "Right. Terrible idea. Nothing we should repeat."

She runs a hand along the leather on the back of the couch. It's indecent, the way she drags that finger along. "But I'm here anyway. And that already doesn't look good."

I scoot closer to her. Just a millimeter. "Nobody's looking, Sloane."

Her lips find mine, soft and warm and tasting of wine, and any remaining restraint I might have had evaporates.

I pull her onto my lap, her knees straddling my thighs, my hands spanning her waist. She makes a soft sound against my mouth, sending heat racing through me. This feels different—less frantic, more deliberate, but no less intense.

"I've been thinking about you," she murmurs against my jaw. "I tried not to, but I couldn't stop."

"Same," I admit, trailing kisses down her neck. "Every day."

Her hands find their way under my shirt, cool palms against the hot skin of my chest. I tug at the straps of her sundress, exposing her shoulders to my mouth. She arches into me, her body remembering mine.

"Last time," she says, her breath catching as I find a sensitive spot, "you said I could have anything I wanted."

"Still true," I reply, meaning it more than she knows.

She pulls back just enough to look at me, her eyes dark with desire but also something more searching. "I want you. Right here. Right now."

I don't need to be told twice. I lift her easily, turning so she's lying beneath me on the sofa, her curls spread across the leather. I kiss her deeply, thoroughly, my hand sliding up her thigh, beneath the hem of her dress.

"Wait," I say, reluctantly breaking away. "Protection."

She nods, her chest rising and falling rapidly.

I reach under the coffee table to the basket full of Thin Ice and some other goodies.

Sloane raises an eyebrow when she sees the branded packaging. "Prepared, aren't you?"

I grin. "This is the Safe and Satisfied basket," I explain. "Even before I was Mr. Thin Ice, my parents were really aggressive about this stuff." I wave my hand at the supplies, and Sloane peeks inside. "It used to be weird that my dad would bring lube when he came to visit."

She arches a brow, and I laugh. "Maybe it's still weird."

Sloane reaches into the pile and pulls out an ultra-thin condom, shaking it at me. I take it from her and watch as she settles back on the couch, spreading her legs and lifting her skirt.

I trail a palm up her beautiful leg and forget every joke I wanted to make.

"I believe you promised to show me your socks," she says. And then her laugh turns into a gasp as my fingers find her center.

"Next time," I promise, focusing on the way her body responds to my touch. I pull aside her panties and inhale the wet scent of her arousal.

What follows is a blur of sensation—her dress pushed up, my jeans discarded, our bodies finding that perfect rhythm we discovered at the ski house. She's responsive, uninhibited, meeting me movement for movement. The glass windows reflect our entwined forms, the city lights creating a backdrop of glittering stars.

I take my time, determined to make this even better than our first night together. If this is my last taste, I'm going to savor it. When I roll the condom on and slide inside her, it really feels like coming home. I should be terrified, but the experience electrifies me. Her nails dig into my shoulders, her breathing harsh against my ear as she tightens around me, repeating my name on ragged breaths. I follow her over the edge, her name on my lips like a prayer.

Afterward, we lie tangled together on the sofa, her head on my chest, my fingers tracing patterns on her bare skin. I feel oddly content, more satisfied than I can remember being in a long time, and it's not just the physical release.

"You okay?" I ask, pressing a kiss to the top of her head.

She nods, her curls tickling my chin. "More than okay."

I tilt her face up to mine, struck by the realization that I want more of this—more of her—and not just in my bed. I want to know her stories, her dreams, her fears. I want to be the one she calls when she's having a bad day. I want to see her smile, hear her laugh, hold her when she cries.

It's too much, too soon, and yet it feels like the most natural thing in the world.

I brush my thumb across her cheekbone, marveling at the softness of her skin, the warmth in her eyes.

"Will you stay, Sloane?" The question comes out rough with an emotion I'm not ready to name.

Her eyes meet mine, and her face shifts, and I know what she's going to say. I feel the crushing weight of her words before she even opens her mouth.

"WILL YOU STAY, SLOANE? PLEASE?"

Tucker's question hangs in the air between us, heavy with an emotion I'm not ready to face. His thumb traces my cheekbone, blue eyes searching mine with unexpected vulnerability.

Reality crashes back. What am I doing? I sit up abruptly, pulling away from his warmth. Tucker's arms fall to his sides, his face already registering the shift in my mood.

"I can't." I look around his apartment with suddenly clear eyes. The place screams single guy with no responsibilities—gaming consoles stacked beneath that massive television, designer furniture that looks barely used, a kitchen with gleaming appliances that probably never see action beyond protein shakes. "I have class in the morning."

I stand, straightening my sundress and searching for my underwear. I spot them on the floor by the coffee table, the delicate fabric torn at the seam from Tucker's eager hands. Great. I grab them anyway and step into them, feeling his eyes on me the entire time.

"You don't have to go," he says, sitting up. He's still naked, his hair mussed from my fingers, looking impossibly gorgeous and entirely too dangerous for my fragile new beginning. "If you stay, we could have breakfast. I make a mean scrambled egg."

I shake my head, collecting my purse from where I'd dropped

it. "This was fun, but I really need to focus on school right now. I can't... I can't do this again."

His face falls, the disappointment unmasked. "Can I call you?"

"I don't think that's a good idea." I'm being cruel, and I know it, but a clean break now is better than messier pain later. Nothing good can come of this. "I'm just starting to rebuild my life, and getting involved with *anyone* right now would be a mistake."

"It wouldn't have to be complicated," he argues, standing now, pulling on his jeans. "We could take it slow."

I almost laugh at that. There's nothing slow about how we combusted together, twice now. Nothing measured or careful about the way my body responds to his.

That's the problem.

"I had a really good time," I say, softening my tone. "You're an incredible lover. But I need to focus on me right now. On school, on figuring out what I want."

"And I'm not what you want." It's not quite a question.

I don't answer directly. "I want my degree. I want to build a career. I want stability."

His eyes flick around his ostentatious apartment, and I can tell he sees it differently now, through my eyes. "Right. And this doesn't fit that goal."

"It's not about your place, Tucker. It's about… I just... can't."

He nods, disappointment evident but accepting. "At least let me walk you down."

"No need." I'm already at the elevator, pressing the button. "Thank you for returning my necklace."

My fingers go to the pendant at my throat, and for a moment, I'm tempted to stay. To return to the warmth of his arms, the safety I felt there. But that's the trap, isn't it? Feeling safe with a man, only to discover you've lost yourself in his world.

The elevator arrives with a soft chime. Tucker stands in the middle of his living room, looking suddenly small against the dramatic city view behind him. As the doors close between us, I see him open his mouth as if to say something more, but it's too late.

Alone in the elevator, I catch my reflection in the mirrored wall. My hair is a riot of curls, my lips still swollen from his kisses, the necklace gleaming at my throat. I look well-fucked and slightly wild.

I also look like a woman about to make the same mistake twice.

"Not this time," I whisper to my reflection. "This time, you choose you."

I think of the years I spent orbiting Josh's life like a moon, reflecting his light, defined by his career. How I'd shrunk myself to fit into the spaces he left for me, until one day I realized there was almost nothing left of the woman I'd been before.

Dr. Rivera, my therapist during the divorce, had made me promise: no serious relationships for at least a year. "You need to remember who you are first," she'd said. "What you want, separate from anyone else's expectations."

I was doing well—getting back into school, building a friendship with Mel, finding my footing. I can't risk that progress, not even for the intoxicating connection I feel with Tucker. Especially not for that. The stronger the pull, the greater the danger.

As I step out into the night air, I take a deep breath. I made the right choice. I know I did.

So why does it feel so much like loss?

———

"He said what?" Mel's eyes widen over her pint of mint chocolate chip ice cream. We're sitting on our small balcony, the city lights twinkling around us. I'd barely made it through the door before she pounced with questions.

"He asked me to stay," I repeat, digging into my own container of cookie dough. "Like, for the night."

"And you said no." It's not a question. She knows me too well.

"Of course, I said no. He works with Josh."

Mel gives me a look. "And that's the only reason?"

I sigh, setting down my spoon. "There's no universe where

this works out. I can't get involved with anyone right now, especially not someone like him."

"Someone like him," she echoes. "You mean gorgeous, clearly into you, and good in bed?"

"Also a fighting brute, party boy with countless women tossing underpants at him." I gesture vaguely in the direction of downtown, where Tucker's penthouse kisses the skyline. "The fancy apartment, the expensive everything, the...superficiality of it all."

Mel studies me for a moment. "Is that really what bothers you? Or are you scared that you might actually like him?"

"I'm not scared," I protest automatically. "I'm being smart. I spent years of my life being Josh Grentley's wife, and you know what I got out of it? A huge betrayal, a pile of divorce papers, and the need for therapy."

"Tucker isn't Josh," she points out gently.

"No, but he's cut from the same cloth." I stab at my ice cream. "I need to focus on my future."

Mel nods, accepting this. "Fair enough. For what it's worth, though, I'm having constant flashbacks to how that man looked at you."

I ignore the flutter in my chest at her words. "Ice cream's melting," I say instead, and she lets me change the subject.

———

The entire week passes in a blur of classes, study sessions, and determined efforts to forget Tucker Stag. I throw myself into schoolwork with renewed vigor, as if acing statistics could somehow erase the memory of his hands on my skin, his voice in my ear.

It almost works. By Saturday, I can go several hours without thinking of him. Progress.

I spread my notes across the kitchen table, highlighters lined up like soldiers ready for battle. The statistics exam on Monday looms large, and despite Mel's patient tutoring, I'm still struggling with confidence intervals and hypothesis testing.

"You can do this," I mutter to myself, flipping through my

textbook. "You used to be good at school. You can be good at it again."

My phone buzzes with a notification, a welcome distraction from the sea of numbers. I unlock it to find a news alert.

FURY GOALTENDER GRENTLEY GRINS AND BARES ALL AT TEAMMATE'S WEDDING

My first instinct is to ignore it. Josh's life isn't my concern anymore. But curiosity—that terrible, persistent human flaw—gets the better of me, and I tap the link.

The article is a fluffy buzz piece. A casual backyard wedding with Gunnar Stag—Josh's nemesis, turned goalie partner. The caption refers to an "intimate ceremony with family and teammates."

Family indeed. There's Tucker and his brothers. Their father —I remember him from the photos in Tucker's apartment. God, I should not know any of this.

I scroll through the images, telling myself I'm just procrastinating on statistics. There's Josh, and the sight of him is less painful than I expected. He's dressed casually in khakis and a blue button-down, actually smiling in a way I rarely saw during our marriage. He looks lighter somehow, more at ease than I remember. But he's still separated from the group, isolating himself even here.

I continue scrolling, past photos of the happy couple, of teammates I vaguely recognize. If things had been different, I would have been there, too.

My brain stutters, snagging on what might have been. Would I have been pregnant by now if Josh hadn't unilaterally stolen that option from us? The room lurches, images flashing through my mind. Tucker above me on his couch, saying all the right things.

Tucker behind me at the ski house, making me feel incredible.

Tucker's hands—rough-textured but so, so gentle.

But then, I see Josh screaming at me in our kitchen, me ripping up documents as I scream right back.

"No," I whisper, scrolling frantically through more photos. There's another—Josh shaking hands with Tucker, both tight-lipped. My ex-husband and the man I've been sleeping with, together in the same frame. I notice that Tucker seems tense, and I hate that I'm able to observe that. I can't be thinking about Tucker at all, let alone reading his moods.

I tried to disconnect from the hockey world during our separation and divorce, precisely because of this kind of thing. Dr. Rivera had encouraged it—a clean break from the environment that had consumed me. I became so resentful, so angry that I allowed myself to be absorbed by that world so profoundly, I lost touch with every friend I'd made. And forget about ties to the Black community in that white world of hockey and hockey fans.

The second I left my marriage, I unsubscribed from Partners and Wives group chats, unfollowed social media accounts, donated or destroyed every piece of Fury merchandise I owned.

Yet I can't seem to quit these news alerts. Even now, my finger hesitates above the checkbox to unsubscribe.

Reading more of the article, I see that Tucker and his brothers joined the team right when Josh and I separated. I had already stopped attending games by then, stopped paying attention to roster changes or team news. I'd been so focused on surviving the shocking news that my husband lied to me, on reclaiming my identity, that I'd effectively erased hockey from my consciousness.

But that doesn't change who Tucker is. Where he works. The fact that he is off limits. It felt delicious at the party.

It feels destructive now.

I nod, determined, and block Tucker's number with shaking fingers. Then I turn back to my statistics textbook, focusing on the one thing I can control—my future.

"Haven't you had enough to drink?" Josh Grentley stands by the galvanized metal tub full of Iron City beer, arms crossed, as if he's been assigned to guard the contents.

"Are you fucking serious right now? This is my brother's wedding." I shove him aside and reach for one of the bottles. I wasn't even planning to have another one until this asshole decided to insert himself.

I was aiming for the cucumber water since I'm already drunker than I wanted to be, sweating in my dress shirt and loose tie.

I twist off the cap and flick it right at Grentley, laughing into the neck of the bottle when the cap bounces off his shoulder and hits the deck with a clink. He scrunches up his face, nostrils flaring.

"You going to do something about it? Here?" I gesture around the sea of Stags and all the rest of our teammates.

He stares at me for long enough that I worry I missed him saying something, but then he stoops, picks up the cap, and slides it into his pocket. "We were both in the team meeting, Stag. It takes sacrifice and discipline to be a champion."

I want to pour my beer on his shoes, maybe pee on his pants while I'm at it. But my mother is here, and I have just enough dignity left to walk away.

"I thought so," he says, when I turn toward the party.

Oh, fuck this guy sideways. I drop the beer and grab his shirt. "You think I don't know how to win, asshole? I already beat you, and you didn't even know there was a prize."

"You're drunk, Tucker." He wrests his shirt from my grasp and runs his hands down his chest while I look around, not sure what to do with the rage throbbing beneath my skin.

A knock on the deck railing behind me makes me jump.

"Tuck? You good?" Alder's voice carries concern. I relax all the way down to my cells and drape an arm around his shoulders. My twin takes one look at my face, and his expression shifts from concerned to alarmed.

"What happened?"

"Nothing. Just—" I run a hand through my hair, making it stand up even more. "I need to get some air."

Grentley shoves past us, striding toward the grass, where he stands facing the river with his hands shoved in his pockets. I move to follow.

"Tucker." Alder blocks my path, using the same immovable presence that makes him an elite defenseman. "What's going on?"

I glance around the party. This isn't the place for this conversation.

"Not here," I say.

He studies me for a long moment, then nods. "Let's walk."

Gunny and Emerson got married in the backyard of their apartment building, right along the Allegheny River. Alder leads me along the gravel path away from the extended Stag family. String lights twinkle overhead, and the setting sun casts everything in gold. But I feel like I'm wearing lead shoes.

"Talk," he says, sitting down on a bench and fixing me with that twin-telepathy stare that says he already knows this is serious.

I stand and stare at the river, thinking about Grentley's stupid face, about Sloane coming around my cock. The water makes me remember the pool, talking to Sloane in the sunshine, thinking I found myself an actual, living goddess.

I can't tell my brother about any of this. And I know he's hiding shit from me, too.

Why the hell did Sloane have to be married to Grentley of all people?

My goalie. The guy on my team who treats everyone like they're gum on his shoe. The guy who's been extra hostile toward me all season, though I'd chalked that up to his general asshole demeanor.

I hooked up with my teammate's ex-wife. Twice.

And I knew it was a terrible idea. And I did it anyway.

And, god, if given the chance, I'd do it again.

"I know you're banging the dentist," I say, rather than air my own hockey gloves.

He kicks me. "Knock it off. Don't talk about her that way."

I kick him back. "Don't pretend like you're not. Not with me."

Alder sighs and stares up at the lamp above the bench. "I asked you what's bothering *you*, man. Come on. You don't pick fights at family functions."

I drop beside him and hang my head in my hands. "I met someone."

"Hey!" His voice brightens, like I'm sharing exciting news or something. "I thought so. You've been—"

"It's Grentley's ex."

Alder blinks at me, then emits a low whistle. "So the incredible woman from Stellan's party—"

"I never told you shit, man. Did Stelly blab?"

Alder nods slowly. "Obviously."

"I know how it looks." I lean forward, elbows on my knees. "But I swear, Alder. We have a connection. I know it's wrong."

Then again, is it really so bad?

Grentley never talks about his personal life. Ever. The guy's a vault, showing up to practice, doing his job, and leaving. I'd heard rumors about a divorce—locker room gossip travels fast—but I'd never heard a name, never seen a photo. It's not like he ever brought his wife to team parties or showed up to the parties himself.

I think about Sloane in the pool at the ski house, the way she looked at me like I was someone worth knowing. The feel of her in my arms, the sound of her laugh, the way she challenged me and pushed back and met me exactly where I was.

Alder sighs, leaning back against the bench. "You're in deep."

"I'm not—" But I stop because he's right. Two nights together and I can't stop thinking about her. Can't stop wanting to know more, to see her smile, to hear her voice saying my name.

"She left," I say quietly. "I asked her to stay, like a sap, and she left."

"Can you blame her? Her divorce is really public. Now here you are, connected to the part of her life she's trying to escape."

The truth of that hits hard. Sloane told me about dropping out of school, about rebuilding her life. She's trying to move forward, and I'm a direct link back to everything she's running from.

"What do I do?" The question comes out more desperate than I intended.

Alder is quiet for a moment, watching the string lights sway gently in the evening breeze. "I wish I knew, brother."

I rest my head on his shoulder, savoring the stillness and unwavering acceptance from the person I've known since conception. "You going to tell me about your love life?"

"Absolutely not," he grunts, resting his head on top of mine. One problem at a time, I guess.

———

We head back up to the deck, where the reception is in full swing. Gunnar and his wife are cutting the cake while the crowd cheers. My parents are laughing with my uncles at a corner table. Odin has somehow convinced one of the bridesmaids to teach him a complicated dance move.

It's all so normal, so happy. And I feel like I'm watching it through glass.

Alder and Lena sneak away like they're about to bump uglies.

I catch sight of Grentley across the yard, talking with one of the forwards. He looks relaxed, almost human, in a way I've never seen him at practice. For a brief, irrational moment, I consider walking over there and demanding to know every detail of his marriage to Sloane. What did he do to make her leave? Why is she so determined to avoid anything connected to hockey?

But Alder's right. That road leads to ruin.

Instead, I grab another beer and find a quiet corner, pulling out my phone to text the last woman I ought to contact.

> I wish we'd met under different circumstances

> I meant what I said at my apartment. You're the most interesting woman I've met in a long time. That hasn't changed.

> I'm not giving up on this. On us. Whatever this is.

———

I hit send on each message, watching them deliver into the void.

"Talking to yourself?" Howie appears at my elbow, drink in hand. "That's a bad sign, man."

"Just checking scores," I lie, pocketing my phone.

"In the summer? What scores?"

"Baseball," I recall that Sloane's grandma liked the Detroit Tigers.

He squints at me suspiciously. "Since when do you care about baseball?"

"Since now. Leave me alone."

Howie laughs and wanders off to harass Spinner, and I stay back, trying to focus on being present for Gunnar's big day.

———

Two weeks crawl by like I'm moving through mud. I start going to the Fury facility daily, using the gym, skating on my own, anything to burn off the restless energy that's been eating me alive since Gunnar's wedding.

I've sent Sloane countless text messages. Drafted a thousand more.

I considered showing up at the café where I'd seen her, but that felt too much like stalking.

Why can't I stop obsessing over a woman I cannot pursue?

Since when do I fucking pursue a woman at all?

I'm in the middle of a punishing workout—my fifth this week, and it's only Wednesday—when my phone buzzes with a text from my uncle Tim.

> Need you to stop by the office this afternoon.
> Contract stuff.

I grin despite my mood. Uncle Tim has been handling legal negotiations for various Stag family members since before I was born. He's brilliant, rigid, and one of my favorite people.

And this will definitely be something to do that takes my mind off the woman who might drive me to destroy my own career.

CHAPTER 11
TUCKER

STAG LAW OCCUPIES THE TOP THREE FLOORS OF A GLEAMING building in downtown Pittsburgh. It's got kick-ass views of Point State Park and, in the winter, the ice rink and giant tree. We have spent a lot of time here as a family over the years.

Parking sucks in the garage, so I pull up near the elevator and leave the blinkers on. I'll just be in there a few minutes, and Uncle Tim gets pissy if I'm late.

I take the elevator to the twenty-third floor, where Uncle Tim's assistant, Donna, has reigned for longer than I've been alive. She still treats all of us nephews like we're still toddlers in diapers.

"Tucker Stag," she says, looking me over with approval. "You seem to have documents with you. I'm impressed."

"Don't get used to it." I wave a folder around. "I'll probably forget this here when I leave."

She smiles and nods toward Tim's office. "He's expecting you. Go on in."

Uncle Tim's office is a strange blend of sterile minimalism and family photos. He's on the phone when I enter, but he waves me toward a chair.

"No, that's not acceptable," he's saying into his headset, typing rapidly on his computer. "My client isn't interested in incentive-based compensation at those rates. We need guarantees." A pause. "Then we'll take our business elsewhere. Get back to me with a real offer." He ends the call and focuses on me. "Tucker. Thanks for coming in."

"What's this about? The endorsement deals? Because if Thin Ice wants me to do another photoshoot, I'm going to need hazard pay—"

"Not the condoms." He slides a folder across his desk. "Your contract extension. The Fury's ready to talk terms for next season, and I want to make sure we're on the same page before negotiations start. Brian has already seen these."

I nod, figuring my agent and my uncle probably spent hours together hashing out details. I flip open the folder, scanning the preliminary numbers. They're offering a two-year extension with a modest raise—not star money, but solid enforcer rates.

"Looks good," I say, though I'm only half-focused. My mind is still on Sloane, on finding a way to talk to her.

"Tucker." Uncle Tim's voice sharpens. "Are you actually reading this, or are you just pretending?"

I force myself to concentrate on the contract terms. Tim walks me through the key points—salary structure, performance bonuses, injury clauses. It's important, I know it's important, but my attention keeps drifting.

"All right, what's going on?" Tim finally asks, leaning back in his chair. "You've been distracted since you walked in."

"Nothing. Just off-season stuff."

He gives me a look that says he doesn't believe me for a second. "Woman trouble?"

I don't answer, which is answer enough.

"Want to talk about it?"

"Not really."

"Fair enough." He taps the folder. "Then let's wrap this up so you can go brood somewhere else."

A knock interrupts him. Donna pokes her head in.

"Tim, your three-thirty is here early."

"Send them to the small conference room. I'll be there in five."

"Actually," Donna says, "they requested to use the large room for accessibility. I thought you'd want to know."

"Of course. Give me five minutes."

Donna disappears, and Tim stands, gathering files. "Sorry,

Tucker. This is a big meeting—potential new superstar hire. Do you feel satisfied?"

"Yeah, no problem." I'm already standing, grateful for the escape from my own distraction.

I follow Tim out of his office and toward the elevator. The main reception area has floor-to-ceiling windows overlooking the city, and I'm admiring the view when I hear voices from the side hallway.

"...really appreciate you taking the time to meet with me, Mr. Stag."

That voice is familiar.

I turn just as Mel Ortega wheels into view, dressed in a sharp business suit, her resume folder balanced on her lap. She looks flustered and out of breath.

And right behind her, holding a briefcase and looking outraged, is Sloane.

Our eyes meet across the reception area.

She freezes. I freeze.

Uncle Tim, oblivious to the sudden tension, extends a hand toward Mel. "Ms. Ortega, wonderful to meet you in person. I've heard excellent things from Stellan."

Mel shakes his hand, but her attention is on me. Recognition flickers across her face—she knows exactly who I am from that awkward encounter at the café.

"This is my friend Sloane," Mel says carefully. "She offered to drive me since parking can be tricky."

"And since someone parked their car directly over the curb cut," Sloane adds, her voice tight with barely controlled anger. "We had to go around to the loading dock entrance. Which, by the way, required going through the service elevator."

Tim's expression shifts to concern. "I apologize. That's completely unacceptable. Donna, can you—"

"It's a McLaren blocking the accessible entrance," Sloane continues, her eyes finding mine for the first time. The accusation in them is unmistakable. "A silver McLaren."

My stomach drops. My car. I'd been in such a rush to get inside, distracted by thoughts of Sloane, that I hadn't stopped to consider the impact of parking in a non-spot.

"That's mine," I hear myself say. "I didn't realize—"

"Of course you didn't." Sloane's voice could cut glass. "Why would you notice something like accessibility when it doesn't affect you?"

Tim's expression shifts from concern to clear disapproval as he looks at me. "Tucker. Move your car. Now."

"I will, I just—"

"Now," Tim repeats, his tone brooking no argument. He turns back to Mel with an apologetic smile. "Ms. Ortega, I'm deeply sorry about this. Let me assure you that Stag Law takes accessibility seriously, even if my nephew apparently doesn't."

The rebuke lands like a slap. Mel looks uncomfortable, clearly not wanting to be in the middle of this.

"It's fine," she says diplomatically. "These things happen."

"They shouldn't," Sloane says firmly. "Not at a law firm that claims to prioritize diversity and inclusion."

"You're absolutely right," Tim says. "Tucker—car. Now. Then we'll finish your contract discussion tomorrow when you've had time to think about how your actions affect others."

He's dismissing me. Uncle Tim, who's always had my back, who's negotiated every major deal in my career, is sending me away in front of Sloane like I'm a kid who got caught spray-painting the garage. And he's right to do it.

Who the fuck have I become?

"I'm sorry," I say, looking at Mel. "I wasn't thinking. I was distracted and I just—I'm sorry."

Mel nods, gracious despite everything. "Apology accepted."

But it's not Mel's acceptance I'm desperate for. I turn to Sloane, who's watching me with an expression I can't quite read —anger, yes, but also something that might be vindication.

"Sloane—"

"Spare me," she says flatly.

Tim is already guiding Mel toward the conference room, and Sloane moves to follow them, but I step into her path.

"Please. Just five minutes after I move the car."

"So, you can explain how you're actually a really considerate person who just happened to block a wheelchair accessible entrance?" Her voice drips with sarcasm. "Or were you going to explain how you don't actually think before you act?"

The accusation stings more because there's truth in it. I didn't think. I was so wrapped up in my own problems, my own desire to figure out how to reach her, that I didn't consider how my parking might affect someone else.

I sent her unreturned messages after she left me with a very clear message.

She thinks everything about Tucker Stag is bad news. And I keep proving her theory.

"You're right," I say. "I fucked up. I should have paid attention. I'm sorry."

"Great. Apology noted. Now move your car."

She tries to step around me, but I shift slightly, not blocking her but making her acknowledge me.

"I really want to talk to you," I say quietly, aware that Donna is absolutely listening to every word of this. "I know how it looks, but I swear to you, I just want to talk."

Something flickers in her eyes—doubt, maybe, or the beginning of belief. But then her expression hardens again.

"It doesn't matter."

"How can it not matter?"

"Because it doesn't change anything." She adjusts her grip on Mel's briefcase. "I'm trying to build a life that has nothing to do with hockey or the Fury or any of that world. And here you are, parking like you own the place, proving exactly why I need to stay away from people like you."

"People like me?"

"People who don't think about consequences. People who take up space without considering who they're taking it from." Her voice drops. "People who are so used to getting what they want that they don't notice when they're making life harder for everyone else."

The words hit harder than any check I've taken on the ice. Because she's not entirely wrong. I parked in that spot without thinking. I've spent weeks trying to contact her without fully considering why she might need space. I've been so focused on what I want—a chance to explain, a chance with her—that I haven't stopped to think about what she needs.

"You're right," I say again. "I've been careless. I'm sorry."

She blinks, clearly not expecting the admission.

"But I'm not sorry for wanting to explain," I continue. "I'm not sorry for wanting a chance with you. I know I don't deserve it right now, but—"

"Sloane?" Mel's voice carries from down the hallway. "You coming?"

Sloane walks past me before I can respond, her footsteps echoing in the reception area.

I stand there for a moment, watching her go, Donna's pointed stare drilling into the side of my head.

In the parking garage, I can see my shitty park job the way others must see it: some pompous, self-centered jerk who just takes what he needs and doesn't think about how his actions impact anyone else. The worst part? This is not the first time I've parked like a jagoff. I honestly never considered the consequences before.

Of course, Sloane told me to fuck off. I'm not someone who deserves a second chance.

Not yet, anyway.

I think about Grentley's admonishment, how I'm drinking away my opportunity to be a leader on this team. When did I become this fuckup, pretentious asshole?

I pull out of the garage without a plan, but with clarity.

I need to become someone worth believing in.

Even if Sloane never gives me another chance, I need to do this. For me.

CHAPTER 12
SLOANE

I settle into a chair in the hall to wait for Mel during her interview, my body trembling slightly with residual anger over my encounter with Tucker Stag.

"Again, my deepest apologies," Tim says, his professional warmth restored now that Tucker has been dismissed. "That sort of thoughtlessness is unacceptable, especially from a family member that should know better."

"It's really okay," Mel says, though we both know it's not. "I appreciate your response."

I open my mouth to add something—probably something less diplomatic—but Mel shoots me a look that clearly says let it go. This is her interview. Her future. I'm just the angry friend who needs to shut up and wait.

Tim shuts the door to the conference room, and I'm alone in the inner office where the admin sits at her desk, eyeing me with curiosity.

"That was quite the scene," she observes as I sink into one of the leather chairs. Her nameplate reads Donna.

"Your boss's nephew parked over a wheelchair accessible entrance."

"I noticed." Donna's tone is dry. "I also noticed you tore into him pretty thoroughly. Good for you."

I don't know what to say to that, so I pull out my tablet, determined to use this time productively. Statistics. Exam on Monday. Focus.

But the numbers blur before my eyes as my mind replays the confrontation. Tucker's face when he realized what he'd done. The genuine shame in his apology. The way he'd said I was right without making excuses.

Josh never said I was right. Not once in five years.

Stop comparing them, I tell myself firmly. *Stop looking for reasons to forgive him.*

My stomach churns—that same unsettled feeling I've been fighting all week. I shift in the chair, trying to find a comfortable position, and catch a whiff of something from the break room. Coffee, maybe. The smell hits me wrong, making bile rise in my throat.

"Restroom?" I ask Donna, my voice tight.

She points down a hallway. "Second door on the left."

I make it just in time, my breakfast making an unwelcome reappearance. When the wave passes, I lean against the cool tile wall, breathing carefully through my nose.

Stress. Has to be stress. Between school, Tucker, and this whole debacle, no wonder I lost my muffins.

I rinse my mouth and splash water on my face, avoiding my reflection. When I finally look up, I barely recognize myself. Dark circles under my eyes. Hair escaping from its ponytail. I look exhausted and unwell, and exactly how I felt during the worst parts of my marriage.

You're not there anymore, I remind myself. *You're rebuilding. You're in school. You're moving forward.*

Even if forward apparently means running into my two-night stand at every turn.

When I return to the reception area, Donna is waiting with a bottle of water and a small pack of crackers.

"You look pale," she says, her tone softer than before. "Figured you might need these."

The unexpected kindness makes my throat tight. "Thank you."

"For what it's worth," Donna continues, her voice low enough that it won't carry, "I've worked for Tim Stag for almost thirty years. I've watched Tucker grow up. That boy can be thoughtless —too used to everything coming easy. But he's not cruel. When he realizes he's messed up, he tries to fix it."

I don't know how to respond to that, so I just nod and open the crackers. The bland taste settles my stomach slightly.

Tries to fix it... Donna's words dislodge a memory of my ex-husband, and his face when I confronted him with the paperwork I'd found after his secret vasectomy.

Josh had been in the kitchen portioning out meals—identical containers of bland chicken, broccoli, and brown rice. I had been digging in a drawer looking for insurance cards when I saw the benefits statement. I asked him what it meant, and he shrugged, not looking up from his containers. "You know my background," he said to me. "I fixed it."

Not angry. Not defensive. Certainly not a man who was open and honest with his wife.

My husband was supposedly a "good man" who overcame a rough start in life. So Donna referring to Tucker as a "good man" does nothing to soften my response.

"We barely know each other," I say, not sure why I'm continuing this conversation with a stranger.

Donna gives me a look that says she doesn't believe that for a second, then returns to her desk, leaving me alone with my thoughts and my statistics notes.

Mel rolls out of the conference room looking like she might explode with whatever news she got in there. We make it to the elevator before she squeals and claps her hands.

"He basically offered me the job!" she says the moment the doors slide shut. "Pending my passing the bar, but he said everything looked excellent and he'd love to have me join the team."

"That's amazing, Mel!" I force enthusiasm into my voice, genuinely happy for her despite the emotional exhaustion dragging at me. "You deserve it."

"I know!" She laughs, bright and unrestrained. "God, I can't believe it. Stag Law. Do you know how many doors this opens?"

I do. I've spent enough time helping her prep to know Stag Law represents some of the biggest names in professional athletics. Including a hockey team I wish I could ignore.

"When do you start?"

"After the bar exam. Probably early August." Her excitement dims slightly. "Which means I'll need to move out sooner than we planned. The firm has connections to accessible housing, and I want to get settled before I start."

My stomach sinks. I'd known this was coming, but hearing it confirmed makes it real. I'll be alone again, trying to figure out how to build a life that doesn't feel like I'm just treading water. Trying to forget a man who was supposed to scratch an itch and has now bored into my psyche.

"That's great," I manage. "You should definitely take advantage of their resources."

"I'm sorry to leave you with the apartment situation," Mel says, her practical brain already problem-solving. "I can help you find a new roommate, or—"

"Don't worry about it. I'll figure something out." I start the car, needing to move, to do something. "Maybe I'll finally use some of the settlement money. Get my own place."

"You should," Mel says firmly. "That money is yours, Sloane. Legally, ethically, completely yours. Using it doesn't mean anything except that you're taking care of yourself."

I know she's right. Dr. Rivera said the same thing in therapy. But every time I think about spending Josh's money, I feel sick. Like I'm accepting payment for five wasted years.

We get situated in the car and drive in silence for a while. My stomach still feels unsettled, and I crack the window, hoping fresh air will help.

"So," Mel says eventually, "are we going to talk about Tucker?"

"No."

"He looked genuinely sorry about the parking."

"He should be sorry. He blocked a wheelchair accessible entrance."

"And then apologized immediately and moved his car."

"After being called out by his uncle."

"True." Mel fiddles with her phone. "But Sloane...the way he *looks* at you."

"Come on, Mel. We can't make life decisions based on people's facial expressions." I focus on the road, careful in the traffic as we head back to our shitty apartment. She's going to leave.

"From what you've shared, he has some pretty good actions, too..."

"It doesn't matter," I insist, but the words feel hollow now. "He's still Josh's teammate. Still part of that world."

"Is it the world you're avoiding? Or the person you became in that world?"

The question stings, because Mel knows me. Knows what my marriage did to me.

"I don't want to talk about this," I say as we pull into our apartment complex.

"Okay." Mel lets it drop, but as we head inside, she adds quietly, "Just think about whether you're avoiding Tucker because of who he actually is, or because of what he represents. There's a difference."

———

That evening, I try to study. I really do. But the statistics formulas blur together, and my mind keeps circling back to the same thoughts:

Tucker's face when he realized what he'd done.

Flashes of fights with Josh.

Visions of Tucker fighting with Josh.

My phone buzzes. I grab it reflexively, half-expecting a text from one of the men I'm obsessing over, but it's just a notification about office hours for my upcoming stat exam.

The thing I should be focused on instead of obsessing over Tucker Stag and his thoughtless parking and his apparent inability to stop thinking about me.

I force myself to return to my notes, but the nausea is back, worse now. I set down my highlighter and press my hands against my stomach, breathing carefully.

This isn't everyday stress. This is something else.

I pull out my phone and open my calendar app, scrolling back through the weeks. When was my last period?

My hand stills as I count backward. Six weeks. Maybe seven.

No. That's not possible. Tucker used condoms. Multiple condoms. Those Thin Ice prototypes he was so proud of.

But condoms aren't foolproof. Nothing is foolproof.

My heart pounds as I do the math again. The party hookup was mid-June. It's now mid-July.

You're being paranoid, I tell myself. *Stress can delay periods. You've barely been eating. You're sleeping terribly. Of course your body is off.*

But the nausea. The sensitivity to smells. The exhaustion that won't quit, no matter how much I sleep…

I should take a test. Just to rule it out. Just to stop this spiraling panic.

But if I take a test and it's positive…

I can't think about that. Can't let myself go there.

Instead, I close my textbook and my laptop, admitting defeat for the night. I'll go to office hours on Friday. I'll ace the exam on Monday. I'll figure out the apartment situation when Mel moves out.

And I'll take a pregnancy test tomorrow, just to confirm that stress is stress and nothing more.

Because the alternative—being pregnant with Tucker Stag's baby after telling him to leave me alone, after blocking his number, after making it abundantly clear that I want nothing to do with him or his hockey world—is too complicated to even contemplate.

I curl up on my bed, my grandmother's necklace warm against my throat, and try not to think about Tucker's hands fastening the clasp, his voice telling me how beautiful I am.

I close my eyes and try to manifest sleep…maybe until after the exam on Monday…maybe until I figure out what to do next. Above all, I pray I have food poisoning instead of a very serious complication involving Tucker Stag.

THE PUCK HITS THE BOARDS WITH A CRACK THAT ECHOES THROUGH the empty Fury facility. I chase it down, my legs burning, lungs screaming for air. I've been skating for two hours straight—sprints, drills, shooting practice—anything to burn off the self-loathing that's been eating me alive since yesterday.

I wind up for another slap shot, channeling every ounce of frustration into the movement. The puck sails wide, missing the net entirely, and clanging off the glass.

"Fuck!" I slam my stick against the ice.

"Easy there, Stag." Mayhem's voice carries across the rink. "That's your third stick this week."

I turn to find him leaning against the boards with Howie and Spinner, all three in workout gear. They must have come in for an optional session.

"What are you guys doing here?" I ask, not bothering to hide my irritation.

"Could ask you the same thing," Howie says, skating onto the ice. "It's July. Training camp doesn't start for another month."

"Just getting some work in."

"Looks more like you're punishing yourself," Spinner observes, gliding past me to retrieve the puck I missed. "What's got you so twisted up?"

I don't answer, lining up another shot. This one finds the net, but there's no satisfaction in it.

"Speaking of twisted up." Mayhem pulls out his phone. "You guys see what resurfaced on Insta?"

Howie and Spinner crowd around him, and I watch their expressions shift from curious to amused to outright gleeful.

"No way," Spinner cackles. "Is that from the Monaco trip?"

"Nah, man, this is older. Look at Tuck's hair—that's at least two years ago."

My stomach drops. "What are you talking about?"

Mayhem skates over, holding out his phone. "Someone dug up your greatest hits, bro. It's making the rounds on socials."

I take the phone, and my own face stares back at me from the screen. It's a carousel of photos—me at various clubs and parties over the past few years. In one, I'm surrounded by women in barely-there dresses, a bottle of champagne in my hand, and a cocky grin on my face. In another, I'm doing shots off someone's stomach. A third shows me stumbling out of a bar with a different woman under each arm.

The caption reads: "Hockey bad boy Tucker Stag living his best life. #PartyAnimal #LivingTheDream #StagNation"

"Classic T-Stag," Howie says, laughing. "You were a legend, man."

"Were?" I hand the phone back, feeling sick.

"Well, you've been pretty tame lately," Spinner points out. "No puck bunnies, barely going out. We figured you were finally growing up or something."

"Or he's got a girl," Howie suggests, waggling his eyebrows. "That's usually what tames the wild ones."

"I don't have a *girl*," I say, but even as the words leave my mouth, Sloane's face flashes in my mind. Her green eyes, hard with anger and disappointment. *People who don't think about consequences. People who take up space without considering who they're taking it from.*

"Then what's your problem?" Mayhem asks, his tone more serious now. "Because you've been off for weeks, man."

I stare at those photos on his phone, at the guy I was. The guy who thought being "T-Stag the Party Animal" was something to be proud of. The guy who parked wherever he wanted because he never considered that someone might actually need that accessible entrance.

"That guy's a fucking asshole," I say quietly.

The three of them exchange glances.

"What?" Howie looks genuinely confused.

"That guy." I gesture at the phone. "He's a selfish asshole who only thinks about himself. Who treats women like accessories and thinks rules don't apply to him."

"Dude, those were just good times—" Spinner starts.

"No." I cut him off, the words coming faster now. "It wasn't good times. It was shallow bullshit. I was shallow bullshit. I still am."

Mayhem studies me with those thoughtful eyes that always see too much. "What happened?"

"I met someone," I admit. "Someone who made me realize what a fuckup I've become. And she was right." I trail off, not sure how to articulate all the ways I've let myself become exactly what Sloane accused me of being.

I tell them about yesterday—about being at Stag Law, parking carelessly, Mel and Sloane, the confrontation. I leave out the part about Sloane being Grentley's ex-wife.

By the time I finish, even Howie looks sobered.

"Shit," Spinner says. "That's rough."

I pick up another puck, turning it over in my gloved hand. "Someone couldn't get to their job interview because of me. Because I was too wrapped up in my own shit to pay attention."

"So pay attention now," Howie suggests. "If you don't like who you've been, be someone different."

"It's not that simple."

"Sure it is." Spinner shrugs. "You're Tucker Stag. If you decide to be better, you'll be better. You're annoyingly good at everything."

I want to tell them it's not a fast process. That I've spent years building this reputation, this identity. That "T-Stag the Enforcer" is who everyone expects me to be—my teammates, my sponsors, even my family to some extent. The wild one. The animal on and off the ice.

Sloane went for me because I looked like a fuck-boy. And I was. But I don't want to be anymore.

"I need to go," I say abruptly, skating toward the bench.

"We just got here," Howie protests.

"So stay. Skate. I'm done."

I'm already unlacing my skates, pulling off my gear with mechanical efficiency. My body is exhausted, but my mind won't stop racing. Those photos. Sloane's face. The way Tim had dismissed me like a child. The realization that I've become exactly the kind of person I never wanted to be.

———

The drive home feels longer than usual. I park carefully in the garage, dead center between the lines, checking twice to make sure I'm not blocking anything or anyone.

Small steps. Maybe that's all I can do. Small steps toward being less of an asshole.

I walk over to the elevator, my duffel bag heavy on my shoulder. I step into the entryway.

And freeze.

Sloane is leaning against the door.

She looks terrible. Her curly hair is pulled back messily, her face pale, dark circles under those green eyes that have haunted my dreams. She's wearing yoga pants and an oversized sweatshirt, and she looks smaller somehow, more fragile than I've ever seen her.

Our eyes meet, and something in her expression makes my chest tight.

"Tucker," she says, her voice rough like she's been crying. "We need to talk."

My heart pounds. I want to ask a thousand questions—how she got past building security, how long she's been waiting, what changed her mind about talking to me. But something in her face stops me.

This isn't about second chances or explanations.

This is something else. Something bigger.

"Okay," I say, keeping my voice steady despite the way my hands are shaking. "Let's talk."

———

I swipe my key fob to open the elevator and gesture for her to enter first. We ride up to the top floor in silence, and she walks past me into my apartment. She doesn't look around, doesn't seem to notice or care about the space. She just moves to the windows, staring out at the city with her arms wrapped around herself.

I set down my bag and wait. Every instinct is screaming at me to fill the silence, to apologize again, to plead my case. But I force myself to stay quiet. To give her the space to say whatever she came here to say.

Finally, she turns to face me.

"I'm pregnant," she says.

The words hit me like a Russian offense. For a moment, I can't breathe, can't think, can't process what she just said.

"What?"

"I'm pregnant," she repeats, and now I can see she's trembling. "With your baby. And before you say anything, I'm keeping it. I've already decided. But I also need you to know that you don't have to be involved. I have money. I can handle this on my own. I just—" Her voice cracks. "I thought you had a right to know."

Pregnant. Sloane is pregnant. With my baby.

Our baby.

I open my mouth to respond, but no words come out. My mind is racing—how, when, what does this mean, what do I do, what does she need—

"Say something," she whispers.

I cross the distance between us in three strides. "Are you okay? Are you healthy? Have you seen a doctor?"

She blinks, clearly not expecting those to be my first questions. "I... yes. I mean, I took a test this morning. I haven't seen a doctor yet, but I will. I'm fine."

"When? When will you see a doctor?"

"I don't know. I just found out today, Tucker. I came here

before I even—" She stops herself. "It doesn't matter. The point is, you know now. And I meant what I said. I don't expect anything from you."

"Don't expect—" I can't even finish the sentence. "Sloane, this is my baby, too."

"I know. But I also know you didn't sign up for this. We barely know each other. And I've already decided I'm keeping it, so if you don't want to be involved—"

"Stop." I reach for her hands before I can stop myself, and she lets me take them. "Just stop. I need a minute to process this, okay? But don't for one second think I don't want to be involved."

She searches my face, looking for something I hope she finds. "You aren't exactly father of the year material."

The comment throws me. I absolutely never thought about myself as a parent before right now, but something deep inside me recoils at the idea that I'd be bad at it. "What?"

"The two of us together are bad news. Look how this child was conceived. What kind of father would—" She stops, pulling her hands away and pressing them to her face. "I'm sorry. That's not fair. I'm just... I'm scared. And you're Josh's teammate, and I promised myself I wouldn't—"

"I'm not Grentley," I say firmly. "And yeah, I fucked up. I've been fucking up a lot lately. But Sloane, I swear to you, I will not fuck this up. I will be the father this baby deserves, even if that means becoming someone completely different than who I've been."

I'm a professional fucking athlete. I know how to work hard, and obviously, I have a tough road ahead of me. But this is my kid. Operation Be A Dad started yesterday, as far as I'm concerned.

She looks at me with those impossibly green eyes, tears streaming down her face now. "I cannot have additional complications, Tucker." She seems so, so angry and determined. "I have to focus everything I have on this baby and on starting my career. I can't lose myself again."

"You won't," I promise, even though I have no idea how to make sure that's true.

CHAPTER 14
SLOANE

I CAN'T STOP SHAKING.

Tucker is staring at me like I just told him hockey season is canceled, his mouth slightly open, those blue eyes wide with shock. We're standing in his ridiculously expensive apartment with its floor-to-ceiling windows and uncomfortable-looking furniture, and I just told him I'm pregnant.

With his baby.

I want to take it back. Not the pregnancy—that feels like the answer to a dream I never imagined could come true after my divorce. But I think I regret telling Tucker about it. I should have waited. Should have figured things out on my own first. Should have—

"Are you okay?" he asks again, and the question surprises me. Not *are you sure*, or *how did this happen*, or any of the dozen defensive reactions I'd braced myself for. Just a genuine concern about my well-being.

"I'm…fine," I manage.

He blows out a deep breath and squints. I stop myself from admitting I haven't told Mel yet, haven't made an appointment, haven't done any of the practical things I should be doing. But I know I want children, and this pregnancy seems like the answer to a lot of hurt I've experienced over the past decade. I just need to focus, study, create some stability. Telling Tucker about this was an item on a checklist, that's all.

"When will you see a doctor?" His voice is urgent, almost demanding.

"I don't know. Soon. I'll make an appointment."

"I'll come with you."

The automatic assumption makes my spine stiffen. "You don't have to do that."

"I want to." He takes a step closer, and I take a step back, maintaining the distance between us. He notices, stopping immediately.

"Tucker." I hold out my hands, palms up. "I think you're a young, professional hockey player whose life is exactly where you want it." I gesture around his apartment. "You're focused on selling shitty condoms that clearly don't work. And I'm telling you it's okay. But you don't have to pretend you're excited about this."

I thought Josh stole my opportunity to be a mother when he went behind my back and stopped his fertility. And now I feel like I'm stealing parenthood from this man, Josh's teammate, who's been nothing but good to me the few times we've been together.

And who also hollers my name, drunk from a riverboat full of equally drunk hockey players, parks in front of the curb cut, and knowingly sleeps with his co-worker's ex-wife–me. The two of us are a bomb about to detonate, and if I don't put my foot down, we will destroy everyone in our orbit.

Tucker runs a hand through his hair, and I notice it's still damp. I know that he showered after a workout. And I know what that body looks like naked and wet. He's wearing athletic shorts and a T-shirt that clings to his chest, and even now, even with everything falling apart, my traitorous body remembers what it felt like to be pressed against him.

"You're right," he finally says. "A baby wasn't part of my plan. But neither were you, and you're changing everything."

I don't know what to say to that.

"I will be involved, Sloane. I am this baby's father. Not just some guy who sends child support checks. An actual father."

The words should be reassuring. Instead, they cause panic to rise in my throat. "I can't recreate the dynamic I had with Josh."

He recoils. "First of all, I don't even know what that means. But this isn't about Grentley. This is about my kid."

"No man will take my choices away from me again." My voice rises despite my efforts to stay calm. "I have already done the song and dance where a man's choices determine my life path. First, the man who killed my father, then my husband. I spent *years* adjusting to a man's needs while all mine got shoved away. Never again." I'm shaking now, outraged.

Tucker takes a step back and shakes his head. "Sloane. I'm not — I would never ask you to change anything."

"Then what are you saying?" I challenge. "Because from where I'm standing, you're already making plans and decisions. 'I'll come to the doctor with you.' 'I want to be involved.' What about what I want?"

Tucker opens his mouth, then closes it. Takes a breath. "You're right. I'm sorry. What do you want?"

The question catches me off guard. Josh never asked what I wanted. He told me what made sense, what was logical, what we should do.

"I want to finish school," I say quietly. "I want to build a career in public health. I want to be the kind of person my grandmother would be proud of." My hand moves unconsciously to the sun pendant at my throat. "And I want to raise this baby without losing myself in the process."

"Okay." Tucker nods slowly. "Then that's what we'll do."

"We?"

"You said you don't want to lose yourself. I get that. But Sloane, I grew up in a family where everyone supported each other. My dad left pro hockey to stay home with my brothers and me when my mom ran for judge. This doesn't have to be you sacrificing everything while I keep living my life."

"Your dad retired to be ... a dad?" I hadn't known that. Hadn't known anything meaningful about Tucker's family.

"Yeah." Tucker laughs. "Family is everything to him." Tucker's expression softens. "I'm not saying I know exactly how this will work. But I'm saying it doesn't have to be like it was when you were growing up. Your grandmother working two jobs, doing everything alone. We have resources. We can figure this out."

The we keeps throwing me. Josh always said we, too, but it usually meant I should do whatever he'd already decided while he kept emotional distance.

"You can't be an active parent when you're on the road twenty weeks a year," I point out, and I watch his face fall.

He sinks onto that fancy couch—the one that's clearly designed for looking at rather than sitting on—and drops his head into his hands. For a long moment, he's silent.

"You're right," he says finally, his voice muffled. "I don't have an answer for that."

The admission surprises me. Josh would have had a dozen answers, a dozen ways to explain why it would all work out, why I was worrying for nothing.

"I just need you to be realistic," I say, more gently now. "I appreciate that you want to be involved. But I can't build my life around your schedule. I can't be the one who adjusts everything while you keep doing exactly what you've always done."

"I hear you." He looks up at me, and there's something raw in his expression. "But I'm not asking you to adjust everything. I'm asking you to let me try. To let me figure out how to be a father even with the travel, even with the complications. Other guys on the team do it. It's not impossible."

"It's not impossible for them because they have wives who handle everything while they're gone," I counter. "I'm not going to be that person, Tucker. I'm not going to be the one who gives up everything while you get to keep being T-Stag the Party Animal."

He flinches at the nickname, and I know I pressed a nerve. "I don't want to be that guy anymore."

I snort. "Sure. Because we met under such wholesome circumstances."

He emits a low growl and stares at his expensive sneakers. "Sloane. This is all coming at me really fast. But I want you to know I will change. I will absolutely become the man who deserves to be this baby's father."

The sincerity in his voice makes my chest ache. I want to

believe him. Want to believe this isn't just panic talking, that he really means it.

But I've been here before. I've believed promises that sounded beautiful in the moment and turned to ash in reality.

"I need time," I say. "To process this. To figure out what I'm going to do."

"Okay." He stands, keeping his distance like he's afraid of spooking me. "But Sloane? I meant what I said. I want to be involved. I want to be at doctor's appointments, I want to help with whatever you need. I know I have to earn your trust. I know I've given you every reason not to believe me. But I'm asking you to give me a chance to prove I'm different than you think I am."

I'm too tired to argue anymore. Too overwhelmed by everything that's happened in the past twenty-four hours.

"I'll text you when I make the appointment," I say. It's not a promise, exactly, but it's something.

"Thank you." The relief on his face is almost painful to witness.

I head for the door, and he doesn't try to stop me. Doesn't ask me to stay, doesn't make any more promises he might not be able to keep. He just watches me go with those blue eyes that have haunted my dreams, and I can't tell if the expression on his face is hope or fear.

The drive home is a blur. I keep expecting to feel something— panic, joy, terror, excitement—but I'm just numb. I told Tucker. He knows. And now I have to figure out what comes next.

Mel's not home when I arrive, which is both a relief and a disappointment. I'm not ready to talk about this yet, but I also desperately need to.

I drop onto my bed, still in my yoga pants and oversized sweatshirt, and pull out my phone. I should call the therapist I was seeing when the divorce process started. Should tell her what's happened and get her professional insight on how to navigate this situation.

Instead, I open my calendar and try to calculate when this baby might arrive. The dates bleed together.

My statistics textbook sits on my nightstand, a silent reminder of Monday's exam. I should be studying. Should be focusing on school, on building the future I keep saying I want.

But all I can think about is Tucker's face when I told him. The way he immediately asked if I was okay, if I was healthy. The way he said *this is my baby*, like it was the most natural thing in the world.

My hand moves to my stomach, still flat beneath my sweatshirt. There's a baby in there. Tucker's baby. And mine. A tiny cluster of cells that will become a person with his blue eyes or my green ones, his blond locks or my curls.

A person who will need me to be strong, to be stable, to be everything I'm not sure I know how to be.

"I can do this," I whisper to the empty room. "I can do this alone if I have to."

But a small voice asks what if Tucker really could be different than Josh, than my own father, different from the playboy persona he's shown me? Tucker speaks of having a father who sounds like make-believe to me, when I never even got to meet mine.

It's always been what's driven me in my studies. I am called to help people make different choices, and I can only do that if I get serious about finishing my degree now that there's a deadline where things are going to get exponentially more complicated.

I reach for my statistics textbook, determined to pretend, at least, that I'm preparing for Monday's exam. The formulas and definitions swim before my eyes, meaningless symbols that have nothing to do with the chaos of my actual life.

I make it through three pages before my eyes start to close. The exhaustion I've been fighting all week finally wins, pulling me under despite the textbook still open on my lap and the late afternoon sun streaming through my window.

CHAPTER 15
TUCKER

Stag family dinner is chaos as usual. My uncle's house on the North Side of the city has plenty of room for all thirty of us, but everyone is crammed in the living room watching my cousin Wyatt on TV, playing in some summer soccer series.

Usually, I'd be invested—trash-talking and scanning the crowd for his girlfriend, Fern. Today, the game might as well be cricket for all I'm following the action.

"Pass it, you idiot!" Odin yells at the screen, throwing a handful of popcorn for emphasis.

"He can't hear you, genius," Alder points out from his spot on the floor, where he's leaning against Lena's legs. She's perched on the arm of the couch, her fingers absently playing with his hair. But we aren't supposed to comment on their touchy-feely vibes.

Odin, oblivious to my inner turmoil, punches my cousin Petey next to him on the couch. "He should be able to feel my psychic energy telling him to PASS THE DAMN BALL."

Wyatt, predictably, doesn't pass. He takes the shot himself and misses.

The room erupts in groans and I-told-you-sos. Usually, I'd be right there with them. Today, I just feel hollow.

"Tuck, you want more potato salad?" My dad appears at my elbow, holding a plate piled high with food. "Your mom made extra."

I glance at his plate—perfectly charred ribs, grilled chicken. My usual Sunday dinner haul. My stomach turns.

"I'm good, Dad. Thanks."

Ty's eyebrows rise. "You feeling okay? You never turn down food."

"Just not hungry."

He studies me for a moment longer, then sets the plate on the coffee table. "Well, here's a plate if anyone's hungry." The food is gone in a flurry of grabby Stag hands. I'm not even sure if my brothers or my cousins are the ones who will win these Hunger Games.

Across the room, Gunnar is arguing with Stellan about something. My mom and one of my aunts are in the kitchen, their laughter carrying over the sound of the game. My Uncle Tim is on the deck with a beer, actually smiling as he talks to his own youngest brother.

It's all so normal. So perfectly, impossibly normal.

And I'm sitting here knowing that in a few months, everything is going to change. I'm going to be a father. Sloane is pregnant with my baby, and she doesn't want me involved, and I have no idea how to fix it. Will my kid even be able to come to Sunday dinner?

"Okay, seriously." Alder twists around to look at me. "What's going on with you?"

"Nothing."

"Bullshit. You've been weird for days. You're working out like a maniac, and now you're turning down food." He pauses. "Did you hear from Sloane?"

Several heads turn at the sound of a woman's name.

"Who's *Sloane*?" Odin asks.

"No one," I say quickly. "Just drop it."

"Is she the one who called you out for parking like an asshole?" Gunnar asks, grinning. "Because Uncle Tim told me and Em that story, and it's hilarious."

"Glad my humiliation is entertaining."

"Oh, come on." Gunnar tosses a piece of popcorn at me. "You fucked up, you got called out, you made it right. End of story."

If only it were that simple.

"He's been moping about this woman for weeks," Alder supplies, clearly trying to help but making it worse.

"Weeks?" My mom appears in the doorway, wiping her hands on a dish towel. "Tucker, you've been upset about a woman for weeks and didn't say anything?"

"I'm not upset—"

"He's definitely upset," Odin confirms. "Look at him. He won't even eat ribs. This is serious."

"Maybe you all forgot that I lost a tooth," I counter, but Lena starts explaining that the temporary crown she placed in my mouth should be entirely up to the task of chewing potato salad.

The attention is suffocating. Everyone is looking at me now, with various expressions of concern, curiosity, and amusement on their faces.

"Some of us have real problems, okay?" The words come out harsher than I intended. "Not everything is a joke."

The room goes silent. On the TV, Wyatt scores a goal and the commentators go wild, but no one here reacts.

My dad sets down his beer with deliberate care. "Outside, Tucky. Let's chat."

———

The back porch overlooks the city. The sun is starting to set, casting everything in gold and amber. My dad leads me to the far end, away from the windows where the family is undoubtedly watching.

"Sit," he says, pointing to one of the Adirondack chairs.

I comply. He takes the chair beside me, not looking at me, just watching the light fade across the glass buildings downtown.

"You want to tell me what's really going on?" His voice is calm, no judgment. Just concern.

"I screwed up."

"Yeah, I got that part. How badly?"

I take a deep breath. There's no point in delaying this. He'll find out eventually, and better he hears it from me first.

"I got someone pregnant."

To his credit, my dad doesn't react. Doesn't flinch or gasp or lecture. He just keeps staring at those skyscrapers, processing.

"The woman your brother mentioned? Sloane?"

"Yeah."

"And she… you're not together?"

"She told me I don't have to be involved. That she can handle it on her own." The words taste bitter. I'm definitely not ready to tell my dad that she's also my teammate's ex-wife. "She has ... she has had a lot of men let her down in the past."

Dad nods slowly. "And how do you feel about a baby?"

"Terrified." The admission comes easier than I expected. "I'm a joke, Dad. I sell condoms on the side—condoms that clearly don't work very well. I party too hard, I travel half the year, I barely know how to take care of myself. How am I supposed to be a father?"

"Do you want to be involved?"

The question catches me off guard.

"Yes," I say without hesitation. "What kind of question is that? It's my kid. But Sloane doesn't trust me. She thinks I'm going to be like her ex-husband—that I'll expect her to sacrifice everything while I keep living my life."

"Are you?"

"No! At least—" I stop, forcing myself to be honest. "I don't want to be. But I don't know how not to be, you know? I'm gone so damn much. How do I be an active father when I'm barely here?"

Dad leans back in his chair, and I can see him choosing his words carefully.

"You know your Uncle Tim practically raised us after your grandmother died, right?"

I nod. It's family lore—how Grandma Laurel died when Dad and his brothers were young, how Grandpa Ted spiraled, how Tim stepped up to hold everything together.

"What you don't know," Dad continues, "is how badly I repaid that sacrifice at first. Tim was working two jobs, trying to keep us fed and in school, making sure we had what we needed. And I thanked him by getting into fights. By being angry at the world. By making his life harder instead of easier."

"Yeah, but you got your shit together and then everything was fine."

Dad laughs. "You think it was some switch that flipped on? You know, I started dating your mom while she was my lawyer, right? We both could have gotten into so much damn trouble." He shakes his head. "Man, I was so irresponsible."

I've never heard this aspect of the story. Dad always talks about his playing days with pride, about his success in the league. Never about being stuck in the minors for fighting.

"What changed?"

"Your mom," he says simply. "Once I met her, I realized what I wanted my life to look like." He turns to look at me. "Being a father isn't about your job or your reputation, Tucker. It's not about being perfect or having all the answers. It's about showing up. Every single day, in whatever way you can."

"But how do I show up when I'm on the road?"

"Same way I did. Same way, plenty of guys do. You make the time you do have count for everything." He pauses. "But Tucker, before you can show up for this baby, you need to show up for Sloane. You need to prove to her that you're not going to be another man who takes her choices away."

The words hit hard because they're precisely what Sloane said. That she can't have another man dictate her life.

"I don't know how to do that."

"Yes, you do." Dad's voice is firm. "You do it by listening more than you talk. By asking what she needs instead of assuming you know. By being patient when she pushes you away, because she will push you away. She's protecting herself, and she has every right to."

"What if she never trusts me?"

"Then you keep proving you're trustworthy anyway. Because that's what we do in this family." He stands, putting a hand on my shoulder. "You can become the man you need to be, Tucker. But you have to prove it through actions, not words. Words are easy. Anyone can make promises. It's the showing up that matters."

I nod, throat tight.

"Does anyone else know?" I shake my head. Dad's brows shoot up. "Not even Alder?"

I swallow. "Sloane said she needs time to process. I'm not telling anyone else until she's ready."

Dad squeezes my shoulder. "Good. That's the right instinct. Respect her timeline, not yours."

I wince. "You're not going to tell Mom? Or the family?"

Dad blows a raspberry. "I'm not going to pretend it'll be easy to keep this news from your mother. She's going to be a Grammy." He nudges me with his shoulder, and I let my head drop back against the wooden chair. Dad pats my arm. "You'll tell me when it's time, okay, kiddo?"

He heads for the door, then turns back. "Tucker, I think you're going to be a great father. You just have to believe it yourself first."

———

After Dad goes back inside, I stay on the porch, watching the last light fade from the sky. I pull out my phone and open a new message to Uncle Tim:

> Can we talk about parental leave policies for pro hockey players? I need to understand what's possible.

His response comes within seconds, and I crane my neck to see him studying his phone in the kitchen.

UNCLE TIM:

> Anything I need to know?

> Just gathering information

UNCLE TIM

> Stop by the office tomorrow, and we'll look over the contracts.

I pocket my phone and head back in, where the family is now arguing about whether Wyatt should have taken a different shot.

Gunnar sees me and holds up his beer in a silent question. I shake my head—no alcohol tonight. I need to stay clear-headed.

Alder catches my eye from across the room and nods slightly. He knows something's shifted. He doesn't know what yet, but he knows.

I sink back onto the couch, and this time, when my mom offers me a plate of food, I take it. The pie feels dry in my mouth, but I eat it anyway, forcing myself to be present. To show up for this Sunday dinner with my family, because showing up is what matters.

And tomorrow, I'll start showing up for Sloane and our baby, whether she's ready to let me or not.

CHAPTER 16
SLOANE

THE SOCIOLOGY EXAM QUESTIONS LOOK LIKE ANTS ON THE PAGE. I'VE read the same multiple-choice question three times now and still can't process what it's asking.

I circle an answer at random and move on. Twenty minutes left. Twelve questions to go. I can do this.

Except I can't stop checking the clock on the wall. The doctor's appointment is at two. It's one-thirty now. The exam ends at one-forty-five. If I leave immediately, I'll have exactly fifteen minutes to get down to the women's hospital a mile away.

And Tucker will be there.

I told him the appointment time, thinking maybe he'd have practice, a workout, or some other hockey obligation. Instead, he'd texted back within minutes: *I'll be there.*

Just like that. No negotiation, no excuses.

My hand moves unconsciously to my stomach. Still flat. Still no visible evidence of the tiny cluster of cells that's turned my entire life upside down.

Focus, Sloane. Finish the exam.

I force myself to read the next question. Something about Durkheim and social solidarity: I know this. Dr. Khan covered it extensively in lecture. But my brain feels like it's wading through fog, every thought taking twice as long as it should.

The exhaustion is constant now. I fall asleep on the couch, at my desk, sometimes mid-sentence while talking to Mel. And the nausea—God, the nausea. I've learned to keep pretzels in my bag, to avoid strong smells, never to let my stomach get completely empty.

Mel still doesn't know. She's been so consumed with bar prep and her upcoming move to the new accessible apartment that Stag Law helped her find. Every time I think about telling her, she launches into another excited monologue about her future, and I can't bring myself to interrupt with my mess.

Five more questions. Ten minutes left.

I speed through them, not caring if my answers are correct, just needing to be done. The teaching assistant collects my exam with a smile that I can't return. Then I'm out the door, practically running to the bus.

———

The OB-GYN office is inside the hospital where people deliver their babies. I've never actually been in here before. And why would I, when Josh took the family option away from us?

I arrive with three minutes to spare, my hair escaping its ponytail, with a light sheen of sweat on my forehead despite the air conditioning.

Tucker's already in the waiting room.

Of course he is.

He's sitting in one of those uncomfortable plastic chairs, dressed in khakis and a navy polo that brings out the color of his eyes. His hair is neat, like he actually made an effort instead of just rolling out of bed. And there's a small bag at his feet—fabric, reusable, the kind of tote bag someone's mother would give them.

He stands when he sees me, his expression somewhere between nervous and hopeful.

"Hey," he says.

"Hi." I clutch my purse strap, suddenly aware of how disheveled I must look compared to his put-together appearance. "I guess I wasn't sure you'd actually come."

"I told you, Sloane. I'm stepping up." He picks up the bag. "I, uh, brought some things. My dad said they helped my mom when she was pregnant. Also, I told my dad."

I peer inside the bag as he holds it open. Ginger ale. Shortbread cookies. Small packets of lavender candies. A tin of peppermint tea.

"I wasn't sure what would help," he continues, his words coming faster now, nervous. "So, I just got everything Dad suggested. The ginger is supposed to be good for nausea, and the lavender is calming, or something? And the shortbread is just... I don't know, easy on the stomach?"

The gesture is so unexpectedly thoughtful that I don't know what to say. Josh would have shown up empty-handed, irritated by having to rearrange his schedule. I really need to stop comparing Tucker to Josh. Or thinking about Josh at all.

"Thank you," I manage. "That's... really thoughtful."

"Sloane Campbell?" A nurse appears in the doorway, clipboard in hand.

Tucker looks at me. "Is it okay if I come back?"

I want to say no. Want to keep this boundary firmly in place. But something about the bag of ginger ale and cookies, about the effort he clearly put into being here, makes me nod.

"Okay."

———

The exam room is small and sterile, with motivational posters about prenatal vitamins and the importance of hydration. The nurse takes my vitals and asks routine questions about my last period and any symptoms I've been experiencing.

"Nausea, fatigue, food aversions," I list off, very aware of Tucker sitting in the corner, listening to every word.

"All completely normal for early pregnancy," the nurse assures me. "Dr. Patel will be in shortly. Go ahead and undress from the waist down, and you can put this sheet over your lap."

When she leaves, Tucker and I sit in silence. The exam table crinkles every time I shift position. The clock on the wall ticks too loudly.

He clears his throat. "Should I step out while you …" He twirls a finger at the sheet.

I shake my head and toss the cloth on my lap as I wriggle out of my pants and underwear. No sense trying to be modest with the man who is deeply familiar with my anatomy at this point. But it's easy enough to cover up with the sheet.

"Are you scared?" Tucker asks, finally.

"Terrified," I admit. "I don't know how to do this. Any of this."

"Join the club."

I look at him, really look at him. He seems smaller in this medical office, less like the confident hockey player and more like… just a guy. A scared guy who has no idea what he's doing.

"I have never even met my father," I say quietly. "And my grandma did her best raising me, but she was exhausted all the time. I remember her falling asleep at the kitchen table, still in her work uniform." I twist my hands in my lap. "I don't know how to do this without becoming her. Without sacrificing everything until there's nothing left of me."

"You have resources she didn't," Tucker points out gently. "Me. Money. Support. You're not alone in this, Sloane. Even if you don't want me romantically, even if we're just co-parents—you're not alone. This baby has a family."

"I don't know what that looks like," I confess. "My whole life, it's just been me and my grandmother until she died. Then Josh and I, but that was just… him making decisions and me going along with them. I've never had people. A network. I don't even know what that means."

Tucker leans forward, elbows on his knees. "It means my mom will probably show up with casseroles. It means ten Stag cousins will be so excited to play uncle, they'll probably drive you crazy. It means you'll have so many babysitters you won't know what to do with yourself."

The picture he's painting sounds surreal. Foreign. Like something from a TV show about families I've never been part of, never dared to dream about.

"That sounds overwhelming."

"It is," he admits with a small laugh. "But it's also… nice? To know people care. To know you're not doing it all alone."

A knock on the door interrupts us. Dr. Patel enters—an Indian woman in her fifties with kind eyes and an efficient manner.

"Sloane, nice to meet you. And you must be...?"

"Tucker," he supplies. "The father."

Dr. Patel nods. "Well, let's take a look and make sure everything is progressing normally. Sloane, if you could lie back on the table and put your feet in the stirrups."

I comply, acutely aware of Tucker in the room as I position myself. Dr. Patel explains what she's doing—measurements, checking my cervix, and preparing for an ultrasound.

"This early, we'll need to do a transvaginal ultrasound," she explains, holding up what looks like a wand. "It's a bit uncomfortable, but it gives us a much better view of the embryo."

Tucker sputters. "Vaginal? Like ... her vagina?"

Dr. Patel looks at him, one brow raised. "I imagine you are familiar with that part of her body?" I cough to cover a laugh. The admin had prepared me for this when I called to make the appointment, but I guess this is an unexpected advancement for Tucker.

"Trust me, you'll be seeing a lot of this over the next eight months," Dr. Patel says with a smile. "Ready?"

I nod, and she guides the probe inside. Tucker stands, his chair scraping against the linoleum tile. "You just went for it. Right on in there. Holy shit, are we seeing inside?"

He's by my side at the exam table, leaning forward toward the screen, which lights up with grainy black and white images and swirling static sounds.

"There we go," Dr. Patel murmurs, adjusting the wand. "Let me just..."

And then I hear it. A rapid flutter, like hoofbeats in the distance.

"Is that—" My voice catches.

"That's the heartbeat," Dr. Patel confirms. "Nice and strong."

Tucker gasps abruptly, moving closer to the screen. His hand finds mine without either of us seeming to decide it should, and I let him hold it because I need something to anchor me to this moment.

That's a heartbeat. A real, actual heartbeat. My baby's heartbeat.

Our baby's heartbeat.

"Wait," Dr. Patel says, her brow furrowing slightly as she adjusts the probe. "Let me check something."

My heart stops. "Is something wrong?"

"No, not wrong. Just..." She moves the wand again, and the sound amplifies. The flutter seems to double in speed. Dr. Patel hums happily. "Yes, I thought so. I'm seeing two gestational sacs. Two heartbeats."

The room tilts. "Two?"

"Congratulations," Dr. Patel says, smiling at both of us. "You're having twins."

Tucker's hand tightens around mine. I can't look at him. Can't look away from the screen where Dr. Patel is pointing out two tiny flickers, two separate miracles that are somehow both mine.

Twins.

"Are you sure?" My voice sounds distant, not quite my own.

"Positive. See here?" She indicates two distinct areas on the screen. "Two separate embryos. Based on the measurements and your last menstrual period, I'd say your due date would be sometime in late February. But twins like to arrive early."

She glances away from the screen. "Do twins run in either of your families?"

Tucker's mouth works open and shut. "I'm a twin." He points a thick thumb at his chest. Dr. Patel nods.

The information is coming too fast. I can't process any of it.

"Both look healthy," Dr. Patel continues, taking measurements, typing notes into her computer. "Heart rates are good. Size is appropriate for gestational age. I'll want to see you back in four weeks for another ultrasound, and we'll need to discuss the specifics of managing a twin pregnancy. Higher risk category, but everything is perfectly normal right now."

She's still talking—about diet, supplements, warning signs to watch for—but I can't focus on any of it. Tucker is squeezing my hand so tightly I'm losing circulation, but I don't pull away.

Twins.

———

Twenty minutes later, we're standing in the parking lot. Dr. Patel printed out ultrasound photos—two tiny bean-shaped blobs that look nothing like babies but somehow are. Tucker is holding his copy like it might dissolve if he grips it too tightly.

"My mom is going to lose her mind." He laughs, but it sounds slightly hysterical. "Once I tell her."

Tucker insists on driving me home and, given the news we just got, I'm not inclined to say no. "You said you told your dad," I start to say, needing something banal to focus on while my brain stops freaking out. "Not the rest of your huge family?"

He sighs and clicks a key fob, unlocking the doors of his fancy car. "I wanted to check in with you before I told the entire crew." He opens my door for me and gestures for me to get in. I stare up at him, surprised he's managing to be thoughtful. "I haven't told my own twin yet. And now I'm having twins. We are, I mean."

Tucker closes my door and walks around to his side. I pop one of the candies from the tote into my mouth as he gets buckled.

"Sloane?" Tucker's voice is gentle. "Are you okay?"

"I don't know." It's the most honest answer I can give. "I thought one baby was overwhelming. Two seems..."

"Impossible?"

"Yes."

He turns to face me fully. "I know it's scary. But I also know my family will help us. I gotta believe this will be okay."

"How, though?" I gesture vaguely between us. "We're not even together. How are we supposed to raise two babies?"

"I don't know," Tucker admits. "We'll figure it out."

I want to believe him and ignore that smug grin on his handsome face. Want to trust that his certainty isn't just naivety, that he understands what he's signing up for.

But I've heard promises before. And they all sounded sincere until they weren't.

Tucker parks effortlessly in a tiny space outside my building. Despite my overwhelm, I appreciate how good he smells when he puts one arm behind my seat as he backs into the spot. And he smiles at me as he turns back around. "Piece of cake." And then his face falls. "Man, I guess this beauty will have to go. Can't be hauling twins around in a two-seater."

"Ha." I push the button to open my butterfly door, imagining curly-haired babies spitting up on his leather interior. "I would think not." I fiddle with the ultrasound photos, the tote bag, and my backpack. Soon I'll be juggling a massive diaper bag, too. And a stroller.

These tiny people will depend on me for everything.

Tucker navigates around the car with his long strides and lifts the bags from my hands, frowning up at the stairs to my front door. "Your building isn't so easy to access. How does Mel manage?"

I point to the side, where there's an accessible entrance and a service elevator she has permission to use. "She gets by." I purse my lips, knowing I need to be open with him, but wanting to protect my privacy all at once. "We're moving. Well, she's moving. Your uncle found her a cool place."

"Sounds like him." Tucker takes the steps two at a time, and frowns when he sees the door to the building isn't locked.

"Well…" I gesture for him to hand me my bags. He hasn't seen my apartment, and I don't want him to, not while it's in chaos and I'm reeling about today's news.

Tucker nods, arranging the straps of the bags on my shoulders. "Text me when we can talk again?" I nod. "Hey." His voice is so soft, his eyes so gentle, I want to cry. "Take care of our guys."

I clutch at my stomach as he walks back to his car, wondering how I'll manage not to lose myself when he keeps saying things like that.

CHAPTER 17
TUCKER

I'M STARING AT THE ULTRASOUND PHOTO FOR PROBABLY THE hundredth time since leaving Sloane's apartment three hours ago.

My babies.

Our babies.

The urge to call someone—anyone—is overwhelming. Alder. My dad. Hell, I want to post it on social media with some caption like "Plot twist!" but I know that would be the worst possible thing I could do.

Sloane needs time. She needs space. She gets to decide when and how to tell people.

But keeping this to myself feels impossible.

I stand, pacing the length of my living room. The space suddenly feels both too big and too small. Three thousand square feet of bachelor pad that will need to become... what? A home? A place where babies live?

I hate that Sloane and my babies are in that apartment building with unlocked doors and no security. I have a really strong urge to barrel over there and scoop her up and bring her here, but obviously that's not the right approach.

I stop pacing in front of the bar cart, staring at the collection of expensive liquor. Glenlivet, Macallan, Japanese whisky I bought because the bottle looked cool. When did I become the guy with a liquor collection? When did that seem like a personality trait worth cultivating?

The weird art on the walls catches my eye next—abstract pieces the decorator chose that I thought looked sophisticated. Now they just look like what they are: empty attempts at appearing grown-up while remaining fundamentally immature.

My place might be secure, but it's not a place to bring a baby, either.

This apartment is a monument to T-Stag the Enforcer. And that douche needs to go.

I pull out my phone and scroll to my designer's number, then hesitate. What am I even asking for? "Make my bachelor pad look less like a bachelor pad"? "I'm having twins, so please remove anything that suggests I've ever had fun."?

I skip texting her and move to my bedroom instead. The California king bed dominates the space, unmade as usual. The closet —bigger than my first apartment, as I once bragged to Sloane—is full of clothes I barely wear: designer labels, expensive fabrics, more shoes than any reasonable person needs.

What do you even wear when you're a father? Do I need different clothes? Or am I overthinking this? My dad always looks pretty slick, but did he when he had four sons pooping their pants all day?

I sit on the edge of the bed and open my laptop, typing "parenting advice" into the search bar. The results are overwhelming —articles about feeding schedules, sleep training, developmental milestones, the importance of establishing routines.

I immediately order the first book that comes up from the American Academy of Pediatrics, because that sounds important. Then I order *Heading Home with Your Newborn*, *The Baby Book*, and something called *What to Do When You're Having Two*.

My shopping cart is up to eight books, and I'm contemplating a ninth when my phone buzzes.

ALDER

You alive? Haven't heard from you since Sunday dinner.

I stare at the message. My twin. The person who knows me better than anyone.

I should tell him. Alder would understand. He'd help me figure this out. And it's been hard talking to him at all, knowing I can't be totally honest with him.

But Sloane asked me to wait. And I promised I'd respect her timeline.

> I'm good. Just been thinking.

ALDER

> About Sloane?

> Yeah. Among other things.

ALDER

> Want to grab dinner? You're being weird, and I'm worried.

I want to say yes. Want to sit across from my brother and unload everything—the pregnancy, the twins, my terror that I'm going to fuck this up spectacularly. But I can't. Not yet.

> Rain check? I've got some stuff to handle.

ALDER

> Tucker. Whatever's going on, you don't have to deal with it alone.

The irony isn't lost on me. I'm about to be responsible for two tiny humans, and I can't even handle my own life without my twin trying to swoop in and help.

> I know. And I will tell you. Soon. Just need a bit more time.

ALDER

> Okay. But I'm here when you're ready.

I set the phone aside and wonder how I'll face the music with the Fury regarding Grentley.

I'm spiraling down a rabbit hole of increasingly gloomy

thoughts when my phone rings. Dad's name flashes on the screen.

"Hey," I answer, closing my laptop guiltily.

"Just checking in," he says. "How'd the appointment go?"

Is it weird for a grown man to cry? Because I feel like crying to my dad right now.

"Good," I manage to say. "Everything looks healthy."

"And Sloane? How's she doing?"

"Overwhelmed, I think. It's a lot to process."

There's a pause. Dad knows I'm holding something back. "Tucker. What aren't you telling me?"

I close my eyes, picturing his face when I tell him. The joy, the excitement. And then the inevitable question: when can he share the news with Mom?

"It's twins, Dad."

Silence. Then: "Twins?"

"Yeah. Two babies. Like me and Alder."

"Holy shit." He laughs, the sound pure delight. "Tucker, that's incredible! Twins! Your mother is going to—" He stops himself. "Crap. She doesn't know yet."

"No. And Dad, you can't tell her. Not yet. Sloane needs time to process. To tell her own people first. I promised I'd respect her timeline."

"Of course. Of course." But I can hear the effort it's taking him to contain his excitement. "But Tucker, twins. That's amazing. Terrifying, but amazing."

"More terrifying than amazing right now."

"Buddy, this is gonna be terrific. I don't mind saying I'm pretty great at twins. Although your mom and I had practice with Odin and Gunny before we got slammed with double trouble." Dad is rambling about how awesome it is being a dad, and I should find it soothing, but somehow it just makes me feel less capable. "Twins are special, kiddo," he adds. "They'll always have each other."

Like Alder and me, we've always been a team, even when we've driven each other crazy.

"I don't know how to do this, Dad. Be a father to one baby, let alone two. Especially when Sloane doesn't really want me involved."

"She let you come to the appointment?"

"Yeah."

"Then she wants you involved more than you think."

"So, what do I do?"

"Keep showing up. Keep being thoughtful. Keep proving you're not going to disappear or make demands or take away her choices."

"Thanks, Dad."

"Anytime. And Tuck? I'm proud of you. For being there today. For respecting Sloane's boundaries. For taking this seriously."

After we hang up, I sit with his words. *I'm proud of you.* When was the last time I did something actually worth being proud of?

I open a new browser tab and search for tea delivery services in Pittsburgh. Something thoughtful but not overwhelming. Ginger tea, maybe. Peppermint. Things that might help with morning sickness.

I find a company that does weekly subscriptions and set up a delivery to Sloane's address. Not extravagant. Just consistent. A reminder that I'm thinking of her, that I'm here even when she needs space.

Then I pull up my interior designer's number again. This time I send a text:

> Need to talk about renovating my place. Making it more family-friendly. Can we meet this week?

Her response comes quickly:

> Absolutely! How family-friendly are we talking?

> Very. Like, babies will be living here, family-friendly.

DESIGN GIRL

> !!! Congratulations! Yes, let's definitely talk. I have some great ideas.

I set the phone down, feeling slightly more in control. Small steps. Tea delivery. Planning renovations. Researching what babies need.

The list keeps growing until I'm overwhelmed again. I close the laptop and grab my gym bag instead. When in doubt, work out. At least that's something I know how to do.

———

Three hours later, I'm drenched in sweat at Fury headquarters and no less anxious. Even as I work my body to the max beside these guys, it's like every breath I take is a lie until I come clean about Sloane.

Josh Grentley is going to find out eventually. The team is going to find out. And when they do, it's going to be a disaster. I knew this when I slept with her at the ski house. I knew it when I went back for more. And now...

I can already imagine the locker room gossip. The looks. The questions about whether I did this deliberately. Grentley's anger —justified anger. The way it'll poison team dynamics that are already fragile after our early playoff exit.

Coach Thompson will pull me aside. Management will get involved. I'll become the guy who knocked up his teammate's ex-wife instead of the guy who protects his teammates on the ice. Fuck—what if they trade me?

My phone buzzes as I'm toweling off. Alder again.

ALDER

Seriously. You're worrying me, Fucker

His nickname has always bugged me, but it hits harder than usual right now. Fucker Stag. I'm deep in the bed I made, and I know how much work it will take to claw my way out. I need to remember the prize here: babies. Family.

I know Sloane has no reason to trust me yet, but I'm going to need the full power of the Stag herd to keep myself on track. I pull out my phone to call her and realize it's late. She's got babies to grow and needs her rest, so I send her a text instead.

> Would you be willing to have dinner with my
> parents? I really need their support so I can
> support you. And the babies.

What I want to say is: I'm wild for you and I'm terrified and excited, and I want to be more than just a co-parent, but I don't know how to prove I'm different from what you think I am.

I want to tell her to move in with me, so I can keep our family safe while she figures out what she needs.

But that shit will scare her off faster than a puck off the boards.

Instead, I save the ultrasound photo as my phone background, so I'll be reminded each time I pull it out. Two tiny beans that will become two tiny humans who will need me to be better than I've ever been.

Even if Sloane never sees me as anything more than a co-parent, I need to be that man anyway.

For those two tiny heartbeats that are counting on me to get this right.

How should I dress to meet the parents of my casual hookup turned twin baby-daddy? A nun's habit feels about right for my mood, but obviously that's too blasphemous. I'm no virginal do-gooder.

After cycling through every item in my closet, I land on a simple dress that doesn't brush against my tender nipples or make me look pregnant. Which I am. I have to keep reminding myself. I look perfectly respectable to meet Tucker's parents. My co-parent's parents.

There's really no reason I should care what Ty Stag and Juniper Jones think of me.

Except they're going to be my babies' grandparents. That word hits a nerve. What would my own grandmother say about this whole situation? She'd probably tell me to hush up and accept the free babysitting Tucker referenced.

And Tucker keeps talking about family support, networks, and all these things I've never experienced. And part of me—a big part—desperately wants what he's describing to be real.

"You look great," Mel says from her doorway, watching me fuss with my hair in the mirror. "But where are you going?"

"Oh." I wave a hand at her. "Just a school thing." Is it totally a lie? The pregnancy is certainly going to impact spring semester, after all.

Mel is clearly not buying it, because she squints at me and

rolls back and forth a few times in the hall. "We haven't had much time to talk lately. I see that this is me being a shitty friend. What time are you getting home?"

I shrug. "I probably won't be late." I have been avoiding this conversation big time, but I know it's the right thing to do—to come clean to Mel, lean in to her advice. Let her boss me around a little. I force my face into an exaggerated smile that makes her giggle. "You going out to study tonight or will you be here later?"

Mel has been such a good friend through all of this—inviting me to move in with her, supporting me through the divorce, celebrating my return to school. And I've been keeping this massive secret from her for weeks.

My phone buzzes. Tucker.

I'm downstairs whenever you're ready. No rush.

Mel hums. "I'll make sure I'm home. Should I get ice cream? Rent a Jason Momoa movie?"

"Oh, great idea. Yes, please." I take a deep breath and check my reflection one more time. The woman staring back at me looks terrified.

"On it," Mel says. "And text me if you need an escape route from whatever this is. I'll fake an emergency."

"Thanks." I hug her quickly, then grab my purse and head downstairs before I can talk myself out of going.

Tucker is leaning against his car—not the McLaren, I notice, but a sensible black SUV. He's dressed in dark jeans and a button-down shirt, his hair neatly styled. He looks nervous, which somehow makes me feel slightly better.

"Hey," he says, straightening when he sees me. "You look beautiful."

"Thanks." I smooth down my dress self-consciously. "You look nice too."

"Thanks. I, uh—" He opens the passenger door for me. "I really appreciate you doing this. I know it's probably weird."

"It's fine." I slide into the car, immediately hit by how clean it is. No fast food wrappers, no gym clothes in the back seat. Just the faint scent of leather and whatever cologne he wears. "Whose car is this?"

Tucker gets in the driver's side and turns toward me with a smile that leaves me breathless. Has he always been this attractive? "It's mine now, baby." He pats the steering wheel. "It's actually my cousin Wyatt's, but he's in the UK for a few more years and said I can use it if I take over the insurance."

We pull away from my building as he rambles on a bit about the extended family system of bartering and favors. Then he seems to run out of things to say. The silence stretches between us, not quite comfortable but not hostile either.

"Do your parents know about the twins or this is a big reveal type dinner?" I ask finally.

"My dad knows. He's terrible at keeping secrets, but he promised he'd let us tell Mom." Tucker glances at me. "Is that okay? If we tell them in person?"

"It's fine. They're your parents." I fiddle with my purse strap. "What did your dad say?"

Tucker's face lights up. "He was excited. Like, really excited. Started talking about cribs and babyproofing and all this stuff I haven't even thought about yet."

The enthusiasm in his voice should be reassuring. Instead, it makes my anxiety spike. His family is going to be so involved, so present. They're going to have opinions and suggestions and expectations.

And I have no idea how to navigate any of that.

"Sloane?" Tucker's voice is gentle. "You okay?"

"Just nervous."

"They're going to love you," he says with such certainty that I almost believe him.

Tucker's apartment building is just as intimidating as I remember —all glass and steel and obvious wealth. As he navigates the parking garage, I tell him, "It was really nice of you to come get me. I could have driven myself."

"And miss out on alone time with you? Not a chance." He

grins and actually winks as he shuts off the engine and springs out to open my car door. "I paid my housekeeper a crap ton of extra money to make something delicious and have it ready to go. So hopefully you can help me pretend I cooked all day."

Despite my nerves, I smile. There's something sweet about that—how much he wants to impress not just me but his parents as well.

The elevator ride to Tucker's penthouse feels endless. I can feel him watching me, probably trying to gauge my mood. When the doors finally open directly into his apartment, I'm surprised by what I see.

The loud art is gone, replaced by framed family photos. The bar cart is still there but pushed into a corner, looking less prominent. The uncomfortable-looking furniture remains, but there are new additions—a bookshelf with actual books on it, a soft throw blanket draped over the couch, small changes that make the space feel less like a bachelor pad and more like... a home.

"You redecorated," I say.

"A little." Tucker rubs the back of his neck. "I'm working with a designer on more changes. Making it more family-friendly."

Before I can respond, a woman appears from the kitchen—petite, with dark hair and warm brown eyes. She's wearing jeans and a casual blouse, an apron tied around her waist.

"Hey, Jamie." Tucker hugs her familiarly and she smiles warmly. "Everything smells amazing."

Jamie pats him on the arm. "Pull the casserole out when the timer dings." She glances at me and lifts a brow until Tucker smacks his forehead. I wince at the word casserole, hoping there's at least some flavor to it. But then remembering that anything with flavor makes me gag these days.

"Oh my gosh, sorry. Jamie, this is Sloane. Sloane, Jamie." He seems like he wants to say more but the doorbell buzzes.

Jamie squeezes my arm as Tucker walks to the intercom to presumably buzz in his parents. "So nice to meet you, dear. We'll talk more, I'm sure." She slips out as Tucker laughs at the wall unit and before I can hyperventilate, I hear the elevator doors and a loud male voice.

"Tucky, this smells way too good for you to have cooked

yourself." An older version of Tucker sticks his head in the apartment. Ty Stag, legendary Pittsburgh hockey player, has graying hair, grey eyes, and a smile that sets me at ease despite the conversation ahead of us. "And you must be Sloane."

He strides toward me as I nod, followed by a statuesque woman with a dark bob haircut and a look of concern. "Tyrion Stag, you know you have to ask permission before you hug—oh. Well, too late I guess." Tucker's dad has his arms around me and … it feels so fatherly, so affectionate, I can't help but lean in until he pulls away, hands on my arms, a smile spreading across his entire face.

"Hey, Mom, Dad." Tucker's voice cuts across the greeting. "This is Sloane."

"Yes, yes." Tucker's mom shoves his dad aside. I know she's going to insist I use her first name, but I feel compelled to think of her as *Judge*. "May I hug you, dear? We're a hugging family."

"Oh, sure, that's—" My words are cut off by a firm embrace that is, again, parental and affectionate and maybe a little magical in that the hug seems to radiate strength and power right into my veins.

"Okay, guys." Tucker again sounds exasperated. "You're being extra."

"Can't help it, buddy." Mr. Stag ruffles his son's hair. I stand awkwardly, not used to family dynamics at all, let alone this type of obvious love.

Judge claps her hands. "Tucker, get us some drinks and invite us to sit down. It's getting weird, right Sloane?" She winks and strides toward the sofa, draping her coat on a peg I hadn't noticed on the wall.

I follow as Tucker grabs bubbly water from the refrigerator, his massive hands each able to hold two cans without much struggle. "Sloane, you want the lime or the strawberry-peach?"

I glance between his parents, who have cuddled into one end of the sofa, and perch on the new armchair. "Oh, lime, please." The chair is incredibly, unexpectedly comfortable and I sink in, remembering to cross my ankles, though I'm tempted to curl up and rub my face against the new throw blanket. Something very odd is happening in this building, to say the least.

Tucker hands out drinks and the hiss and pop of cans opening drowns out the sound of my heartbeat rushing in my ears. "So," Mr. Stag says, gesturing with his can and biting his lip expectantly. I guess we're just diving in.

Tucker nods. "Yeah." He scratches the back of his neck. "Mom, Sloane and I met at Stelly's graduation party."

Judge smiles. "That's lovely. And you've been seeing each other?" Her brows lift into her hairline. I sip my drink, grateful for the bubbles as my stomach roils.

"Not exactly," Tucker says. He glances at me. "Do you want to ...."

I shake my head and gesture. These are his parents. It should be him doing the big reveal. He knows them best, and I don't trust myself not to throw up if I say the words aloud.

"Hoooo," Tucker sighs, perching on the arm of the chair where I'm sitting. "So, Mom, Dad already knows this, and I obviously want you to know that..." Judge looks between her husband and Tucker. I can feel her confusion and discomfort, and it intensifies my own. Tucker meets my eye and then smiles. I can almost forget that this is a nightmare. That nothing can happen between us other than shared responsibility. That he will probably flame out of even that. Because that smile is the sort of thing that could fool a woman as fast as it melts her underwear.

He looks back at his mother. "Sloane's pregnant. We're having twins."

The room falls silent apart from the heartbeat that's back pounding in my ears. Is my blood pressure dangerously high? Maybe I should leave and go right to the hospital and hide for seven months.

But suddenly I hear a shriek, and I'm jolted back to reality by the sight of Juniper Jones jumping and clapping her hands. "Really? Babies? My gosh, Ty, does this make us grandparents?" Mr. Stag nods as she starts smacking his chest. "And you knew! Oh, baby, I'm glad you felt like you could go to your father with something big. Ty, I really thought it would be Gunnar and Emerson first, didn't you? Twins. Twins!"

Once she runs out of electricity, she sinks into the couch, head on her husband's shoulder. Tucker laughs quietly and looks like he wants to pat my arm, but doesn't. "Yeah. Twins." A series of beeps emerges from the kitchen, and he downs the rest of his drink, crushing the can as he stands. "Let me grab the casserole, and we can talk about it more while we eat."

I'm not sure how I manage to move from the armchair to the high back chair at Tucker's table, but before I know it, I have a plate of steaming rice and mushrooms and savory chicken to go with my bubbly water.

I am surprised by how amazing everything smells, and despite my anxiety, my stomach growls appreciatively.

"Dig in," Judge says, sitting across from me. "Please, don't be shy."

For a few minutes, everyone focuses on serving themselves and passing dishes. The silence is punctuated by the clink of silverware and appreciative murmurs about the food.

Then Mr. Stag sets down his fork and looks at me with those kind eyes. "So, Sloane, Tucker mentioned you're in school. Public health?"

"Yes." I swallow my bite of casserole. "I'm just starting up again. It's been... challenging, getting back into student mode after so long. I'm going to be doing a research project with social safety net programs locally."

"Oh, that does sound interesting." He glances at Tucker. "Our family has always valued social safety nets. Juniper's a judge in family court, as Tucker probably mentioned."

"He did." I look at Judge. "That's impressive."

"It's demanding," she says with a smile. "But rewarding. And Ty made it possible by being the primary parent when our boys were young."

"You really stayed home with all those boys? Instead of playing pro hockey?" I hope my curiosity doesn't come across as judgmental. It's such a foreign concept for me that I truly cannot imagine that level of commitment from a man.

Mr. Stag's expression is proud. "Best job I ever had. Don't get me wrong—I loved playing. But being there for my sons' child-hoods? Nothing compares."

The conversation flows more easily than I expected. They ask about my classes, my goals, what drew me to public health. They share stories about raising four boys, about the chaos and joy of a full house. Tucker chimes in occasionally, but mostly he just watches, a small smile on his face.

I'm starting to relax, starting to think maybe this won't be so bad, when Judge sets down her water glass and leans forward.

"So, twins," she says, her eyes bright with excitement. "That's going to be quite the adventure."

"Yeah." I touch my stomach instinctively. "It's still sinking in."

"Well, the good news is you'll have plenty of support." Tucker's mom pulls out her phone. "I've already been thinking about schedules. If we coordinate properly, you'll have around-the-clock help."

"Schedules?" I ask uncertainly.

"For babysitting rotations," Mr. Stag explains. "Between us and Tucker's brothers and cousins, we can make sure you're never without help. Especially those first few months when you're sleep-deprived and overwhelmed."

"We'll set up a shared calendar," Judge continues, scrolling through her phone. "I can take Tuesdays and Thursdays. Ty can do Mondays and Wednesdays when I have night court. That gives you weekdays covered, and then—"

"Wait." I hold up a hand, my chest tightening. "The babies aren't due for months."

"Oh, I know," Judge says, still scrolling. "But it's good to plan ahead. And with twins, you're going to need all the help you can get. Trust me, it's no joke."

"My brothers will want to help too," Tucker adds. "Alder especially. He's great with kids."

"And your aunts," Tucker's dad jumps in. "Imagine Lucy taking them out in her jogging stroller?"

They keep talking—about cribs and diaper services and the best pediatricians in Pittsburgh. About how Mr. Stag will build the nursery furniture himself because he's currently obsessed with woodworking. About how Judge knows a wonderful doula who helped them with the twins.

Each suggestion is well-meaning. Each offer is genuinely kind. But with every word, I feel smaller. More trapped. Like I'm disappearing into their plans, their schedules, their perfectly coordinated family system.

"We should probably set up a nursery at our house too," Judge says. "For when the babies stay over. It'll be easier if we have everything they need."

"Stay over?" My voice comes out sharper than I intended.

"Well, yes." She looks surprised. "So, you and Tucker can have date nights. Or so you can rest. New parents need breaks."

"Tucker and I aren't dating," I manage to say.

"Of course, of course." Mr. Stag waves a hand. "We're getting ahead of ourselves. It's just—we're excited, you know? A grandchild. Two grandchildren! It's wonderful news."

"You're going to be a Pappy," Judge grins. "I think I'm a Mimi."

Mr. Stag throws a napkin at her. "Whatever you say, Meemaw."

"Ugh." She laughs. "Can you imagine?"

I can't imagine. Can't imagine being part of a family this large, this involved, this... present.

"It's been a long time since we had a baby at Stagsgiving," Tucker's dad continues and then, realizing he's said a confusing word, he turns to me. "We do our own version of Thanksgiving dinner since half the kids have professional sports games on the actual day. Alice always manages to find a few hours where all of us can make it. Total chaos."

"You'll need to come to those," Judge adds. "It's important the babies grow up knowing their family."

"I haven't agreed to any of this," I say quietly.

The table goes silent. Three sets of eyes turn to me—Tucker's worried, his parents' confused.

"Agreed to what?" Judge asks gently.

"Any of it. The schedules, the sleepovers, the family dinners." My voice is shaking now. "You're making all these plans about my babies without even asking what I want."

"Sloane—" Tucker starts, but I cut him off.

"No. This is exactly what I was afraid of." I stand abruptly, my chair scraping against the floor. "Everyone deciding what's best for me, what my life should look like, how I should raise my children. I didn't agree to be absorbed into your family system. I didn't agree to weekly dinners and coordinated schedules and—"

"We're just trying to help," Mr. Stag says, looking genuinely bewildered.

"I know." And that's what makes it worse. "I know you mean well. But I already spent five years in a relationship where everyone made decisions about my life. Where I disappeared into someone else's world." I look at Tucker, tears burning my eyes. "I told you I couldn't do that again."

"This isn't the same thing," Tucker says, standing. "Sloane, we're not trying to control you. We're offering support."

"It feels like control." My breath is coming too fast now. "It feels like you're all planning out my life without me. Like I'm just supposed to smile and nod and be grateful."

"I think we came on too strong—" Judge starts.

"I know what you meant!" The words come out too loud, too sharp. "I know you're trying to be kind. But I can't—I can't do this. I can't be part of this."

I grab my purse from where I'd set it on a side table. Tucker reaches for me, but I step back.

"I need to go."

"Sloane, please—"

"I'm sorry." I look at Juniper Jones and Ty Stag, who both look shocked and hurt. "Thank you for dinner. I'm sorry I—I just need to go."

I'm already moving toward the door, toward the elevator. Tucker follows.

"Let me drive you home."

"I'll take an Uber."

"Sloane—"

The elevator doors open and I step inside, jabbing the lobby button repeatedly until the doors close. Through the gap, I see Tucker standing in his hallway, his parents behind him, all three of them looking concerned and confused.

The last thing I see before the doors shut completely is Tucker's face—devastated.

I make it to the lobby before the tears start. I'm crying in the back of an Uber, still crying when I stumble into my apartment, still crying when Mel finds me curled up on my bed.

"What happened?" she asks, wheeling close.

"I ruined everything," I manage between sobs.

"Oh, Sloane!" I feel the mattress dip as she transfers herself into bed beside me. "Tell me."

Through sputtering, choking sobs, I tell her how Tucker's stupid promotional condoms resulted in me pregnant. With twins. And his family wants to take control of all our lives.

By the time I get it all out, she's nodding robotically and slumped against my pillow. I watch her expression shift from confusion to shock to something like understanding.

"Oh," she says softly. "Oh, Sloane."

"And now his whole family wants to be involved, and I don't know how to do any of this and I'm so scared I'm going to lose myself again."

Mel reaches for my hand, squeezing tight. "You're not going to lose yourself."

"How do you know?"

"Because you're already fighting for yourself. That's what tonight was about, right? Setting boundaries. Protecting yourself." She squeezes again. "That's not losing yourself, Sloane. That's finding yourself."

I want to believe her. Want to believe that running out of Tucker's apartment was self-preservation and not self-sabotage.

My phone buzzes with a message.

> **TUCKER**
>
> Please let me know you got home okay.

I stare at the message, fresh tears blurring my vision.

> I'm home.

> **TUCKER**
>
> I'm so sorry. This is on us. On me. I should have warned them to go slower.

It's not your fault.

TUCKER

Can we talk tomorrow? When you're ready?

I don't respond. Don't know what to say. Instead, I curl up against Mel's shoulder, let her stroke my hair, and cry until I have no tears left.

CHAPTER 19
TUCKER

HOCKEY IS BRUTAL TODAY.

I almost wish I were fighting instead. Give me a huge, angry guy from Montreal with his fist in my teeth instead of this feeling of dragging my legs through sand.

Coach has us running defensive scenarios—breakouts, gap control, transition defense—and I'm going through the motions like a robot.

"T-Stag! What the hell was that?" Coach Thompson's voice booms across the ice. "You're supposed to be closing the gap, not giving them a highway to the net!"

I skate back to position, jaw clenched. Beside me, Alder shoots me a concerned look but doesn't say anything. He's been shooting me those looks all week.

It's been a week since Sloane ran out of my apartment, and I've been staring at my phone like an idiot ever since. And it's affecting my work.

"Again!" Coach blows his whistle. "And T-Stag, I need you present. Not whatever the hell that was."

We run the drill again. And again. And again. Mayhem glowers at me while Howie pukes in a trash can. By the time Coach finally blows the whistle for the end of practice, my legs are screaming and my lungs are burning, but my mind won't shut off.

The locker room is loud with the usual post-practice banter.

Guys peeling off gear, talking about plans for the evening, the normalcy of it all feels alien.

"You coming to Howie's tonight?" Spinner asks, tossing his gloves into his bag. "He's got that new grill he won't shut up about."

"Pass," I mutter, unlacing my skates.

"Come on, man. You've been weird."

"I'm fine. Just exhausted."

Across the room, Alder is packing up his gear, moving with deliberate slowness. Watching me. Always watching me. Gunnar is nearby, whispering on his phone—probably to his wife.

"I'm heading out," Gunnar says, pocketing his phone. "Em made dinner."

"Of course she did," Alder teases. "That's what they're calling it these days?"

"Don't be jealous." Gunnar grins. "You'll get there eventually."

Alder's ears redden slightly, and I know he's thinking about Lena. My twin and the team dentist finally came out as a couple during a huge press conference. I was too mired in my own shit to be there for him.

"Yeah, yeah." Alder shoulders his bag. "I'm heading to the dental office to help Lena with some paperwork."

"Paperwork. Right." Gunnar winks. "See you guys tomorrow."

I fiddle with my skate laces and shoulder pads while they file out with the rest of the team, until suddenly I'm alone in the locker room. The silence is deafening after all the noise, both inside and outside my head.

I should leave. Should go home. Should do literally anything productive.

Instead, I just sit there on the bench, staring at my phone. At the last message I sent Sloane three days ago—ignored.

"Fuck," I whisper to the empty room. Panic builds in my chest. I feel like I'm about to explode. I sense something in my bones howling.

I think about calling my dad for advice, but for some reason, I head for the showers, still in my base layers. The water is scalding, but I don't adjust it. I just stand there, letting it pound against my shoulders, my back, soaking through the fabric, clinging to my skin.

I press my forehead against the tile wall, water streaming down my face, and finally let go. The tears come hot and fast, mixing with the shower spray. My shoulders shake with the effort of staying quiet, but it's useless. A sob escapes, then another.

I'm losing her. I'm losing them. And I don't know how to fix it.

"I'm so fucked," I choke out. "I fucked everything up."

Suddenly, Alder's voice cuts through the sound of the water.

"Tuck?"

I straighten immediately, swiping at my face like that will hide anything. "I'm fine. Just—"

"You're crying in the shower." Alder appears in the doorway, his expression somewhere between concerned and determined. "Fully clothed. You want to tell me that's fine?"

"Go away, Alder."

"Not a chance." He leans against the doorframe, arms crossed. "Talk to me, Fucker."

"There's nothing to—"

"Bullshit." His voice is firm.

He turns off the water, and I stand there dripping, my base layers plastered to my skin. "I fucked up, man."

He nods. "Okay. Tell me and we'll fix it. That's what we do, right?"

I shake my head, water droplets flying off me. "Not this time." My teeth start chattering, and my brother wraps me in his arms. I should care that I'm drenching him in a gross shower. I should care that he's probably come here fresh from banging his dentist, and now I'm a mess and interrupting his mojo. But instead, I just cry into his shirt while he pats my back.

"Is this about Sloane?" He holds me at arm's length and tilts his head til he can meet my eyes.

I shrug. "Yes and no. I...um." I blow out a breath and close my eyes. I can't even look at him when I say this. "She's pregnant."

He produces a noise somewhere in between a whoop and a question mark. "No. Way."

"With twins." I sink back onto the floor of the shower with a squelch as Alder starts to laugh maniacally.

"Twins!" He gestures between us. "We've got mutant sperm, don't we? Where we only duplicate? Or something?" Alder sits beside me with a laugh. "But okay, this isn't like *cry in the shower* bad. Babies are kind of awesome."

I shake my head and tell him everything. About the dinner with our parents, about how they overwhelmed her with schedules and plans, about how she said she can't lose herself again like she did in her marriage.

"Fuck."

"Yeah."

Alder is quiet for a long moment, and I brace for judgment or lecture or I-told-you-so. Instead, he stands and pulls me up with him, both of us embracing in the shower stall, me still soaking wet.

He rests his forehead against mine and laughs quietly. "You're a dad."

I nod. "I'm going to be a dad."

Alder slaps the tile, the sound echoing through the locker room. "You're going to be okay," he says quietly. "We'll figure this out."

The comfort of my twin—my other half—is almost too much. I hug him back, feeling some of the tension in my chest loosen.

"I don't know how to be a dad," I admit. "I don't know how to prove to Sloane that I'm not going to disappear or let her down. I don't know how to—"

"Hey." Alder pulls back, hands on my shoulders. "You're already doing it. Showing up. Trying. That's what matters."

"But she won't let me."

"Then you keep trying. Keep showing up. Even if she doesn't respond." He squeezes my shoulders. "That's what Stags do. We don't give up."

"When did you get so wise?"

"I've always been the smarter twin." He grins, then sobers.

"But Tucker, you need to tell the team. Or at least talk to Coach. Before Grentley finds out another way."

"I know. I just—"

"Too late for that."

The voice comes from behind Alder, low and furious. We both turn to find Josh Grentley standing in the locker room doorway, his expression twisted with rage.

Grentley's hands are clenched into fists at his sides. "You fucked my wife, Stag?"

"Josh—" I start, but he's already moving.

He grabs Alder—mistaking him for me like everyone else does when we're standing side by side—and yanks him backward. Alder stumbles, caught off guard.

"You son of a bitch!" Grentley roars. "You had to ruin everything, didn't you? Couldn't leave well enough alone!"

"Hey, man, that's not—" Alder tries to say, but Grentley's fist is already flying.

The punch connects with Alder's jaw with a sickening crack. My twin goes down hard, blood immediately streaming from his mouth.

"NO!" I launch myself at Grentley, tackling him away from Alder. We crash into the lockers, metal clanging. "That's not me, you fucking idiot! That's my brother!"

Grentley's eyes widen as he realizes his mistake, but he doesn't stop fighting. "I don't care which of you goes down. You're both assholes!" He screams and shouts, fists flying. I leave my twin bleeding on the ground so I can get a few hits in on this puckered-up asshole.

We're grappling, both slipping on the wet floor, when suddenly someone is pulling us apart.

"What the hell is going on?" Gunnar's voice booms through the locker room. He's got Grentley in a bear hug, dragging him backward. "Josh, what are you doing?"

"He got her pregnant!" Grentley struggles against Gunnar's hold. "Your piece of shit brother fucked my wife!"

Gunnar snorts. "I think I'd know if my brother was having a baby."

I shoot a death glare at Gunnar and try to get to Alder, who's sitting on the floor, hand pressed to his mouth, blood seeping between his fingers.

"Tuck, I'm calling you later, man." Gunnar grunts, barely maintaining his grip on Grentley. "Take Alder to Lena. Now!"

I don't argue. I drop beside Alder, hauling him to his feet. His face is already swelling, blood dripping down his chin.

"Come on," I say, wrapping his arm around my shoulders and dragging him toward the dental suite.

Behind us, I hear Grentley howling as Gunnar drags him toward the exit.

"This isn't over, Stag! You hear me? This isn't over! All of you Stags are going to pay for this!"

The threat follows us as I move my brother. I'm soaking wet, leaving a trail of water. Alder is bleeding, stumbling beside me. Everything is falling apart faster than I could have imagined.

I shoulder through the door to Lena's office, startling her from whatever she was doing at her desk.

"Tucker? What—" She sees Alder and immediately springs into action. "What happened?"

"Grentley," I say, helping Alder into the dental chair. "He thought Alder was me. Punched him."

"Jesus." Lena's already putting on gloves, gently tilting Alder's head back. "Let me see, babe."

Alder removes his hand from his mouth, revealing a mess of blood and—

"Tooth's out," Lena says grimly, examining his mouth. "Upper right lateral incisor. Damn it, Josh."

"We match now," Alder mumbles, trying for humor despite the pain. His words are slurred around the swelling.

I sink into the chair, my head in my hands. Everything is ruined. The team knows. Grentley attacked my brother. And Sloane—

Sloane is going to hear about this. Probably from Grentley himself.

"Tucker." Lena's voice is gentle. "I need you to call team medical. Alder needs proper treatment. And—" She hesitates. "You need to call your agent. This is going to get back to Coach Thompson."

I pull out my phone, shaking, and dial my dad.

"Hey, kiddo," he answers cheerfully. "What's up?"

"Dad." My voice cracks. "I need help. Everything just fell apart."

The cheerfulness vanishes instantly. "Where are you?"

"We're at the practice facility, Ty," Lena shouts above Alder's groan of pain. Tooth stuff makes me queasy, and I try not to barf while explaining to my dad that I need him to call Brian for me. Hopefully, our agent isn't on a flight somewhere.

"I'm on my way." Dad's voice is calm, like he's used to managing colossal fuckups like this. "We'll figure this out."

But as I watch my twin spit blood into a basin, as I hear Grentley's threats still echoing in my head, as I think about Sloane finding out about this disaster, I'm not sure anything is going to be okay ever again.

I turn my head to the side and puke up bile all over the floor. My insides truly evacuate my body as I think about my career imploding, my brother's ruined face, and the mother of my children who will now most certainly never speak to me again.

Alder reaches out with his non-bloody hand and squeezes my shoulder. Even injured, even caught in the middle of my mess, he's still trying to support me.

For the first time, I'm really not sure I deserve it.

CHAPTER 20
SLOANE

Professor Khan's office smells like old books, and the dust is making my eyes water. Or is that the impending sense of doom from the red-marked exam on her desk? Either way, my eyes are leaking.

"Sloane." Her voice is kind, which somehow makes this worse. "I can see you're struggling."

"I'm fine," I lie. "Just need to study more."

"That's not what concerns me." She leans forward, hands folded. "You've missed three classes in the past two weeks of a six-week summer intensive. Your assignments have been incomplete. And this exam—" She taps the paper with its damning 47% circled at the top. "This isn't someone who doesn't understand the material. This is someone who's overwhelmed."

The tears come despite my best efforts. I swipe at them angrily. "I'm sorry. I'll do better. I can retake the exam, or—"

"I'm not trying to punish you." Dr. Khan's expression softens. "I'm trying to help you succeed. Talk to me. What's going on?"

I open my mouth to lie again, to say it's just stress, just adjusting to school. But the words that come out are: "I'm pregnant. With twins. And everything is falling apart."

Dr. Khan doesn't look shocked. She nods slowly, like this explains everything. "Okay, so you have some options for a medical exemption."

She sits back, studying me. "Sloane, I've seen your work when you're focused—you're bright, capable, passionate about public health. But right now, you seem unable to give this your best effort. What about an incomplete—"

"I can handle it."

"Can you?" Her tone is gentle but firm. "Because from where I'm sitting, you're drowning. And that's not good for you or your babies."

The truth of her words settles heavily in my chest. I am drowning. Between the pregnancy exhaustion, the nausea, the stress with Tucker, and Mel moving out—I can't keep all the plates spinning.

Dr. Khan continues. "You can withdraw from the class with a medical exemption. No penalty. Or—" She pauses. "You can take an incomplete and finish the coursework in the fall term..."

I spit out a laugh. "In the fall, I'll have 12 credits and even more appointments."

"Sloane, I think you need to be realistic about your capacity right now." She slides a form across the desk. "Think about it. You have until Monday to decide. But whatever you choose, please— take care of yourself first. The degree will still be here when you're ready."

I nod, taking the form with shaking hands. How can she possibly know that I'm the first person in my family to go to college at all, and I already interrupted that process once. "Thank you."

"And Sloane?" Dr. Khan waits until I meet her eyes. "Ask for help. Whatever support systems you have—use them. I don't know your situation, but if you need suggestions, I personally benefited from a support group for Pittsburgh parents of color. Let me know if I can make connections, okay?"

I'm walking out of the building, Dr. Khan's words still echoing in my head, when my phone rings. Josh's name flashes on the screen.

For a moment, I consider not answering. But whatever he has to say, I'd rather hear it now than wonder about it all night.

"Hello?"

"You're pregnant." His voice is cold, clipped. "By Tucker Stag."

My stomach drops. "How did you—"

"How did I find out that my teammate knocked up my ex-wife?" He laughs bitterly. "He said something weird at his brother's wedding, and then I hired the same chatty decorator he uses. I confronted him while he was crying in the shower like a child."

I stop walking, pressing my phone tighter to my ear. "Josh—"

"Were you ever going to tell me? Or were you just going to let me find out online?"

"Why would I tell you?" The words come out sharper than intended. "We're divorced. What I do isn't your business anymore."

"It is when it's with someone at my work!" His voice rises. "Do you have any idea what kind of position this puts me in? What people are saying?"

"What are people saying?" Anger flares hot in my chest. "You're worried about gossip? About your reputation?"

"I'm worried about how this looks! My ex-wife, pregnant with my teammate's kid. It looks like you used me, Sloane. Like you were just biding your time until you could trap someone else."

The accusation steals my breath. "Trap someone? Are you serious right now?"

"What else am I supposed to think? You told me you didn't want kids. We agreed—"

"We didn't agree!" I'm shouting now, not caring who hears. "You got a vasectomy without telling me! You made that decision for both of us!"

Silence on the other end of the line. Then: "I did what was best. For my career."

"For YOUR career. Not ours. Yours." My hand moves instinctively to my stomach as I stand shouting in the middle of campus. "You lied to me, Josh. For years. I was a *teenager* when we first discussed kids."

"I was protecting our future—"

"You were controlling my future. There's a difference." I take a shaky breath. "And now I'm moving on with my life. And it has nothing to do with you."

"It has everything to do with me when it's with someone on my professional sports team!"

"Then that's your problem to deal with." My voice is steadier now. "Not mine. I didn't plan this. I didn't trap anyone. And I sure as hell don't owe you an explanation."

"I should have figured you'd—" He stops himself.

"Figured what, Josh? Say it."

"Nothing. Forget it."

"No. You started, so finish. What did you assume about me?"

Another pause. When he speaks again, his voice is quieter but no less cutting. "You have no idea how to make things last. You just cut and leave when there's a disagreement."

The words hit like a city bus. As if what he did was a silly little misunderstanding.

"Fuck you." My voice shakes. "You don't get to know about my life anymore. Not after what you did."

"Sloane—"

"Do not contact me again." I'm crying now, hot, angry tears streaming down my face. "Don't call me. Don't text me. Whatever you need to work out with Tucker, work it out with him. But leave me out of it."

"Wait—"

I hang up, hands shaking so badly I nearly drop the phone. Around me, the university continues its late afternoon bustle—students heading to dinner, professors locking up offices. Everyday life, carrying on while mine implodes.

Part of me—the part that spent five years trying to make Josh happy—wants to apologize for hanging up. To smooth things over, to make it easier for him.

But the rest of me, the part that's carrying two babies and fighting for her future, knows better.

I block his number and shove my phone in my pocket.

Then I pull it back out and open my Uber app. I need to see Tucker. Need to know what happened, what Josh meant about the locker room. Need to see if we're about to face an even bigger disaster than I thought.

I might not want a relationship with Tucker Stag. I no longer get to have casual flings post-divorce. But I'm tied to him, and I want our children to see parents who talk to each other like adults.

———

The ride to Tucker's building takes 20 minutes through rush-hour traffic. Twenty minutes of my mind spiraling through worst-case scenarios that continue as the doorman waves me into the lobby. What if the team kicks Tucker out? What if this ruins his career? What if Josh makes good on his threat to make everything impossible?

What if I've ruined Tucker's life with my uber-fertile womb?

The thought sits heavy in my chest as I ride the elevator to Tucker's penthouse. The doors open directly into his apartment, and I step out, calling his name.

"Tucker?"

"Huh?" His voice comes out rough and tired.

I follow the sound to find him in the living room, and my heart clenches at the sight. He's sitting on the couch in sweatpants and a wrinkled t-shirt, hair disheveled like he's been running his hands through it for hours. His eyes are red-rimmed, face pale. I see bruises on his cheek, and his knuckles look raw.

He looks destroyed.

Another man is gathering papers from the coffee table—tall, sharply dressed in a suit, looking distinctly unimpressed.

"Oh." I stop in the doorway. "I'm sorry, I didn't know you had company."

"Just leaving." The man straightens, giving Tucker a pointed look. "Brian Klein, Tucker's agent. You must be Sloane."

"Yes. Hi."

Brian shakes my hand, his grip professional but his expression skeptical. "Well, T-Stag, looks like you've got your hands full. Remember what we discussed—shape up, lean into this family man thing. It's your only play right now."

"I know," Tucker says quietly.

"Do you?" Brian's tone sharpens. "Because you just torched a very lucrative endorsement deal and picked a fight with one of your teammates. The family angle is the only thing that might salvage your reputation."

"It's not an angle," Tucker says, his jaw tight.

"Then start acting like it." Brian nods to me. "Nice meeting you, Sloane. Do not go easy on him. He needs all the help he can get right now."

The older man leaves, the elevator doors closing behind him with a soft chime. The silence that follows is heavy, loaded with everything we need to say and don't know how to start.

"Josh called me," I say finally, looking around this apartment that will become an important part of my life, no matter what I think of its occupant.

Tucker's swollen eyes drift closed. "What did he have to say?"

"A lot of things. Most of them angry." I move closer, sinking into the chair across from him. "He said you have the same decorator and that you were crying in the shower."

Tucker's face flushes. "I didn't think to tell her it was a secret. I bet that fucker didn't tell you he attacked Alder."

"He did what?"

Tucker's hands clench into fists. "Thought he was me. Punched him. Knocked out his tooth."

"Jesus." I lean back, processing. "How is Alder?"

"Okay. Pissed. Lena's taking care of him—the team dentist. Wasn't sure who all you know." He looks at me, and I see fear in his eyes. Raw, genuine fear. "Sloane, I'm so sorry. I never wanted it to come out like this. I was trying to respect your timeline, to wait until you were ready. Think of the right way to tell the team…"

"I know."

"And now Coach has me on probation. I have to do anger management therapy with Grentley. Team building exercises. The whole thing." He laughs bitterly. "My agent just told me the condom company dropped me. Apparently, getting your hookup pregnant is bad for the 'Thin Ice' brand."

Despite everything, I feel a small laugh bubble up. "I guess that makes sense."

"It's a disaster." Tucker drops his head into his hands. "Everything I touch turns into a disaster."

I watch him for a moment, this man who's usually so confident, so sure of himself. Seeing him like this—vulnerable, scared, beating himself up—does something to my heart.

Josh never looked like this. Never showed this kind of raw emotion, this kind of self-awareness about his mistakes. When things went wrong in our marriage, he'd retreat into cold silence or redirect blame. He'd act first and tell me later, presenting his decisions as the right and only way forward.

Tucker acts impulsively, too. But he tells everyone. Announces his intentions, asks for help, doesn't hide when things fall apart.

It's a subtle difference. But maybe it's an important one.

I stand and move to the couch, sitting beside him. Close enough that our shoulders touch.

"It's not all a disaster," I say quietly.

He looks at me, hope and disbelief warring in his expression. "How is any of this not a disaster?"

"You have a job. You have a family who supports you. You have—" I gesture around the apartment. "All of this. And you have two babies on the way who are healthy and growing."

"I have the twins because you let me." His voice cracks. "And I'm terrified you're going to take them away."

"I'm not taking anything away."

"Then why are you here?" The question is desperate. "Grentley called you. I'm sure he said terrible things. I'm sure he told you to stay away from me. So why are you here?"

I think about Dr. Khan's words, and I think about Josh's accusation.

And here on this couch sits Tucker, destroyed but owning it.

"I'm here because I'm drowning," I admit. "And I need help."

Tucker's eyes widen. "What do you need?"

"I'm failing statistics. My professor basically told me I need to either drop the class or take an incomplete. Mel's moving out in two weeks, and the lease is ending, and I can't have babies in that building." I take a shaky breath. "And I'm pregnant with twins and I'm terrified and I can't do this alone."

"You're not alone." Tucker's hand finds mine. "Sloane, you're not alone."

"I know. Theoretically, I know that. But—" My voice breaks. "I'm so scared of losing myself again. Of disappearing into someone else's life. Of staying cut off from community. I did that with Josh for five years, and I can't—"

"You won't." Tucker shifts to face me fully, both hands holding mine now. "I promise you won't. Whatever you need, whatever boundaries you want—I'll respect them. You want your own space? Done. You want to keep working on your degree? We'll figure it out. You want to make your own decisions about the babies? They're your decisions."

"But you'll have opinions."

"Of course I'll have opinions. But I'll tell you my opinions and then we'll decide together." His shoulders tense, like he's anticipating a blow.

I close my eyes, and a single tear rolls down my cheek. "He got a vasectomy," I whisper. I owe it to Tucker to come into whatever this is with wide eyes. "He never told me. Not until years later. That was the beginning of the end."

Tucker squeezes my hand, and I let myself feel the comfort and warmth of his touch.

"We'd talked about kids when we first got together—I was nineteen at the time. I said I wanted them someday. He said..." I pause, remembering. "He said, 'Maybe.' I thought that meant yes, eventually. But three years into our marriage, I found the paperwork. He'd done it without telling me."

Tucker's jaw tightens. "That's fucked up."

"The worst part?" My voice cracks. "When I confronted him, he didn't apologize. He just said, 'I told you I wasn't sure.' Like 'not sure' meant 'absolutely never' and I should have known." I wipe my eyes. "He wasn't cruel about it. He was just... blank. Like he'd already decided I'd either accept it or leave, and either way, he'd be fine."

Josh was always distant with his emotions. He suffered his own trauma as a kid—something we bonded over initially. My mistake was believing our love would heal him. And me, I guess.

Tucker growls. "That's *really* fucked up, Sloane. He had no right."

"He thought he was protecting his future."

"He was controlling yours." Tucker's voice is firm. "And that's not the same thing."

The validation—someone seeing it, naming it, being angry on my behalf—breaks something open in my chest.

"He said I use people," I whisper. "On the phone today, he said I take what I can get and move on."

"He's wrong." Tucker's voice is fierce now. "You're nothing like that. You're strong and smart, and you're trying to build a life for yourself. That's not taking—that's creating."

I want to believe him. Want to believe I'm not repeating harmful patterns, not using people, not running from one disaster into another.

"About my living situation," I say slowly. "You got room here for a few more people?"

Tucker goes very still, striking blue eyes dancing in the fading light. "Yes. God, yes. But Sloane, I don't want you to feel pressured. If you're not ready—"

"I'm not ready," I interrupt. "But I'm also out of options. Failing school. Living alone. It's not safe."

"Okay." He nods quickly. "Okay. We can make it work. Whatever you need—"

"Boundaries," I say firmly. "This is temporary. Just until the babies come, and I figure out something more permanent. We're roommates. Co-parents. Nothing more."

Something flickers in his eyes—hurt, maybe, or disappointment—but he nods. "Whatever you need."

"I need my own space. My own room."

"Done. Easy. The main bedroom even has a full bathroom, walk-in closet, sitting area. I'll move my crap down the hall to the guest room."

"You don't have to give up your room."

He waves a hand. "All the bedrooms have an ensuite in this

place. You need the bigger room because you are growing Stag babies." He gestures to his frame. "We make 'em big, Sloane." Then he winces, as if just realizing the implications of that declaration. I clutch my midsection and breathe through a twinge of panic, reminding myself that the babies will not start out as massive Vikings like their father.

"There are some things I won't bend about," I tell him. "Like vaccines."

He holds up a hand. "We are pro-science in the Stag family. No worries there."

I purse my lips. "We'll be raising Black kids."

He sits up, fully alert, and looks me in the eyes. "Of course, Sloane. I want to learn all I can and make sure these nuggets feel whole." Tucker stops himself. "You have my word. Your autonomy, your independence—that's non-negotiable."

I study his face, looking for any sign that he's just telling me what I want to hear. But all I see is sincerity. Determination. Fear that I'll say no.

"Okay," I say. "I'll move in."

Tucker's whole body seems to sag with relief. "Thank you. I promise you won't regret this."

"I already regret it a little," I admit. "But I also don't have a better option right now."

He laughs, the sound almost breaking with emotion. "I'll take 'better than nothing.' It's more than I thought I'd get after today."

We sit there for a moment, hands still clasped, the weight of this decision settling over us.

CHAPTER 22
TUCKER

I'M SITTING IN AN UNCOMFORTABLE CHAIR ACROSS FROM JOSH Grentley, with my brother Odin perched on a stool in the corner, and a woman named Paulina Rodriguez settled in the chair between us like a referee at a boxing match. Given the physical altercation from the other day, everyone thought it was safest for Odin to observe as a bouncer.

I guess this is therapy.

"Thank you both for coming," Paulina says, like the two of us are at a party and she's the host. She's probably in her forties, Latina, with dark hair pulled back and an expression that suggests she's seen it all. "I know this isn't easy, but Coach Thompson and team management feel that mediation is necessary given recent events."

Grentley snorts. "Mediation. That's what we're calling it?"

"What would you call it?" Paulina asks evenly.

"Damage control. PR bullshit." He leans back in his chair, arms crossed. "The Stags fuck up, and the rest of us have to sit through therapy."

I bite the inside of my cheek to keep from responding. Odin shifts slightly in the corner—he's not allowed to participate since he's family. I can feel his tension as he slips out of the room.

"Josh," Paulina says, "that's not a productive way to—"

"Productive?" Grentley laughs bitterly. "You want productive? How about we talk about nepotism? About how there are four

Stags on this team because Daddy played here twenty years ago?"

I snort before I can stop myself. "We earned our spots."

"Did you?" Grentley leans forward. "Or did management just figure having the Stag name would sell jerseys?"

"Gentlemen—" Paulina tries to interject.

"I've led the team in penalty minutes and fighting majors for two seasons," I say, my voice tight. "I do my job."

"Your job is to protect the team. Not fuck your teammates' wives."

The room goes silent. Paulina's eyes dart between us, assessing.

"Josh," she says carefully, "I'm not sure you're in the right headspace for this session today."

"I'm fine."

"You're clearly not fine." I can't help myself now. "You're pissed that Sloane ditched you when you're the one who got your balls snipped without telling her."

Grentley's face goes red. "The fuck did you just say?"

"You heard me. You made that decision—"

Grentley lunges across the space between us. I'm on my feet instantly, chairs clattering backward. Odin bursts back into the room and grabs Grentley from behind while Paulina shouts something about stopping, but I'm ready to fight, adrenaline pumping—

A whistle pierces the air, directly in my ear. Sharp, shrill, and probably causing permanent hearing loss.

We all freeze.

Coach Thompson heaves me back into my chair, whistle still at his lips, his face purple with outrage.

"What the hell is wrong with you two?" He looks between us. "This is a therapist's office. A place where you're supposed to be working out your problems like adults. And you're about to throw punches?"

"He started—" Grentley begins.

"I don't care who started it." Coach's voice is deadly calm now. "Get out of my building. Both of you. Go home. Come back when you're ready to act like professionals instead of fucking children."

"Coach—" I start.

"Out. Now." He points toward the door. "Before I suspend you both."

Grentley shoves past me, shoulder-checking me hard as he goes. Every instinct screams to retaliate, but I force myself to stay still.

Coach watches him leave, then turns to me. "I expected better from you, T-Stag."

"I know. I'm sorry."

"Sorry doesn't fix this. Your family name means something in this organization. Live up to it." He shakes his head.

I grab my jacket and leave, Odin following me into the hallway.

"That was bad," he says quietly once we're out of earshot.

"You think?" I flick my brother in the nipple, and he smacks my shoulder.

"Tuck, you can't let him bait you like that. He's looking for a reason to make you the villain."

"I'm aware." I run a hand through my hair. "I just—fuck. He makes it so easy."

"I know. But you're better than that." Odin squeezes my shoulder. "Go home. See Sloane. Remember what you're fighting for."

Home. Except Sloane specifically asked me not to be there while she was moving in. Said she needed to set up her space on her own, establish her territory before I was around.

So instead, I find myself driving to BabyLand—where apparently, I can get everything from cribs to car seats to snot suckers.

The automatic doors whoosh open, and I'm immediately overwhelmed. Rows and rows of tiny clothes, furniture, gear. A woman pushing a stroller passes by, twins asleep inside, and something in my chest clenches.

That's going to be me. In a few months, that's going to be my life.

"Can I help you find something?" A cheerful employee appears at my elbow, name tag reading "Sandra." She's a petite white woman who looks like she could be everybody's grandma.

"I need—" I look around. "Everything. I'm having twins."

Sandra's face lights up. "Congratulations! First time, Dad?"

"Yeah."

"Okay, let's start with the basics." She grabs a cart, not seeming to recognize me, which is a small mercy I will gladly accept right now. "Cribs, stroller, car seats, changing table..."

For the next hour, Sandra guides me through the store while I say yes to almost everything. Bamboo crib sheets because they're supposed to be hypoallergenic. An obscenely expensive European double stroller because it has the highest safety ratings. Uncle Tim will be so proud.

"You're going to want multiple changing pads," Sandra says, loading another item into the growing pile. "Trust me, with twins, you'll be grateful for backups."

"Add it."

By the time I'm done, my cart looks like I'm preparing for the apocalypse.

"Your partner is lucky," Sandra says as she processes the payment. "Not every dad gets this involved before the babies arrive."

"I'm trying," I say.

"That's all anyone can do."

———

I pull into my building's garage, Wyatt's back seat loaded with the smaller bags, with the rest of it getting delivered later this week. I take the elevator with all my loot, suddenly nervous.

What if she's changed her mind? What if being here made her realize this was a mistake?

But when the doors open into my apartment—our apartment now—I find Sloane curled up on the couch, fast asleep. A statistics textbook is open on her chest, rising and falling with her breath. Her curls are pulled back in a messy bun, and she's wearing yoga pants and one of those soft-looking sweaters that makes her look impossibly small and vulnerable.

My heart does something complicated in my chest.

I leave the bags by the elevator and move quietly into the kitchen. The sink is full of dishes—I really should have cleaned up before I left for work. I roll up my sleeves and start washing, careful to keep the water running softly so I don't wake her.

Dish by dish, I work through the pile. Plates, glasses, silverware. It's meditative somehow. Calming after the disaster of the therapy session.

"Tucker?"

I turn to find Sloane sitting up, rubbing her eyes. The textbook has fallen to the floor.

"Hey there, gorgeous." The words slip out before I can stop them.

She groans, but there's no heat in it. "What time is it?"

"Almost five. You hungry?"

"Starving. And my feet are killing me." She looks down at them with betrayal. "Since when is unpacking so exhausting?"

"Since you're growing two Stags." I dry my hands and move to the couch. "Here. Let me."

Before she can protest, I lift her feet into my lap and start rubbing. Her eyes close immediately, a slight sound of relief escaping. I will my crotch not to respond to that sound, and that's probably the most challenging task of my day. And that's saying something.

"Oh my god. That's amazing." She practically purrs.

"My dad said he used to do this for my mom when she was pregnant." I work my thumbs along her arch.

"Your dad's a smart man."

We sit like that for a while, me rubbing her feet while she relaxes into the couch cushions. The late afternoon sun streams through the windows, painting everything gold.

This feels right. More right than anything has felt in a long time.

"I bought some stuff," I say eventually. "Baby stuff. It's by the elevator. I can put it in your room or wherever you want."

"What kind of stuff?" She talks with her eyes closed, and it's familiar. Comfortable. I like it.

"Crib sheets. A stroller. Some other things Sandra said we'd need."

"Who's Sandra?"

"Lady at BabyLand. She was very helpful."

Sloane opens one eye. "How much stuff?"

"Some stuff."

"Tucker."

"A reasonable amount of stuff for someone having twins."

She tries to sit up to look, but I press gently on her ankle. "Stay. You're comfortable. I'll show you later."

"I can't believe you went baby shopping."

"I can go again. With you. We can take everything back if you want."

She laughs, the sound sleepy and warm. "That's excessive even for you."

"Nothing's excessive for our babies."

The words hang between us. Our babies. Not my babies or her babies. Ours.

Sloane doesn't correct me. She just settles back into the cushions, her feet still in my lap, and closes her eyes again.

"This is nice," she murmurs.

"Yeah?"

"Yeah. Don't get used to it, though. Still just roommates."

"Right. Roommates who co-parent."

"Exactly."

She falls back asleep within minutes, her breathing evening out. I sit there, one hand resting on her ankle, watching her.

I should probably get up. Start putting the baby things away, make dinner, and do something productive. But I don't want to move. Don't want to disturb this moment.

My eyes drift to the framed photo on the wall—me, Alder, and Gunnar in our Fury gear after our first pro game. We're all grinning, arms around each other, on top of the world.

Hockey has been my life since before I was conceived. The ice, the team, the game—it's shaped everything I am.

But sitting here with Sloane, her feet in my lap, thinking about the twins growing inside her—this feels important in a different way. Essential in a way hockey never quite has been.

I think about my dad leaving the pros when Mom had Odin. I never really understood it before. How do you walk away from something you love? Something you've worked your whole life for?

But now, looking at Sloane, I'm starting to get it.

My family isn't just hockey. My family is here, asleep on this couch, trusting me enough to let her guard down.

My family is two tiny heartbeats I can't stop thinking about.

My family is this life I'm trying to build, this future I'm trying to be worthy of.

Except... hockey is family too. Alder, Gunnar, Odin. The team. The ice that's thick in my veins.

How do I choose between those things? How do I balance them when they both matter so much?

The thin ice I'm skating on right now feels weaker by the day. One wrong move and everything will crack, sending me plunging into water I'm not sure I can swim out of.

Coach's words echo in my head: *Your family name means something in this organization. Live up to it.*

But which family? The one I was born into or the one I'm trying to create?

CHAPTER 23
SLOANE

I WAKE UP FEELING WELL-RESTED FOR ONCE, UNTIL I REALIZE TUCKER must have carried me to bed last night. I check the time on my phone and see that it's nearly eight. Tucker Stag really does have magic fingers if he can massage me into deep slumber and transfer me without waking me.

I bite my lip and listen to see if he's up or moving around, but all I hear is silence.

He must have already gone to hockey practice.

I sit up slowly, my hand moving to my stomach. Still flat, but not for much longer, according to Dr. Patel. I try not to think about Tucker's assertion that Stag babies grow big.

Better to focus on the physical space.

The bedroom is gorgeous in the morning light. Enormous, with that sitting area Tucker mentioned, the walk-in closet, the ensuite bathroom with a tub big enough to swim in. The bed is absurdly comfortable—some fancy mattress that manages to be the exact perfect firmness I like.

But what gets me are the small details I missed last night when I was too exhausted to notice.

As I wander around, I notice a basket on the dresser brims with snacks—crackers, dried fruit, those lavender candies from the doctor's office.

He thought of everything.

I make my way to the bathroom. The counter has been cleared

—empty except for a note in Tucker's handwriting propped against the mirror:

> Towels in the closet. Make yourself at home. - T

I open the drawers to find them lined with that fancy shelf paper, completely empty and waiting. The medicine cabinet's the same—cleared out, ready for my things.

He gave me his bedroom and moved himself into the guest room without complaint.

I brush my teeth and head back out to explore.

The living room looks different in daylight—less intimidating, more lived-in. My boxes are stacked neatly by the wall, labeled in my own handwriting. But what catches my eye are the shopping bags piled by the door.

So many bags.

I move closer, peeking inside the first one. Bamboo crib sheets in soft neutrals—gray, cream, sage green. I pull out another package. More sheets. A third bag has receiving blankets, also bamboo, also expensive.

"Jesus, Tucker," I mutter, moving to the next bag.

A sound machine. Swaddles. A baby bathtub. Hooded towels with little animal ears. Everything is high-quality, thoughtfully chosen, ridiculously expensive.

And then I see the box.

It's huge, leaning against the wall, and the picture on the side shows a sleek double stroller. I recognize the brand—European, featured in all the "best of" lists I've been secretly reading at 2 AM when I can't sleep. A four-figure gadget.

I sink onto the couch, staring at the pile of supplies. He went shopping. By himself. And bought everything we might need and then some.

My phone buzzes.

TUCKER

Morning. How'd you sleep?

I stare at the message, then at the shopping bags, then back at the message.

Good. You bought a lot of stuff.

TUCKER

Too much? I can return things.

A $2,400 stroller might be a little extra.

TUCKER

It has the highest safety ratings. And it converts from infant car seats to toddler seats. We'll use it for years.

We could use it to drive the babies to college.

TUCKER

Exactly. Practical.

Despite everything, I smile.

Thank you. For all of it. It's really thoughtful.

TUCKER

You're welcome. Appointment at 2, right?

Yes.

TUCKER

I'll be home by 1:30 to pick you up.

I set the phone down and look around the apartment again. Our apartment. With all these baby supplies. With Tucker thinking ahead, preparing, making space for me and the twins.

This is real. This is actually happening.

I'm having babies with Tucker Stag.

And I'm living with him and his expensive tastes.

I need coffee. Or tea. Something with caffeine that won't make me puke.

———

Dr. Patel's office is becoming familiar—the same motivational posters, the same exam table, the same sterile smell. Same Tucker Stag sitting beside me, note app open on his phone, recording everything from my vitals to my comments on the temperature of the room.

"Blood pressure is good," the nurse says, making a note on her own tablet. "Weight is up three pounds since last visit, which is perfect. Any concerns?"

"She's exhausted all the time," Tucker says before I can answer. "Like, falling asleep sitting up. Is that normal?"

The nurse looks at me for confirmation. I nod reluctantly.

"Very normal, especially in the first trimester going into the second." She makes another note. "Are you able to rest when you need to?"

"I'm trying," I say. "I have school—"

"She's taking an incomplete in one class," Tucker interrupts again. "But she's still stressed about it. And she just moved. Is there anything I can do to help?"

The nurse frowns. "I need Sloane to answer her own medical questions, sir."

His eyes widen. "I'm doing it again. I'm sorry. I'm just worried."

Something in my chest softens at the genuine concern in his voice. He's not asking for himself—he's advocating for me.

"He's right," I assert. "I moved in with Tucker, hoping to ease stress and get more rest."

"Rest is crucial," the nurse says. "Especially with twins. If you're feeling overwhelmed, don't push through it. Listen to your body."

"She has coursework to finish," Tucker presses. "How can I help her balance that with needing rest?"

The nurse looks between us, a small smile forming. "It sounds like you're already helping by being aware. Make sure she's eating regularly—small meals throughout the day. Encourage naps. Take over household tasks so she doesn't have to worry about them." She looks at me. "And Sloane, let him help. Pride doesn't grow healthy babies."

"I'm not—" I start, then stop because she's kind of right. I am being proud. Stubborn about accepting help.

"I'll make sure she rests," Tucker says firmly, typing furiously on his phone. Has he always looked this good when he's concentrating?

"Good." The nurse finishes her notes. "Dr. Patel will be in shortly for the exam."

When she leaves, I look at Tucker. "You didn't have to do that."

"Do what?"

"Ask about helping me. I can manage."

"I know you can manage," he says. "But you don't have to manage alone anymore. That's the whole point." He gestures vaguely between us.

"The roommate arrangement?"

"The co-parenting partnership." He leans forward, elbows on his knees. "Sloane, you're growing two humans. My humans. The least I can do is make your life easier while you do it."

Before I can respond, Dr. Patel enters with her warm smile.

"Good to see you both again. How are we feeling?"

"Tired," I admit, eyeing Tucker. "But okay."

"Excellent. Let's take a listen to these babies."

She squirts the gel on my stomach—still cold, still startling—and presses the doppler wand against my skin. Static fills the room, then that rapid flutter of a heartbeat.

"There's Baby A," Dr. Patel says, moving the wand slightly. The heartbeat changes pitch. "And Baby B. Both sound strong and healthy."

Tucker reaches for my hand without seeming to think about it, his fingers threading through mine as we listen to our babies' heartbeats. I should pull away, maintain boundaries, but I can't make myself do it.

"Heart rates are excellent," Dr. Patel continues, making notes. "Growth is on track. Everything looks great. You'll start feeling movement any day now if you haven't already."

I grin at the thought of that, of feeling my babies swim and turn inside my body. What will that be like? And then I'm hit with a wave of sadness wondering if my own mother was even aware enough to appreciate my internal gymnastics.

"What about the exhaustion?" Tucker asks, his voice cutting through my melancholy. "The nurse said it's normal, but it seems extreme."

Dr. Patel gives him an appraising look. "Twin pregnancies are demanding. Her body is working overtime. The exhaustion should improve in the second trimester, which she's entering now, but with twins it might persist longer."

"So rest, small meals, and what else?"

"Hydration is crucial. Prenatal vitamins. And Sloane—" She looks at me seriously. "Don't try to maintain your pre-pregnancy schedule. Your body has different priorities now."

"I have school," I repeat weakly. It's all I have right now. A few classes and shacking up in a fancy palace full of designer baby gear. I need to recalibrate. Remember my mission. I'm building the experience of the people I said I want to help, right? First-hand knowledge.

Dr. Patel taps her fingers on her leg. "Well, I would say whittle your days down to absolute must-dos and use the rest of your time sleeping and hydrating. There's no prize for pushing yourself to exhaustion."

Tucker squeezes my hand. I squeeze back.

"Any other questions?" Dr. Patel asks.

"When will we be able to tell what they are?" Tucker asks. "Like, boy or girl?"

"We should do an ultrasound to check things out visually. We'll schedule that for your next appointment."

I tune out as Dr. Patel goes through the now-familiar litany of what I should expect for the next round of appointments. My belly will be goo-ed up, the babies will be on screen, and I will double in size. Tucker helps me off the exam table with a gentle arm that dances across the small of my back as we make our way to the parking garage. I realize I like the feel of it, the warmth of his skin, the quiet support of his physical strength.

———

In the car on the way home, Tucker is quiet. I watch the city pass by the window, settling in to the growing comfort of being around him.

"Thank you," I say finally.

"For what?"

"For asking about the exhaustion. For caring about whether I'm okay."

He glances at me, then back at the road. "Of course I care. You're—" He stops himself. "You're carrying my kids. Your health is their health."

Right. It's about the babies, not me. I shouldn't feel disappointed by that, but I do anyway.

Back at the apartment, Tucker disappears to his room and returns with a printed Fury calendar. He spreads it on the kitchen island.

"I want to show you my schedule. So, you know when I'll be gone."

I study the calendar. It's color-coded—green for home games, red for away games, blue for practices. The away games are clustered in brutal stretches.

"Four days here," Tucker says, pointing. "Three days there. The longest stretch is six days in December."

"That's a lot of travel."

"Yeah." He runs a hand through his hair. "I hate it. Hate the idea of being gone that much when you're pregnant."

"It's your job."

"I know. But—" He stares at the calendar. "I'm going to miss things. Appointments, maybe. Important moments."

"We'll FaceTime," I offer. "And lots of people have jobs that take them away from home. We'll figure it out."

"My dad managed it," Tucker says, more to himself than to me. "When he was still playing. He made it work."

"Then so will we."

He looks at me, something unreadable in his expression. "You keep saying 'we.'"

"Isn't that what this is? Co-parenting?"

"Yeah. It is." But he sounds uncertain, like he wants to say something else.

The moment stretches between us, loaded with something I'm not ready to name. Then Tucker's phone buzzes and he breaks eye contact to check it.

"Almost time for anger management part deux," he says. "You okay if I go?"

"Of course. Your job is important."

"So is yours," he says. "And I don't want to leave if you need something."

"I'm fine. I'm just going to work on my statistics coursework."

"Okay." He hesitates. "But text me if you need anything. I can come back."

———

After he leaves, the apartment feels too quiet. I settle on the couch with my laptop and statistics textbook, determined to make progress on the incomplete.

But I can't focus. My mind keeps drifting to Tucker asking the doctor about my exhaustion. To his hand holding mine during the doppler. To the way he keeps saying "our apartment" like he's trying to convince himself I belong here.

I give up on statistics and start unpacking boxes instead, claiming space in this enormous remodeled factory loft. My books go on the built-in shelves. My clothes in the walk-in closet that's bigger than my entire bedroom at the old place. My toiletries in those empty drawers Tucker cleared for me.

By the time he gets back, I've made significant progress. He finds me in the kitchen, arranging my mismatched mugs in the cabinet.

"You're nesting," he says with a grin.

"I'm unpacking."

"You're nesting. It's cute."

I throw a dish towel at him. He catches it, laughing, and that's when I notice how good he looks post-workout. Gray t-shirt clinging to his chest, hair damp, face flushed.

I look away quickly, focusing on the mugs.

"Mel's coming over tomorrow," I say. "To see the place. That okay?"

"Of course. She's welcome anytime." He moves to the fridge, pulling out a protein shake. "You eat lunch?"

"I had crackers."

"Sloane. That's not lunch."

"I wasn't hungry."

He gives me a look. "The doctor said small meals throughout the day. Crackers don't count."

"I'll eat later."

"Let's eat now." He opens the fridge again, surveying the contents. "I've got stuff for sandwiches. Or I could make pasta. Or we could order something."

"You don't have to feed me."

"Someone has to." He's already pulling out bread, turkey, cheese. "You like mustard or mayo?"

"Both."

"Weirdo."

But he makes the sandwich exactly how I like it—both condiments, extra pickles, chips on the side. He even microwaves the deli meat so it's safe for me to eat. He sets it in front of me at the island and leans against the counter, drinking his shake while I eat.

"This is good," I admit. "Thank you."

He grins, taking huge bites of his own food, which I suspect is more of a pre-meal snack for him, given his size and my experiences with Josh.

"How was anger management?" I take a swig of water and am pleased that everything seems to be staying put in my stomach.

Tucker grunts and keeps eating. He wipes his mouth with a napkin eventually and says, "Maybe we can table talking about that? I'm beat and you seem like you have a lot of work."

I nod, ceding his point. We fall into comfortable silence, me eating, him watching once he finishes. It should be weird, having him watch me eat, but it's not. It's... nice.

Domestic.

Dangerous.

The next afternoon, Mel wheels into the apartment and immediately starts exploring.

"Holy shit, Sloane. This place is huge."

"I know."

"And fully accessible." She rolls a big circle around the living room, into the kitchen, toward my room. "The hallways are wide enough, the bathroom has a roll-in shower—did Tucker do this on purpose?"

"I think the building is just fancy."

"No, look." She points to the kitchen. "The counters have different heights. The cabinets have pull-down shelves. This was designed for accessibility."

Tucker always talks about his designer being a genius. I guess I just felt so comfortable that I never noticed the kitchen's unique features. But she's right.

"That's..." I trail off, not sure how to finish the sentence.

"Hot," Mel supplies. "That's hot, Sloane."

"It's considerate."

"Same thing." She wheels further down the hall, peeking into the guest room where Tucker has moved his stuff. "This is his room now?"

"Yeah. He gave me the primary."

"Also, hot."

"Stop saying that."

She grins and continues exploring, finding the door to what will be the nursery. "Can I?"

"Go ahead."

She opens the door, and I follow. The room is empty except for the shopping bags Tucker moved in here—all those supplies, carefully stacked.

Mel starts going through them, pulling out items. "Bamboo sheets. Nice. Oh, this stroller—Sloane, do you know how much this costs?"

"Yes, in fact I do."

She whistles and runs her hands over the box. "He's serious about this."

"I know."

She turns to face me, expression thoughtful. "Are you okay? Like, really okay with all this?"

"I think so?" It comes out as a question. "It's a lot. Living with him, seeing how much he's preparing, how invested he is. It's not what I expected."

"What did you expect?"

"I don't know. That he'd offer money and show up for big moments but otherwise stay distant. That I'd be doing this mostly alone, like my grandmother did."

"But Tucker's not distant."

"No. He's..." I gesture helplessly. "He's here. He's present. He asks the doctor questions, makes me sandwiches, and buys ridiculously expensive strollers."

"And you thought he was just a party hookup."

The observation lands heavily. This was going to be the year of me going back to school. Finally stepping out of the cycle of having babies too young, with too little support. Tucker was a little treat on the way to bigger things. "He was supposed to be..."

Mel snorts and pulls out another item—a book. "Parenting Twins: The First Year." She sets it aside and grabs another. "What to Expect: The First Year." Another. "The Baby Book." She pauses, pulling out a pamphlet tucked between the books. "Black Hair and Skin Care: A Guide for New Parents."

We both stare at it. I'm immediately transported back to elementary school, when one of the Black neighbors took Grandma aside and offered to show her how to comb my hair. It was the beginning of a daily ritual of moisturizing and wrapping.

"He got a pamphlet," Mel says slowly, "about Black hair care."

"He's ... binge reading."

"He's doing the *work*, Sloane." She hands me the pamphlet, which has notes in the margins like I've seen him take on his phone during doctor appointments. "This isn't performative. This is him actually trying to understand what your kids will need."

I flip through the pamphlet. It's detailed—information about different hair textures, product recommendations, how to moisturize, protective styles for babies. Someone has highlighted sections in yellow.

Tucker highlighted sections about caring for our babies' hair.

"Okay," I admit. "That's kind of hot."

Mel laughs. "Finally! She admits it."

"Don't—"

"You have the hots for your baby daddy."

"I do not—"

"You absolutely do. Look at your face right now." She wheels closer. "Sloane. It's okay to be attracted to him. He's hot."

"We're supposed to be roommates. Co-parents. I set boundaries."

"Boundaries can adjust," Mel points out. "If both people want them to."

"I don't know what I want."

"Don't you?"

I look at the pamphlet again. At the highlighted sections. At the stack of parenting books, at the expensive stroller, at all the evidence of Tucker's preparation.

I think about his hand holding mine during the ultrasound. About him asking the doctor how to help me. About him giving me his bedroom, clearing out his drawers, and making sure the apartment is accessible for Mel.

I think about how he looks post-workout. About his hands on my feet, working out the soreness. About the way he called me gorgeous, like he couldn't help himself.

"I might," I admit quietly. "Want the boundaries to adjust."

"Then tell him."

"I can't just—"

"Why not? You're adults. You're attracted to each other. You're having babies together. What's stopping you?"

Fear, I think. Fear that I'm repeating patterns. Fear that I'll lose myself again. Fear that this is just pregnancy hormones and proximity, and not something real. This is all happening very fast. A few short breaths ago, he was day drinking on a tiki boat, hollering at me when I was trying to jog.

"I need time," I tell Mel. "To figure out what I'm feeling."

"Fair enough. But Sloane?" She picks up the hair care pamphlet again. "Don't take too long."

———

After Mel leaves, I sit in the nursery surrounded by baby supplies, holding that pamphlet. I think about the man I was attracted to at that party—cocky, sexy as sin, carefree. And Tucker is still those things. I hear him laugh on the phone with his brothers and see him smile when he writes texts to his mom.

He's not performing. He's not trying to control me. He's just... showing up. Consistently. Thoughtfully.

And I'm attracted to him.

Not just physically, though God knows that's there too. But attracted to who he is. How he's trying. The man he's becoming.

Despite my vow to take space and time, to make up for what I lost during my marriage … I'm attracted to my baby daddy.

And I have no idea what to do about it.

CHAPTER 24
TUCKER

Coach Thompson's voice cuts through the locker room chatter. Everyone goes quiet.

I look up from buffing my dress shoes. Grentley is across the room, already shaking his head.

"Coach, that's not—" he starts.

"Not a request." Coach's tone leaves no room for argument. "Management wants to see progress on team cohesion. You two sitting together for three hours is a good start."

"This is bullshit," Grentley mutters, but loud enough for everyone to hear.

"Watch it, Grentley." Coach doesn't even look up from his tablet. "Stag, you have a problem with this?"

I think about Sloane back at the apartment, probably curled up on the couch with her statistics textbook. About the babies growing inside her. About not making this situation worse than it already is. They are what matters. The rest of this is nothing.

"No problem, Coach."

"Good. Spruce up, gentlemen. Straight ties and zippered flies."

He walks out, leaving me and Grentley staring at each other across the locker room. The silence is oppressive until Mayhem breaks it with a low whistle.

"Damn, T-Stag. Three hours next to your baby mama's ex? That's cold."

"Shut up, Mayhem," Alder says from beside me.

"I'm just saying." Mayhem grins. "Better you than me, man. I'd rather sit next to Spinner's smelly feet."

"My feet don't smell," Spinner protests.

"They absolutely do," several guys chorus.

The tension breaks slightly as everyone returns to packing their gear and checking out their suits. But I can feel Grentley's eyes on me, and when I glance his way, his expression is pure hostility.

This is going to be a long flight.

———

The bus ride to the airport is mercifully short. I sit with Alder, both of us quiet. My twin knows me well enough not to push conversation when I'm in my head.

But as we board the plane, there's no avoiding it. Grentley is already in our assigned row—window side—arms crossed, jaw tight.

I stow my bag in the overhead compartment and slide into the aisle seat. The armrest between us might as well be the Fort Pitt Bridge.

For the first twenty minutes, neither of us speaks. I pull out my phone and check messages. Nothing from Sloane yet, but it's still early.

"So," Grentley says finally, his voice low enough that only I can hear. "How's domestic life treating you?"

I don't take the bait. "Fine."

"Must be nice. Playing house with my wife."

"She's not your wife anymore." I keep my voice even. "And we're not playing anything."

"Right. You just knocked her up and moved her into your place. That's totally different."

"It is different." I turn to look at him. "Because I'm not lying to her. I'm not making decisions for her. And I'm sure as hell not going to—"

"What? Say it." His eyes flash. "You're not going to what? Fuck up like I did?"

"I didn't say that."

"You didn't have to." He turns back to the window. "Everyone thinks it. Poor Sloane, married to that mopey asshole. Thank God Tucker Stag swooped in to save her."

"That's not what happened."

"Isn't it?" He looks at me again. "You saw an opportunity and you took it. Got her drunk at a party, got her pregnant, now you're the hero."

"She wasn't drunk." My hands clench into fists. "And I didn't plan any of this."

"Sure, you didn't."

I take a deep breath, forcing myself to stay calm. This is what he wants—to provoke me, to make me the bad guy again.

"Look," I say carefully. "I get that this sucks for you. I do. But taking shots at me isn't going to change anything."

"What's going to change is you realizing that Sloane isn't going to stick around." His voice is bitter. "She'll get what she needs from you, and then she'll move on. That's what she does."

"You don't know her."

"I know her better than you ever will." He turns away again. "But go ahead. Play happy family. See how long it lasts."

The flight attendant arrives with the beverage cart, mercifully ending the conversation. I order water. Grentley orders nothing.

We don't speak again for the rest of the flight.

———

The hotel in St. Louis is nice—one of those places with a lobby full of modern art and staff who are too polite to acknowledge when hockey players trash their rooms. Not that we do that anymore. We're professionals now.

Most of us, anyway.

I'm unpacking when Alder knocks and lets himself in.

"How was the flight?" he asks, though his tone suggests he already knows.

"Terrible."

"Figured." He sits on the other bed, his tongue clicking his removable fake tooth, which matches mine. "Grentley say anything useful?"

"Just the usual. That I'm using Sloane. That she's going to leave me. That I'm a piece of shit." I shove clothes into a drawer. "Standard stuff."

"He's projecting."

"I know."

"Do you?" Alder leans forward. "Because you look like you're letting it get to you."

"I'm not."

"Tucker."

I pause unpacking and turn to face my twin. "What if he's right?"

"About what?"

"About Sloane leaving. About this not lasting." I run a hand through my hair. "What if once they're born, she realizes she doesn't actually want me around?"

"Have you asked her?"

"She keeps saying we are co-parents. But ... we don't have any paperwork or anything."

"And you're okay with that?"

"I don't have a choice."

"You always have a choice." Alder stands, moving to the window. "But you have to actually tell her what you want. Not just go along with whatever she says because you're scared."

"I'm not scared."

He gives me a look. "You're terrified. I can see it. You're afraid that if you push for more, she'll run. So, you're playing it safe, being the perfect roommate, hoping she'll realize on her own that she wants you."

"That's not—"

"That's exactly what you're doing." He crosses his arms. "And it's not working. Because she probably thinks you're fine with the roommate thing. That you don't want more."

I sink onto the bed. "What am I supposed to do? If I ask for an official custody document, she'll think I'm being controlling. If I don't, I'll walk around constantly scared she's going to bail."

"Or she'll realize you're being honest about what you want. Which is the opposite of what Grentley did, by the way." Alder sits beside me. "Tucker, you can't keep waiting for permission to want things. At some point, you have to take the risk."

I know he's right. But the thought of telling Sloane how I feel, of risking the fragile peace we've built—

"Come on," Alder says, standing. "Let's go to the rink. Get your head in the game."

———

The energy in the locker room is familiar, and despite the anxiety and superstitions flying around, it feels calming to me. Better than fretting over my misguided romantic urges.

Guys taping sticks, checking equipment, talking shit to each other.

I'm sitting in my stall when Alder settles into the one beside me. We're both in our base layers, gear laid out in front of us.

"You ready for this?" he asks.

"As ready as I'll ever be."

He grins and reaches up to his mouth, carefully removing his false tooth. I do the same with mine. We turn to face each other, both grinning with matching gaps.

"We look ridiculous," I say.

"We look like hockey players." Alder's grin widens, and he takes a selfie, sending it to the family group chat. "Mom's going to kill us when she sees the photos."

"Worth it."

We sit there for a moment, two grown men with missing teeth, and I think about my twins. Will they be like this someday? Goofy together, comfortable in a way that only comes from sharing everything?

God, I hope so.

"What are you thinking about?" Alder asks.

"The babies." I set my flipper tooth in a cup in my locker. "Wondering if they'll be weird like us."

"They're Stags. Of course, they'll be weird." He claps me on the shoulder. "But they'll be lucky. They'll have you."

"And Sloane."

"And Sloane," he agrees. "Who, by the way, you need to tell that you're crazy about."

"One crisis at a time."

My phone buzzes. I grab it, hoping—

SLOANE

Good luck tonight!

My chest tightens. She's reaching out. This has to be progress, right?

SLOANE

Also got my stats exam back. C minus. Not great but not failing!

I grin, typing quickly.

That's amazing! See? My sandwich-making skills are clearly helping.

SLOANE

You might be right about that.

I'm about to set my phone down when another message comes through.

SLOANE

I'm going to celebrate by swimming in your tub. This thing is massive. Pretty sure I could fit a dolphin in here.

The image hits me like a punch to the gut. Sloane, in my tub. Naked. Water sliding over her skin, her curls piled on top of her head, her hand resting on her stomach where our babies are growing.

"Fucker? You good?"

I look up to find Alder watching me with amusement.

"Yeah. Fine."

Alder punches me in the arm. "Oh man. You've got it bad."

"Shut up."

"Talk to her. When you get back. Tell her you want more than roommates."

I stare at my phone, at Sloane's messages. At the proof that she's comfortable in my space, in my life.

I want her. God, I want her so badly it's hard to breathe.

But first, I have to get through this game. Have to survive three periods on the ice with Josh Grentley, who hates me.

I can do this. I can keep my head in the game, focus on hockey, not think about Sloane in my tub.

Except I'm absolutely going to be thinking about Sloane in my tub.

"T-Stag!" Coach Thompson's voice booms through the locker room. "You with us?"

"Yes, Coach."

"Good. Because I need you sharp tonight. Chicago's bringing heavy hitters, and Mayhem's already nursing a shoulder injury. You're my primary enforcer. Don't let me down."

"I won't."

I send one last text to Brian and Uncle Tim. I need an update on the parental leave policy, and the players' union is dragging their ass.

Then I start suiting up, piece by piece. Shin guards. Pants. Shoulder pads. Each piece of equipment is familiar and comforting. This is what I know. This is what I'm good at.

Protecting people. Fighting when necessary. Being the guy who makes sure his teammates can play without fear.

But tonight, there's an extra layer of complication. Because Josh Grentley is one of those teammates. And I'm supposed to protect him, too.

Even though he hates me.

Even though the woman I love used to be his wife.

Love feels like the wrong word, but I can't figure out another one. Not when I need to get my head in the game.

I lace up my skates and stand, testing my weight. Everything feels right. Solid. Ready.

Across the locker room, Grentley is suiting up too. Our eyes meet for a moment. His expression is unreadable.

We start filing toward the tunnel. The sound of skates on concrete echoes off the walls. Somewhere above us, the crowd is already roaring.

This is it. Game time.

Sloane is at home, in my apartment, in my tub. Nope—I absolutely cannot focus on that mental magnificence.

All I have to do is survive the next three periods without getting killed.

Then I can go jerk off about it.

I follow my teammates into the tunnel, the roar of the crowd getting louder with each step. The lights, the ice, the game—it all waits ahead.

Here we go.

CHAPTER 25
SLOANE

TUCKER'S BEEN GONE FOR DAYS ON A LONG SERIES OF AWAY GAMES, but he's coming back tonight.

After he plays at seven.

Despite saying I would never watch another one of these games, I'm on the couch by six-thirty with the pre-game show on Tucker's massive television. I have my laptop open like I'm going to work on my sociology coursework, but really, I'm just waiting.

When the broadcast starts, I close the laptop.

The St. Louis arena is loud, the camera panning across a sea of blue jerseys in the crowd. The announcer runs through the line-ups, and I hold my breath until I hear "Number 41, another Stag—Tucker, right wing."

There he is, skating onto the ice with the rest of the team. Even through the TV screen, I can pick him out—something about the way he moves, confident and loose.

Number 34 skates past him. Josh Grentley. They don't look at each other.

Well, I don't want to look at Josh, either. I try to ignore him as the game gets going, and it goes about as well as me trying to ignore the swoops in my belly as I watch Tucker glide around the ice, swoops that have nothing to do with his babies inside me.

The first period is fast, aggressive. Pittsburgh scores early, then St. Louis answers back. I find myself leaning forward, tracking Tucker every time he's on screen.

He's not a scorer—I've tangled myself with another defender. But Tucker's also an enforcer. His job is different. Harder to see unless you're looking for it.

Halfway through the second period, I see it.

A St. Louis player—huge, mean-looking—slams into Alder near the boards. Tucker's twin goes down hard and doesn't get up immediately. Before I can even process what's happening, Tucker is there.

He drops his gloves. The other guy does too. And then they're fighting—actual fighting, fists flying, crowd roaring.

My stomach lurches. I should look away but I can't.

Tucker takes a hit to the face but lands two solid punches in return. The refs finally pull them apart, both players breathing hard, Tucker's face already swelling from the look of things as he skates toward the box.

I should know more about the strategy of it all by now. I realize that in a few years, these kids will ask what it means if Tucker gets a five-minute penalty for fighting. They'll want to know if his team is angry with him. The camera catches his face as he sits in the naughty chair, hand on a hockey stick. He's smiling while he gnaws on a mouthguard, split lip and a rising bruise on his cheek.

"Damn," I whisper to the empty apartment.

This is his job. This is what he does.

I watch the rest of the game with my hand on my stomach, feeling the babies flutter. They're moving more now, little tumbles and kicks that Dr. Patel says are perfectly normal.

Are they feeling my anxiety? Can they sense when I'm scared?

Pittsburgh wins 4-2. Tucker's aggression was a big part of that victory. The announcers call him "a force out there tonight" and "exactly what this team needs."

I turn off the TV and sit in the quiet apartment, processing.

Tucker protects people. That's his role. And it's violent and dangerous and I watched him get punched in the face on national television.

But he was also protecting Alder. Making sure his teammate could play without fear.

It's complicated. He's complicated.

I try to go about my bedtime routine, rubbing lotion into my skin, trying not to remember what it felt like when Tucker's hands slid along my legs in much the same way.

I'm still thinking about it when I hear the elevator at almost midnight. I'm in the bathroom, wrapping my hair for bed—the silk scarf carefully positioned to protect my curls overnight.

I freeze. Tucker hasn't seen me like this yet. Other white guys I've dated haven't understood the ritual, the care required, and I brace myself to explain.

But I hear Tucker moving around the kitchen and I need to see if he's okay after that fight.

I step out of the bathroom, scarf tied securely, wearing one of his old t-shirts left behind in the dresser in what's now my bedroom.

Tucker's at the sink, drinking water straight from the tap. He's still in his suit from the flight—tie loosened, jacket discarded somewhere. When he straightens and turns, I see the bruise on his face.

His beautiful face now blooms purple, blue eye swollen.

"Tucker—"

"Hey." His voice is rough, tired. His eyes track from my head wrap to my shirt, and something in his expression softens. "I wake you?"

"No. I was up." I move closer, instinct overriding self-consciousness. "Your face."

"It's fine. Just a bruise." He sets down the glass. "Fighting is part of the job."

I reach up without thinking, my fingers hovering near the bruise but not quite touching. "Does it hurt?"

"Not really. I've had worse." He's studying my face like he's looking for something. "You okay? You look upset."

"I am worried. I watched you get punched."

"It's part of the job."

"I know. But—" I drop my hand. "It's different seeing it. Understanding what you do out there."

Tucker's quiet for a moment. Then: "You want me to stop? Fighting?"

"I don't know." It's the honest answer. "I don't know what I want."

We stand there in the dim kitchen, both of us showing parts of ourselves we usually keep hidden.

"Your hair..." Tucker says quietly. "I was reading about bonnets and silk pillowcases."

"Yeah." I smile. "I saw you were doing some studying."

"Purple is a good color on you." His voice is firm. "I want you to feel comfortable here."

Something in my chest loosens. "I am. Comfortable, I mean."

"Good." He adjusts his stance, and we're suddenly very close. Close enough that I can smell him—ointment and soap and something underneath that's just Tucker.

His eyes drop to my mouth. Mine drops to his split lip.

This would be a terrible idea. He's injured. We're both exhausted. We're supposed to be roommates, co-parents, nothing more.

But I want to kiss him so badly I can barely breathe.

"Sloane," he says, and there's a warning in his voice. Or maybe a question.

"I should go to bed." I don't move.

"Yeah. Me too." He doesn't move either.

The moment stretches between us, loaded with everything we're not saying. Everything we're not doing.

Then Tucker steps back, putting space between us. "Goodnight, Sloane."

I shouldn't love the sound of my name in his mouth, the way his tongue moves against his teeth when he says it. I shouldn't want this man. "Goodnight."

I flee to my room—his room, that he gave me—and close the door.

My heart races. The babies are tumbling around like they can feel the adrenaline coursing through me.

This is getting complicated.

No—this has been complicated from the start. I'm just finally admitting it.

I climb into bed, the sheets expensive and soft, and stare at the ceiling.

Down the hall, I hear Tucker's door close. Hear the shower start up.

I imagine him in there, washing off the flight, the violence. Taking care of his bruised face. Being alone when maybe he doesn't want to be.

Is he touching himself in there, the way I touched myself in his tub, just thinking about the lightning that struck when we slept together?

I could go to him. Could knock on his door. Could tell him I don't want to be just roommates anymore.

But fear keeps me frozen. Fear of losing myself again. Fear of making the same mistakes. Fear that this is just proximity and pregnancy hormones and not something real.

So, I stay in bed, hand on my stomach, feeling his babies move and wondering how much longer I can resist their father.

CHAPTER 26
TUCKER

She's staring at me again.

I pretend not to notice, keeping my eyes on the TV where my cousin Wyatt and West Ham are getting demolished by Liverpool. But I can feel Sloane's gaze tracking across my shoulders, down my bare chest, lingering on my stomach.

It's been happening for weeks now.

Ever since that night I came home from St. Louis with a bruised face and she looked at me like she wanted to jump my bones.

At first, I thought she thought I looked weird, especially as the bruise shifted to a weird yellow-green.

But something shifted. I see it in the way she watches me move around the apartment. The way her eyes drop to my mouth when I'm talking. The way she bites her lip when I walk past her in the hallway.

I've had my nose to the ice, totally focused on working out, keeping my cool around Grentley, and calling the players union every fucking afternoon to talk about actual time off for when these babies show up.

And all the while, Sloane's been looking at me like she's starving and I'm a bowl of ice cream.

It's driving me insane.

"How was class?" I ask, not taking my eyes off the game, adjusting myself before I spring a chub in my sweats.

"Fine." Her voice sounds strained. "Lots of reading."

"You need help with anything?"

A pause. Then: "No. I'm good."

I glance at her. She's standing by the kitchen island in leggings and an oversized sweater, her backpack still on one shoulder. Her curls are loose today, framing her face. Her cheeks are flushed.

She's staring at my sweatpants.

The ones I threw on after my workout this morning because I didn't think she'd be home until later.

Her tongue darts out, wetting her bottom lip.

Christ.

I turn back to the TV, willing my cock to cooperate and stay soft. "Game's almost over if you want to watch something else."

"No, it's fine. I'll just—" She doesn't finish the sentence.

I hear her walk toward her room, then stop. The apartment goes quiet, except for the announcers commenting on Liverpool's third goal.

"Tucker?"

"Yeah?"

Another pause. "Never mind."

Her bedroom door closes.

I drop my head back against the couch and stare at the ceiling.

———

More weeks pass in a haze of tension and restraint.

Sloane's belly has bloomed, and it's so fucking sexy. But it's also my babies in there, and all I want to do is feel them and talk to them. I'm trying to keep my distance like a good co-parent respectfully. Lord knows, I'm trying.

Sloane is full-time at school, determined to prove she can handle it. I watch her leave in the mornings with her backpack, watch her come home tired but animated, talking about her professors and assignments.

Sometimes she has Mel with her, and they roll around the apartment talking about my uncle and uptight lawyers. My cousin Pete, Tim's oldest, is back in town after his fellowship and he's been working with Mel, so sometimes he comes over to rag on me for becoming boring.

Like, Pete hasn't always been boring.

He doesn't seem to think it's boring to get a law degree, and write for some law journal, and move back to Pittsburgh to write boring contracts.

I should be grateful that boring people like Pete and Mel exist, since they tell me they're making progress with the hockey players' association and getting me some parental leave in my contract. Pete keeps pointing out that Stag Law has a good record with this sort of thing for women's pro sports already.

Meanwhile, Sloane seems less exhausted. The second-trimester glow everyone talks about is real—her skin looks amazing, her energy is up, and her belly is finally starting to show.

She's beautiful. She's always been beautiful, but now—

Now I can't stop staring at her.

And she can't stop staring at me.

The apartment is thick with want. With everything we're not saying, not doing.

I think about asking her to come to a game. Want her there, want her to see me play, want to look up in the stands and know she's watching.

But Grentley and I are still navigating our forced therapy sessions, our mandatory team-building exercises. Things are better—less hostile, more professional—but fragile. I don't want to risk that progress by parading his ex-wife around the arena.

So, I keep my distance on both fronts, and my dick suffers for it.

———

In mid October, I have a rare day off and I'm sprawled on the couch watching West Ham play Chelsea in men's soccer. It's a lazy afternoon—no practice, no commitments, and I already jerked off in the shower, so I'm treating myself to sports on TV.

Sloane's at class, so I'm shirtless in gray sweatpants, barefoot, wondering if I should grab one of Wyatt's jerseys for luck since the game is tied 1-1. But then I hear the elevator.

Sloane steps into the apartment, backpack on her shoulder, keys in her hand. She looks tired, distracted, like she's had a long day of classes.

Then she sees me.

Her eyes go wide. Her keys clatter onto the side table. The backpack slides off her shoulder and hits the floor with a thud.

She just stares.

I raise my eyebrows, unable to help the small smile tugging at my mouth. "Something you need?"

She shakes her head. But she doesn't move. Doesn't look away.

Enough of this shit.

I stand slowly, letting her look. Letting her see exactly what she's been staring at for weeks. "You sure about that?"

Her chest rises and falls, breath coming faster.

I take a step toward her. Then another. Moving slowly, giving her time to stop me, to tell me to back off.

She doesn't.

"I read somewhere," I say, my voice low, "that pregnant women have a high libido in the second trimester."

Her lips part. Her eyes are huge, dark with want.

"Is that true, Sloane?" I take another step. "You feeling that?"

She nods.

"I need words, Sunshine. You need to tell me what you want."

Her voice comes out breathless, desperate. "Please fuck me. For the love of God, Tucker, please."

Something in me snaps.

I close the distance between us and scoop her up, one arm under her knees, one supporting her back. She wraps her arms around my neck, burying her face against my shoulder.

"I've got you," I murmur against her hair. "I've got you."

I carry her to her room and lay her on the bed carefully. She's breathing hard, her hands already reaching for me.

"Wait." I catch her wrists gently. "What's comfortable for you? I don't want to hurt the babies. Or you."

"Ugh," she says immediately. "My belly—it's too much pressure if I'm on my back. And I can't—I need—"

"Show me."

She rolls onto her hands and knees, that perfect ass in the air, and looks back at me over her shoulder. "Like this. Please, Tucker. I need you like this."

I'm going to die. I'm actually going to die from wanting her this much.

I move behind her, my hands spanning her hips. "Sloane, I need you to know—I haven't been with anyone else. Got a physical last month, everything's clear."

"Good." Her voice is strained, and she starts ripping off her clothes, revealing so much golden brown skin I'm actually drooling. "Now please—"

"Use your words."

"Fuck me. Now. Please."

I hook my fingers in her panties, dragging them down. She kicks them off impatiently. She's naked and on her knees and the most beautiful thing I've ever seen.

My sweatpants hit the floor. I stand behind her, one hand steadying her hip, the other guiding myself to her entrance.

"You sure?" I ask one more time.

"Tucker, I swear to God—"

I slide into her in one long thrust.

She gasps, her back arching, her hands fisting in the sheets. I freeze, terrified I've hurt her.

"Don't stop," she breathes. "Don't you dare stop."

I don't stop.

I fuck her the way she asked—fast and hard and desperate, like our very first time together. My hands grip her hips, probably too tight, but she's pushing back against me, meeting every thrust. The sounds she's making are going to live in my head forever—little gasps and moans and my name, over and over.

"Tucker. Tucker. Oh God, Tucker—"

She comes, her whole body shaking, clenching around me and I didn't even touch her. It's so fucking hot that I follow seconds later, burying myself deep and spilling inside her, my vision going white at the edges.

I slump forward, careful not to crush her, my forehead resting against her back. Her skin is hot, slick with sweat. Her breathing is ragged.

I should move. Should give her space. Should say something.

But all I can think is: How am I ever going to stop wanting this?

I press a kiss to her spine, right between her shoulder blades. She shivers.

"You okay?" I ask quietly.

"Yeah." Her voice is soft, sated. "More than okay."

I ease out of her carefully and help her roll onto her side. She curls up immediately, one hand on her belly, her eyes heavy-lidded.

I lie down beside her, not touching but close. Close enough that I can see the freckles on her shoulder, the way her curls are tangled and wild, the satisfied smile playing at her lips.

"That was—" she starts.

"Yeah." I look at the rounded globe of her stomach, knowing half of my heart is inside there. I can't resist the urge to touch, so I rest my hand there gently. "Is this okay?"

She purrs and nods, so I rub and hold her. And I feel ... like everything in my life has been pointing to this. All my fucking around, partying, letting myself be the irresponsible Stag child... all of it has led to this perfect moment with this woman and these babies I can't wait to meet.

Sloane pushes up on one arm and meets my gaze. "We should probably talk about—"

"Later," I say. "Just... let me look at you for a minute."

Something passes between us. Something bigger than sex, bigger than co-parenting, bigger than any of the boundaries we've tried to maintain.

But I don't say it. Don't push.

I just lie there beside her, watching her drift toward sleep, knowing that everything just changed and there's no going back.

And wondering how the hell I'm supposed to protect my heart when it's already hers.

CHAPTER 27
TUCKER

Sloane is extra beautiful when she's annoyed.

She's standing in front of the full-length mirror in the bedroom, scowling at her reflection, adorably frustrated. She's wearing one of my t-shirts—again—and a pair of leggings that are riding low under her belly.

"These don't fit anymore," she announces, tugging at the waistband.

"I can see that." I'm sprawled on the bed naked, supposedly checking my phone for team updates but really just watching her. "You know what would help?"

"Don't say it."

"Maternity clothes."

"You said it." She turns to glare at me. "I'm not ready for maternity clothes. That feels too... official."

I bite back a laugh. "Sunshine, you're visibly months pregnant with twins. It's pretty official."

"I know that." She tugs at the shirt—my shirt—which is also getting snug around her middle. "But maternity clothes are so... frumpy."

"They make cute maternity clothes now. I've seen them online."

Her eyes narrow. "You've been browsing maternity clothes?"

"Research." I sit up, swinging my legs over the side of the bed.

"Come on. Let me take you shopping. We'll find you stuff that fits and doesn't make you feel frumpy."

"I have schoolwork—"

"Which you can do later. I'll help you. I'm very smart." I stand and move toward her, wrapping my arms around her from behind, my hands settling on her belly. "Besides, you need pants. Unless you want to start wearing my sweatpants everywhere."

She leans back against me, and I feel the tension in her shoulders start to ease. "Your sweatpants are comfortable."

"They're also enormous on you." I press a kiss to her neck. "Let me do this. Let me take care of you in a non-suffocating way that respects your independence and also results in you having pants that fit."

She laughs, the sound warm and genuine. "That was a very carefully worded request."

"I've been practicing."

"Fine." She turns in my arms to face me. "But I'm not buying anything with ruffles or bows."

"Deal."

———

I take her to Nordstrom, where my brother hooked me up with his personal shopper and a private entrance so no hockey fans would swarm us. I like being out with her, like we're a real couple. We still haven't had a big conversation. With the holidays approaching, it seems like we really ought to. But we've been fucking every time we're both home and awake, and then she is too tired.

Sloane touches fabrics with deep suspicion. "These are basically regular pants with a stretchy panel," I point out, holding up a pair of dark jeans.

"The stretchy panel goes all the way up." She makes a face. "I'll look like I'm wearing a tube top on my stomach."

"Or you could try the under-belly ones." I grab another pair. "See? Normal waistband, just sits lower."

She takes them, examining the construction like she's looking for hidden flaws. I bend low to whisper in her ear, "Or you could just stop wearing pants. Make things easier for me."

Sloane swats at me while a middle-aged woman with sepia skin and a warm smile approaches. "You must be Gunnar's brother," she says warmly, extending a hand. "Kamila."

"Tucker." I smile and gesture at my baby-mama. "And Sloane here is uncomfortable but terrified of looking dumpy."

Sloane bites her lip and Kamila smiles. She gathers options for Sloane in a whirlwind—filling a cart with leggings and stretchy tanks I can't wait to peel off later.

"Those are nice," she admits grudgingly.

"Right? And look—no bows."

She takes them from Kamila, feeling the fabric. "Okay, these are actually really soft."

"And they have pockets," our shopper adds.

Sloane's eyes light up. "Pockets?"

"Pockets," I confirm, showing her. "Deep ones."

"I'm trying these on."

———

I settle onto the bench outside the fitting rooms while Sloane disappears inside.

"She's lucky to have you," Kamila says, organizing the clothes on the rack. "A lot of men won't even come to the maternity section, but I know you Stag men are made different."

"I like shopping with her." It's true. I like watching Sloane make decisions, like seeing what catches her eye, like being part of these small moments.

"Well, she's lucky anyway." Kamila heads back to the floor, leaving me alone with my phone.

I scroll through messages—Alder asking about dinner later this week, my mom sending photos of baby shoes she found, Mayhem sharing a ridiculous meme. Everyday life, carrying on.

The fitting room door opens. Sloane steps out wearing the dark jeans I picked, paired with a soft burgundy top that drapes over her belly without clinging.

I forget how to breathe.

"These actually fit," she says, turning to check her reflection. "Like, really fit. They're comfortable."

"You look incredible."

She glances at me, and something in my expression makes her blush. She toys with the sun locket at her throat. "It's just jeans and a shirt."

"It's you." I stand, moving closer. "You look beautiful. Happy."

"I am happy." She says it like she's surprised. "These pants don't dig into my sides. That makes me very happy."

"Good." I kiss her forehead. "Try on more things. I want to see everything."

———

Over the next twenty minutes, Sloane models outfit after outfit. The leggings with pockets make her squeal. A soft gray dress makes her look ethereal. She declares the joggers "life-changing." A denim jacket fits over her belly.

With each outfit, she relaxes a little more, and my own pants grow a little tighter. Smiles come easier. She even does a little spin in one particularly flattering dress, laughing when she nearly loses her balance.

"Okay," she finally says, emerging in her original clothes with an armful of selections. "I'm getting tired."

"Then we should head home," I tell her, adjusting myself as I stand. At the register, I pull out my credit card before she can reach for hers.

"Tucker—"

"My treat. For putting up with my nagging you to come shopping." I hand the card to Kamila before Sloane can argue. "Besides, I like buying you things."

"That's not—" She stops, takes a breath. "Thank you. I'll pay you back—"

"You absolutely will not." I take the bags from Kamila and steer Sloane toward the exit. "You're growing my children. The least I can do is buy you pants."

"Your giant children are the reason I need new pants in the first place."

"Exactly. My responsibility."

She's quiet on the walk to the car, but it's a comfortable silence. I load the bags in the back while she settles into the passenger seat.

"That was actually fun," she says as I start the engine.

"Yeah?"

"Yeah." She's smiling, small, and genuine. "I haven't done something that normal in a long time. Just... shopping. Like a regular person."

"You are a regular person."

"You know what I mean." She rests her hand on her belly, where the babies are clearly moving. "Everything feels so big and scary and complicated. But today was just... nice."

I reach over and take her free hand. "We can do nice. We're good at nice."

"We really are."

Back at the apartment, Sloane disappears into the bedroom to put away her new clothes. I'm in the kitchen pulling together a snack when she emerges wearing the leggings with pockets and a soft tank top.

"Comfortable?" I ask.

"So comfortable." She moves behind me, her arms wrapping around my waist. "Thank you for today."

"Anytime." I turn in her embrace. "Seriously. We should do more stuff like this."

"I'd like that." She goes up on her toes—not far, given her current center of gravity—and kisses me.

It starts soft. Sweet. A thank you kiss that tastes like happiness.

Then her hands slide under my shirt.

"Sloane—"

"I need you," she says against my mouth. "Right now."

"Right now?"

"Right now." Her fingers work at my belt. "Tucker, please. I've been thinking about this since you called me beautiful in the store."

"You are beautiful—"

"Less talking. More sex."

I don't need to be told twice.

I lift her onto the kitchen counter, and she immediately wraps her legs around my hips, pulling me closer. Those new leggings hit the floor in record time. My jeans follow.

"Bed?" I manage, even though the counter is right here and she's already reaching for me.

"No time." Her breathing is ragged. "Just—Tucker, please—"

I slide into her in one smooth motion, and she gasps, her head falling back. I grip the counter on either side of her hips, giving her what she needs—fast, hard, exactly how she wants it. Although, I might like it slow and gentle. Maybe with her cuddling me and falling asleep together, my hands on her stomach.

"Yes," she breathes. "God, yes, just like that—"

It's quick and desperate, and this is what she needs. She comes first, her whole body tensing around me, my name on her lips. I follow seconds later, burying my face in her neck, breathing her in.

We stay like that for a moment, both catching our breath, her fingers threading through my hair.

Eventually, she slides down and pats my chest, heading toward the bedroom. "I'm going to take a nap now. That was exhausting."

"Which part? The shopping or the sex?"

"Yes."

I watch her go, this woman who's building my future, who lets me buy her pants, who pulls me into spontaneous kitchen sex and then announces naptime like it's nothing.

Something in my chest expands, warm and certain and almost frightening in its intensity.

This is it, I think. This is what I want, every day, for the rest of my life.

Shopping trips. Kitchen sex. Laughter and normalcy and the simple pleasure of being together.

I'm on the cusp of something perfect.

And for once, I'm not going to fuck it up.

CHAPTER 28
SLOANE

Tucker's mouth is on my neck, his hands gripping my hips as he thrusts into me from behind. We're in the kitchen, my palms flat on the cool marble island, my belly hanging heavy in front of me.

"God, Sloane," he groans. "You feel so fucking good."

I should stop doing this. Should remind him we have things to do today—I have reading for my epidemiology class, he has a team meeting later. We shouldn't be doing this again.

But then he hits that spot inside me, and I stop thinking altogether.

"Tucker—" His name comes out as a gasp. "More. Please."

"Yeah," he promises against my shoulder. "Never stopping."

I come hard, my whole body shaking with it. He follows seconds later, his fingers digging into my hips as he spills inside me.

We stay like that for a moment, both breathing hard. Then he eases out carefully and helps me straighten up.

"You okay?" he asks, turning me to face him. His hair is disheveled, his face flushed. He looks thoroughly satisfied.

"Yeah." I lean against the island, my legs still shaky. "We really need to stop doing this."

"Do we?" He grins, completely unrepentant. "Because it's pretty great..."

"We've had sex in every room of this apartment."

"Not every room." He counts on his fingers. "We haven't done the laundry room yet. Or the guest bathroom. Or—"

"Tucker." But I'm smiling despite myself.

He pulls me close, mindful of my belly between us. "What's wrong with enjoying each other? The sex is incredible."

"It is," I admit. "But that doesn't mean—"

"Doesn't mean what?" His blue eyes search my face. We've been putting this conversation off for way too long. "Are we together, Sloane?" He seems so vulnerable despite being the size of a lumberjack. "Because you live here, you're pregnant with my kids, and we fuck six times a day…we're sort of together."

Yes. That's exactly what I mean. But I can't seem to make myself say it.

Because the truth is, I want him all the time—morning, night, in between. It's like pregnancy has turned me into someone I don't recognize, someone who can't keep her hands off Tucker Stag.

"We should get dressed," I say instead. "Don't you have that team thing?"

"Yeah." He doesn't move, still holding me. "But I'd rather stay here with you."

"Tucker—"

"I know, I know. Responsibilities." He kisses my forehead and steps back. "But for the record? I really like what we've got going. And I want more."

I watch him walk away toward his bedroom, completely naked and utterly comfortable. And I think: This is dangerous. This is so, so dangerous.

———

My epidemiology class is going better than I expected. Professor Newman handed back our midterm exams today, and I got an A-.

"Nice work, Sloane," she said as she placed the exam on my desk. "Your analysis of the outbreak data was particularly strong. Have you thought about what you want to focus on for your final project?"

"Maternal health disparities," I said immediately. It's been on my mind lately—how Black women are three times more likely to die from pregnancy complications than white women. Access to quality prenatal care is still dependent on zip code and income level.

How I'm lucky to have excellent care, and how wrong that is.

"Excellent choice," Professor Newman had said. "Come to my office hours next week and we'll discuss scope."

Now I'm in the library, reading articles about preeclampsia rates and making notes for my project proposal. My phone buzzes with a text from Mel.

MEL

Dinner at my place tonight? Pete's bringing Thai food, and we need a third to referee our legal arguments.

I smile, typing back.

Can't. Tucker has a thing. Rain check?

MEL

You've said that the last three times I've invited you over. Beginning to think you're avoiding me.

Not avoiding. Just busy.

MEL

Busy having sex with your baby daddy?

I nearly drop my phone. Look around the library to make sure no one saw.

Mel!

MEL

I'm right, though, aren't I? You mentioned you were "busy" when I called at 2 pm on Tuesday. Very suspicious.

We're not talking about this.

I promise her I will, even though I'm not sure when. Between school, doctor appointments, and Tucker—

Tucker. Who's always there. Always wanting me as fiercely as I want him. Always making me feel good.

Too good.

I push the thought away and go back to my reading. I'm not going to help other women when I spend all my waking energy fantasizing about blue eyes and hard abs.

———

His mother calls Thursday evening while I'm curled up on the couch with my laptop, working on a response paper for my health policy class. Tucker is at practice.

"Sloane! I'm so glad I caught you." Judge's voice is warm, energetic. "I asked Tucker for your number so I could apologize about dinner. I know we came on strong."

"Oh." I am totally caught off guard by this, not sure how to respond. "Thank you. I … am … not used to people making a fuss over me."

She laughs, a sound that echoes off the walls of wherever she's calling from. "Look, I know Tucker said things are … well, that you two are still figuring things out, but I wanted to see if you would come to a baby shower."

My stomach clenches. "The what? Sorry—I mean, I wasn't expecting—"

"The family is so excited, Sloane! You're having twins! And everyone is dying to meet you." She sounds genuinely excited. "Now, I know Tucker's been buying things—Ty tells me he's been very... enthusiastic about shopping. But there must be things you still need. Have you made a registry?"

I look around the apartment. At the nursery down the hall, it is already fully stocked with everything two babies could possibly need. The snot suckers and nail clippers, the mountains of tiny clothes Tucker keeps bringing home.

"We really have everything," I say. "Tucker's been kind of relentless about it."

"That's my boy." Judge laughs. "Well, what if we do a helping shower instead? The Stag family is very good at providing support—meal prep, childcare commitments, that sort of thing. Would that work?"

A helping shower. Where Tucker's enormous family descends with their schedules and plans and well-meaning suggestions about how I should raise my babies. But they're also Stag babies, aren't they? It's not like I can keep them from his family.

"That sounds great," I hear myself say. My voice sounds normal, enthusiastic even as I panic inside. "Thank you."

"Perfect! How about Sunday? My boys are all off that day, and I think Wes and Cara are both in town. You can meet everyone properly."

Everyone. I've been avoiding Tucker's large 30-person family gatherings, mainly because it feels overwhelming. I keep imagining dozens of white people, all enormous like Tucker, all with thoughts to share about my "exotic" appearance.

Still, I find myself saying, "Sunday works."

"Wonderful. I'll text you the address. We're so happy you and Tucker are doing this together. He's different lately—more settled. You're good for him."

After we hang up, I sit there staring at my laptop screen, the words of my health policy paper swimming in front of my eyes.

You're good for him.

Not: This is good for you. Or: We're excited to support you.

You're good for him.

I close my laptop and go to bed, even though it's only eight o'clock.

CHAPTER 29
SLOANE

Sunday arrives too quickly.

"You're going to love everyone," Tucker says as he drives us to his parents' house. His hand rests on my thigh, warm and familiar. "They're all excited to meet you officially. As my—" He pauses. "As the mother of my kids."

Not as his girlfriend. Not as his partner. As the mother of his kids.

Which is accurate. That's all we are, and it's my choice.

So why does it sting?

He glances at me and must notice something in my facial expression. "What's up?"

I sigh and close my eyes, gathering my thoughts. "Am I going to be the only person of color? I just need to prepare myself if there are three dozen white people."

He scratches his chin as he waits for a light to turn. "Well." He proceeds through the intersection. "Cara is Latina. But yes, everyone else is white."

"Did you tell anyone?" The question comes out sharper than I intended. "About me?"

"They've seen pictures." He glances at me, confused. "I didn't think I needed to make an announcement."

"You didn't." I look out the window, watching the pristine Squirrel Hill houses pass by. Of course, he didn't think about it. Why would he? "I just like to know what I'm walking into."

My babies are going to be Black, like me. They're going to grow up in this family, surrounded by all this whiteness, and I'll be the one making sure they know how to navigate that safely. I need to find community. The pressure of all of this feels heavy.

"They're going to love you," Tucker says for the third time.

———

The Stag house is huge—a sprawling colonial in one of Pittsburgh's nicest neighborhoods. Expensive black sports cars are already parked along the driveway. Through the windows, I can see people moving around inside.

"Ready?" Tucker asks, squeezing my hand.

No. "Yes."

The house is chaos.

That's the only word for it. People everywhere—dogs, too. Voices overlapping, laughter, someone singing Taylor Swift songs off-key in another room. Tucker's hand is on my lower back, guiding me through the crowd, making introductions.

"Sloane, this is my brother Odin. Odin, Sloane."

"Nice to officially meet you," Odin says. He's a psychologist on the Fury's behavioral health staff—but has mostly been a referee for Tucker and Josh's ... interactions. "How are you feeling?"

"Good. Tired, but good."

"I'm pretty clueless about parenting stuff, but let me know if you need any resources for anxiety or—"

"She's fine," Tucker interrupts. "Not everyone needs therapy, O."

They bicker good-naturedly, and someone else is pulling me toward the kitchen. Judge Juniper, smiling and warm, put a glass of sparkling cider in my hand.

"Sloane! Come meet everyone. This is Tim's wife Alice—"

A short woman with graying hair and kind eyes. "Lovely to meet you, dear. Tucker's been gushing about you for months."

"And some of the gals, Cara and Thora—"

Two women in their twenties, both athletic-looking. Cara

grins. "We've already volunteered to babysit. I'm going to take them jogging in one of those fancy running strollers."

"They'll be infants," I say weakly.

"Babies love jogging!" Cara insists. "Right, June?"

I recall that Judge is a rower. She shares stories about jogging through all of her pregnancies while other women file into the kitchen for snacks.

"And I'll teach them to bake," Thora adds. "Cookies, cakes, bread—"

"They'll be babies," Aunt Alice interjects. "Maybe start with purees."

"Details." Thora waves a hand.

My head is spinning. More introductions—Tucker's brother Alder, and his girlfriend, Lena, the team dentist. His other brother Gunnar and his wife Emerson, who's glowing and can't stop touching her own barely-there baby bump.

"We just found out!" Emerson smiles. "Twelve weeks! I feel so great."

The kitchen erupts in conversation. Mr. Stag makes his way into the kitchen and starts giving out bear hugs.

"Another grandkid!" Mr. Stag booms. "I'm totally winning this race, Tim-bo. Three to nil!"

Uncle Tim and Tucker's Uncle Thatcher start arguing that this isn't the sort of thing they should compete over. I silently wonder if there's anything this family doesn't compete over.

"Congratulations," I say to Emerson, who beams at me.

"Thank you! I'm so excited. I think I'm going to take some time off when the baby comes. Really be present for those early months, you know?"

"That's wonderful," Judge says warmly. "There's nothing wrong with prioritizing family."

Mr. Stag nods enthusiastically. "Best decision your mother and I ever made, me staying home with you boys. You can't get that time back."

My chest tightens. I smile and nod, like this is fine, like I'm not drowning in the implication that good parents stay home. Neither Tucker nor I have any plans to leave the workforce.

More people. Tucker's cousin Stellan mentions that he met

someone. More cheers. Someone's brought another dog. The noise level is overwhelming.

"Sloane?" It's Judge, touching my arm. "Are you okay? You look pale."

"I'm fine. Just—it's a lot of people."

"Let's sit down." She guides me to the living room, to a comfortable chair. People gather around—well-meaning, loving, overwhelming.

"So about childcare," Mr. Stag says, pulling out his phone with a calendar app. "I'm thinking Tuesdays and Thursdays, I can take the babies. Juniper has court those days, but I'm free."

"And I can do Mondays," Aunt Alice offers. "Cara, you're off Mondays, right?"

"In the off-season, yes."

"We should set up a rotation," Judge says. "Make sure Sloane and Tucker have consistent support."

They're planning. Making schedules. Deciding when they'll take my babies without asking if I want that.

"What about nighttime?" someone asks. "We should set up a night rotation."

"I can help with that," Lena volunteers. "Especially when the Fury are on the road."

"And I can set up laundry service," Emerson says. "This company, Green Cheeks, does cloth diaper delivery—"

"Wait." My voice comes out too loud. Everyone stops and looks at me. "I appreciate all this, but—we haven't even discussed —I mean, Tucker and I need to figure out what we want first."

"Of course," Judge says smoothly. "We're just offering options. You don't have to use any of this."

But the planning continues. Who's good with infants. Who has experience with twins. Someone mentioning their friend who had preemie twins, and here's what worked. Someone else bringing up sleep training.

I know this is the point of a helping shower. Apparently. But it all just feels like a hot mess. I'm out of control, and I'm sweating. How am I going to be a present parent? Will I even see these children with 30 other people fighting over who gets to raise them? This is the total opposite of what I'm familiar with, and it doesn't feel right, either.

I'm a damn Goldilocks with no idea what "just right" would even look like.

Tucker is across the room, talking to his brothers. He's laughing at something Alder said, entirely at ease in this chaos.

He doesn't notice I'm drowning.

"Sloane," Odin says quietly, sitting down next to me. "You okay? You seem overwhelmed."

"I'm fine."

"You don't look fine."

I force a smile. "Just tired. Pregnancy is exhausting."

He studies me for a moment, then nods. "If you ever want to talk—professionally or just as Tucker's brother—I'm here."

"Thank you."

The afternoon drags on. More food, more conversation, more plans being made for my life. Someone asks about names. Someone else asks if I'm hoping for boys or girls. Someone mentions Tucker's childhood and how wild he was.

"But he's settling down now," Ty says proudly. "Having kids does that to a man. Makes him grow up."

Like I'm a life event that's happening to Tucker. A catalyst for his maturation.

Not a person with my own dreams, my own goals, my own life.

By the time we leave, I have a headache, and the babies are kicking like they can feel my stress.

"That was so great," Tucker says in the car. "Everyone loves you."

"Mm."

"You okay? You're quiet."

"Just tired."

He squeezes my hand. "Let's get you home. I can give you your afternoon O, charge your batteries."

Home. His apartment. That I live in. That he pays for.

"Actually," I hear myself say, "I have a lot of reading to do tonight. For class."

"Oh. Okay." He sounds disappointed. "Want me to pick up dinner anyway? You need to eat."

"I'll grab something later."

We drive in silence. Tucker's hand stays on my thigh, but it feels heavy now. Possessive rather than comforting.

Back at the apartment, Tucker heads to his room to change. I go to my room—his room that he gave me—and close the door.

Then I sink onto the bed and try to breathe.

The walls are closing in. This beautiful apartment, this comfortable life, this family that wants to absorb me—it's all closing in.

I pull out my laptop and open my epidemiology reading. Try to focus on mortality rates and statistical analysis. Try to remember who I'm supposed to be.

Sloane Campbell. Future public health professional. Someone who helps others, who makes a difference, who doesn't need to be rescued.

But when I look around this room—at the expensive furniture, the closet full of maternity clothes Tucker bought when he noticed I was crammed into his shirts, the drawer full of prenatal vitamins and snacks he keeps stocked—all I see is dependence.

I haven't paid for anything in months. Haven't bought my own groceries. Haven't made a major decision without Tucker's input.

The babies kick. I put my hand on my stomach, feeling them move. They're getting so big. In a few months, they'll be here. Real, actual humans that I'll be responsible for.

How am I going to take care of two babies when I can barely take care of myself?

I close my laptop, lie back on the bed, and stare at the ceiling.

There's a soft knock on the door. "Sloane? I ordered Italian anyway. It's here if you want some."

"Thanks. Maybe later."

A pause. "You sure you're okay?"

"Just tired."

"Okay. I'll be in the living room if you need anything."

His footsteps retreat. The apartment goes quiet.

I should get up. Should eat dinner with him. Should have sex with him because that's what we do now, that's what we've been doing every day for weeks.

But I can't move.

I'm pinned here by the weight of everything—school, pregnancy, Tucker's family, Tucker himself. By the slow, creeping realization that I've done it again.

I've disappeared.

Not into Josh's controlling demands this time. Into Tucker's overwhelming generosity instead.

But the result is the same.

I'm not Sloane Campbell anymore. I'm Tucker's baby mama. The mother of his children. The woman living in his apartment, eating his food.

I'm becoming one of those women. The ones my grandmother warned me about. The ones who need a man to survive.

The thought makes me feel sick.

I roll onto my side, curling around my belly. The babies kick against my hand.

I'm supposed to be different. Supposed to finish school, get a good job, help people. Supposed to prove that I'm not my mother, that I can take care of myself and my children without needing a man to rescue me.

I walked into this with my eyes open. I chose this.

Which somehow makes it worse.

I cry until I'm exhausted, until the babies stop kicking, until I finally fall asleep fully dressed on top of the covers.

And I dream about running away.

———

The next morning, Tucker is gone before I wake up. There's a note on the kitchen counter.

> Morning skate, then team meeting. There's breakfast in the fridge. Text me if you need anything. -T

I throw the note away and make my own breakfast—eggs and toast that I force myself to eat even though my stomach is churning.

I have class at ten. Professor Newman's office hours at two. Then a study group at four.

My life. My schedule. My goals.

I cling to that thought all day.

During Professor Newman's office hours, we discuss my final project.

"Maternal health disparities are a huge topic," she says. "You'll need to narrow it down. What specifically interests you?"

"Access to quality prenatal care," I say immediately. "How income and race affect outcomes. How could we improve the system."

"Excellent. Very timely, given your personal experience." She smiles at my belly. I had meetings with my professors at the beginning of the semester to talk about my health and any accommodations I might need.

Everyone wants to support me.

But their support feels like another word for dependence.

I leave her office feeling worse than when I arrived.

I go home—to Tucker's apartment—and find him in the kitchen cooking dinner.

"Hey!" He turns, smiling. "How was your day?"

"Fine."

"I'm making chicken and vegetables. Thought you might want something light." He moves toward me, clearly intending to kiss me. "Missed you today."

I step back before he can reach me. "I need to work on my project proposal."

His smile falters. "Oh. Okay. I'll save you a plate."

I retreat to my room and close the door.

———

A few hours later, Tucker knocks on the door. "Sloane? You haven't eaten. I'm worried."

"I'm fine."

"You're not fine. Talk to me."

"I'm just stressed about school."

A long pause. "Can I come in?"

No. "Okay."

The door opens. He stands in the doorway, looking uncertain. It's strange, seeing him like this—he's usually so confident.

"Did I do something wrong?" he asks. "You've been distant."

"You didn't do anything wrong."

"Then what's going on?"

Everything. Nothing. I'm drowning and I don't know how to tell you.

"I'm just tired," I repeat. "And I have a lot of work to do."

He studies my face. "Is this about my family? Were they too much?"

Yes. "They were fine."

"Sloane—"

"Tucker, I really need to work on this proposal. Can we talk later?"

He looks like he wants to argue. But then he nods. "Okay. I'll be in the living room if you need me."

The door closes.

I'm alone again.

And I realize: this is how it's going to be. Me pushing him away because I don't know how to need him without losing myself. Him giving me space because he doesn't understand what's wrong.

We're going to keep circling each other, getting closer and pulling apart, until the babies come and force us to figure out what we are to each other.

But by then, it might be too late.

CHAPTER 30
TUCKER

Sloane hasn't let me touch her in eight days.

She pulls away when I reach for her, doesn't smile when I make jokes about dicking her down. Instead of eager smiles, I get closed doors and shouted "I'm tired" responses.

I feel like I'm losing something, but not understanding what.

I thought maybe she just needed space after the family shower. My family can be a lot—I get that. But it's been over a week and she's still distant, still locked behind walls I can't break through.

"You going to bed?" I ask, standing in her doorway. She's at the desk, laptop open, surrounded by textbooks.

"I have a lot of reading to do."

"It's almost midnight."

"I know what time it is." Her voice is sharp, then softens. "Sorry. I'm just stressed about this project."

I lean against the doorframe, studying her. She's wearing one of my old t-shirts, her hair in a wrap, her shoulders tight with tension. "Sloane, talk to me. What's going on?"

"Nothing's going on."

"You've barely spoken to me in over a week. You won't—" I stop myself. "You won't let me near you."

She closes her laptop, turns to face me. Her eyes are tired, with shadows underneath. "I'm just overwhelmed right now. School, the pregnancy, everything. I need space."

Space. She needs space. From me.

"Okay," I say, even though nothing about this feels okay. "I'm here if you need anything." It feels so inadequate, but what else can I say?

"I know."

I retreat to my room and lie in bed staring at the ceiling. Down the hall, I can hear her moving around. The bathroom door closing. Water running.

I want to go to her. Want to hold her, make her tell me what's wrong. Rub her shoulders at least. But she asked for space, and I'm trying to respect that.

Even though it's killing me.

———

Morning practice is brutal.

"T Stag! Where's your head?" Coach Thompson yells as I miss an easy pass. "You're playing like you're asleep!"

"Sorry, Coach."

"Sorry doesn't win games." He blows his whistle. "Line drills. Everyone. Again."

I catch Alder's eye. He gives me a concerned look but doesn't say anything, just licks at the gap in his upper teeth. We run the drills until my legs are screaming, until I'm too tired to think about Sloane pulling away from me.

After practice, I'm headed to the showers when Brian catches me in the hallway.

"T-Stag. Got a minute?"

"Sure."

We step into an empty office. Brian looks serious, which is never a good sign.

"The parental leave advocacy," he says. "It's getting push-back." I texted him about this weeks ago at my father's advice. I should have been following through on this ... been a thorn in their side.

"What kind of pushback?"

"Management's concerned about your commitment. There's talk that you're becoming a distraction."

My stomach drops. "Seriously? Mayhem just wrecked a motorcycle. I'm just trying to be a good dad…"

"Your play's been off lately. Everyone's noticed." Brian leans against the desk. "And with all this talk about wanting time off—some people are questioning if you still have the edge."

"I'm still doing my job."

"Are you?" He raises an eyebrow. "Because from what I've seen in the last few games, you *are* distracted. Slow. Not protecting your teammates the way you used to."

"That's not—"

"Tucker." His voice is gentle but firm. "I'm on your side. But you need to figure out what's going on. Because if your play doesn't improve, management's going to start asking harder questions."

He pats me on the arm with a folder. "I gotta go snag one of your brothers before he leaves me high and dry over a dog food endorsement."

Brian breezes down the hall like we were just casually chatting about the weather.

Meanwhile, I feel like I got hit with a monsoon.

My play is suffering. I know it is. But it's not because I'm soft or distracted by family. It's because Sloane won't talk to me, and I don't know how to fix it. One thing I do know: Sloane has enough on her plate, and worrying about my job isn't going to relieve any of the stress she's feeling. I have to keep this shit on lock until I find a solution.

———

On Thursday, I have to leave for a short road trip—just two days, games in Columbus and Detroit. Sloane has a doctor's appointment while I'm gone.

"Text me after?" I ask before I leave. "Let me know how it goes?"

"Sure."

"And if you need anything, my parents are around. My mom said she'd be happy to—"

"I'll be fine, Tucker. Go and win, okay?"

I kiss her forehead. She lets me, but doesn't lean into it. Doesn't kiss me back. Definitely not the time for me to tell her I don't even know if I'll get play time on this trip.

I need to make progress with the parental leave policy pronto. What's the point of being related to your lawyer if he can't even rattle the bars with the big guys? It occurs to me that my cousin Pete is working at Stag Law now that he's back in town. He can help me figure out what's up with my negotiations.

I call him on the team bus, hoping no one can hear my conversation over their Showgirl sing-along.

"Tuck? Where the hell are you?" Pete sounds like I just interrupted him while he was working out.

"Hey, man. This is a genuine work question."

He sighs, and I hear a door close. Wonder where he actually is. But that's a personal question, and I'm calling him as a client right now. "What's up?"

"I need you to go full Stag on the players' association about my contract amendment. They're being dicks about giving me leave."

"Hm." The line crackles, like Pete's scratching beard stubble. Which shocks me because my straight-laced cousin is as fastidious as his father when it comes to grooming. "That project isn't on my docket."

"Well, can you put it on there? I want family handling this, Pete. Honestly, I thought your dad was on it."

Another growling sound, more scratching. Pete finally says, "Dad's dealing with a crisis from a player injury. But … yes. I've added this to my workload." My cousin guffaws. "Oh, man, they're setting themselves up to be sued. Do they even see how gendered this is? It's discrimination."

"That's what I thought!" Pete says something about precedent with the women's national team and calling up Ortega, so I know he and Mel are going to actually get on this. By the time I get him off the phone, I'm feeling a lot more confident that I'll actually get to see these babies while they're babies, without putting an end to my hockey career.

———

The road trip is terrible, though. I'm still not playing my best. I play badly in Columbus, take a stupid penalty that costs us the game. In Detroit, I'm benched for the third period after missing an assignment.

Coach pulls me aside after. "What the hell is going on with you?"

"Nothing. I'm fine."

"You're not fine. You're playing like shit." He crosses his arms. "Is this about the baby mama drama? Because I need you focused, Stag. I can't have you playing like this."

"I'll figure it out."

"You'd better. Because right now, you're a liability."

On the bus back to the hotel, Sloane texts.

Appointment went fine. Babies are good.

That's it. No details. No "wish you were there" or "miss you."

That's great! What did Dr. Patel say? Any updates?

SLOANE

Just the usual stuff.

I stare at my phone, that uneasy feeling growing stronger.

I might be keeping my worries from Sloane, but she's clearly holding something back from me, too.

———

Friday night, we're back in Pittsburgh for a home game against Philadelphia, and my entire family is there. I can see them in the stands during warm-ups—Mom, Dad, all my brothers, uncles, cousins. A whole Stag section, loud and proud.

But Sloane's not there.

I knew she wouldn't come. She's been avoiding anything that feels too couple-y, too public. But seeing that empty seat hits harder than I expected.

"You good?" Alder skates up beside me.

"Yeah. Fine."

"Liar." He knocks his stick against mine. "She'll come around. Just give her time."

But what if time isn't what she needs? What if she's pulling away because she's decided this isn't what she wants?

The game starts, and I try to focus. Try to be present, to do my job.

But I keep looking up at the stands. At my whole family cheering, and that one empty seat.

Halfway through the second period, Philadelphia's enforcer—a huge guy named Morrison—goes after Grentley behind the net. It's a dirty hit, late and high. Grentley goes down hard.

I should move. Should drop my gloves, should protect my teammate.

But I'm watching my family in the stands. Watching my dad jump to his feet, watching my mom cover her mouth. And I'm thinking about Sloane at home, alone, pulling further away from me every day.

I'm too slow.

By the time I react, Morrison has already gotten in two more hits. By the time I reach them, the damage is done.

The refs blow the whistle. Grentley is on the ice, holding his shoulder. The trainer is rushing out.

And Coach Thompson is screaming at me from the bench.

"STAG! WHAT THE HELL WAS THAT?"

I help Grentley up. He's favoring his left side, face twisted in pain.

"You okay?" I ask.

"Peachy." He skates off toward the bench, and I follow.

Coach is waiting. "My office. After the game."

The rest of the period is a blur. Grentley is meaner than usual. We lose 3-1. And I know I'm fucked.

———

Coach's office is small and cold. He sits behind his desk, arms crossed, looking at me like I farted on his pillow.

"You want to tell me what happened out there?"

"I was slow to react."

"Slow?" His voice rises. "You were asleep! Morrison went after Grentley, and you just stood there!"

"I know. I'm sorry."

"Sorry doesn't cut it, T-Stag. Your job is to protect your teammates. That's the whole reason you're on this team." He leans forward. "So either you start doing your job, or we find someone who will."

"It won't happen again."

"It better not. Because I'm this close—" He holds up two fingers an inch apart. "—to benching you permanently."

I swallow my pride, my excuses, and nod at Coach, who waves me out of his office.

He's right. I am somewhere else entirely. I'm with Sloane, who won't let me in. I'm in that empty seat in the stands. I'm lost in all the ways I'm failing—at hockey, at being there for her, at everything.

And tomorrow I leave for a six-day road trip—the longest of the season. Columbus, Detroit, Boston, New York. Six days away from Sloane when she's pregnant with fucking Stag babies and trying to go to school full-time.

Six days when everything could fall apart.

I want to go to her now. Want to drive home and demand she talk to me, tell me what's wrong, let me help. But she's pregnant, and fragile, and stressed about school. I need to handle this shit and go to her with a solution once I find it. That's my only route to protecting my family right now.

Back in the locker room, I peel off my gear slowly, every movement feeling heavy. Around me, the room is quiet. Most guys have already left. It's just me and the equipment manager, and the sound of my own breathing.

CHAPTER 31
SLOANE

TUCKER LEFT FOR THE ROAD TRIP THIS MORNING.

Six days. Boston, New York, Philadelphia, Columbus. Six days of games and hotels and team dinners while I'm here, alone in his apartment, trying to pretend everything is fine.

It's not fine.

I've been having back pain since yesterday. Not contractions—I know what those are supposed to feel like from all the books Tucker keeps leaving around the apartment. Just pressure. Tightness. A low ache in my spine that won't go away.

It's probably nothing. Braxton Hicks, maybe. Or just my body adjusting to carrying two babies who seem determined to take up every available inch of space.

I tell myself this as I sit at the kitchen table, laptop open, trying to focus on my epidemiology reading. Professor Newman wants a draft of my project proposal by next week, and I haven't written a single word.

The cramping gets worse. I shift in my chair, trying to find a comfortable position.

There isn't one.

My phone buzzes. I know without looking that it's a message from Tucker.

Made it to Boston. Hotel is nice. Miss you.

I stare at the message. Miss you. Like this is normal. Like we're a typical couple, and he's away on a normal business trip.

Like I'm not sitting here balanced on a hockey stick.

On one hand, I moved in here so I'd have help and support from my co-parent.

On the other hand, he's in another state and not even around to learn the sex of our babies. I have it in an envelope on the table, waiting for when he gets back.

When will that be? I've lost track.

We aren't together, not really, and all the sex and cohabitating is just blurring lines I need to sharpen instead. I have to get out before I disappear completely.

The problem is, I have nowhere to go.

No apartment lined up. No plan beyond "I can't do this anymore."

And even more persistent than the pain in my lower back is the dread of winding up just like my mother—a woman who can't make it on her own, who needs to be rescued.

It's a mindset at odds with what I hope to learn in school. If my grandmother hadn't raised me, I could easily have been a woman with no options. I want to help create policies and design the social safety nets. And now I see just how impossible it feels to access them. And I have financial resources!

The cramping intensifies. I put my hand on my belly, feeling the tightness. I'm only five months and some change. Everyone needs to calm down and grow some more lungs.

"It's okay," I whisper to the babies. "We're okay."

But I don't feel okay.

I feel trapped. Suffocated. Like the walls of this beautiful apartment are closing in, and I can't breathe.

I need to get out. Need to find myself again before I'm lost completely.

But where would I go?

The question circles in my head, over and over, no answer appearing.

I try to go back to my reading. Maternal health disparities. Access to prenatal care. All the things I wanted to study, wanted to fix, wanted to dedicate my life to.

Before I became someone's baby mama. Before I moved into someone's apartment and started living off someone's resources.

Before I lost track of who Sloane Campbell was supposed to be.

Another cramp, stronger this time. I gasp, gripping the edge of the table.

Okay. That one hurt.

I stand up slowly, one hand on my belly. Maybe I should lie down. Rest. Drink some water.

The cramping eases slightly. See? Nothing.

I make it to the bedroom—my bedroom, Tucker's bedroom, I don't even know whose bedroom it is anymore—and lie down on top of the covers.

The babies kick. Strong, insistent movements that make my whole belly shift.

"I know," I say to them. "I know you're there."

I close my eyes and try to sleep.

———

I wake up to pain.

Real pain, not just cramping. Sharp and low and insistent, radiating through my belly and down my legs.

I sit up carefully, breathing through it. It passes after a moment, leaving me shaky and scared.

Okay. That was different.

I check the time. It's been two hours. I slept through the afternoon.

Another cramp hits, harder than before. I curl onto my side, waiting for it to pass.

It doesn't pass.

I need to use the bathroom. Maybe that will help.

I make it there slowly, one hand on the wall for support. Everything aches. Everything feels wrong.

I pull down my underwear and freeze.

Blood.

Not a lot. But enough. Red against white cotton, unmistakable and terrifying.

"No," I whisper. "No, no, no."

The babies. Something's wrong with the babies.

I should call Tucker. He should know. He should be here.

But he's not here. He's hours away.

My hands shake as I pull out my phone and scroll to a different name.

Mel answers on the second ring. "Hey, what's up?"

"I need help." My voice cracks. "I'm bleeding. I'm scared, Mel."

"Bleeding? Sloane, where are you?"

"Home—Tucker's apartment. He's in Boston and I'm bleeding and—"

"I'm calling an ambulance."

"No, I don't need—"

"Sloane." Mel's voice is firm. "I can't drive. I can't get you to a car. You need an ambulance. I'm calling now, and then I'm coming over. Which hospital?"

"Magee Women's, I guess. Where Dr. Patel is."

"Stay on the phone with me. Don't move. I'm calling 911."

I sink to the bathroom floor, phone pressed to my ear, and start to cry.

———

The paramedics arrive with the doorman and, despite their professionalism, I feel embarrassed.

They find me still on the bathroom floor, phone in hand, trying to explain that I'm fine, that it's probably nothing, and that I'm so sorry to bother them.

"Ma'am, you're pregnant with twins and you're bleeding," the taller one says. He looks biracial like me. Like how my babies might look when they're grown. I feel so dizzy. "This isn't nothing."

They help me up, check my vitals, ask me a hundred questions. How far along? Any pain? When did the bleeding start?

I answer automatically, my brain floating somewhere outside my body.

The ambulance ride is a blur of beeping monitors and reassuring voices and pain that comes and goes in waves. I keep my hand on my belly, feeling the babies move.

They're okay. They have to be okay.

Mel is waiting when we arrive at the ER. She wheels alongside the gurney, her hand finding mine.

"I'm here," she says. "You're okay. All three of you."

Everything is beeps and shouts until I'm hooked up to monitors and wires, and finally, mercifully, I hear the melody of heartbeats.

Two steady rhythms that make me cry with relief.

They're alive.

Mel sits in the chair beside my bed, her hand holding mine, and I sob. I didn't realize how afraid I was until I saw that all is well.

Although I do hear Dr. Patel muttering something about tests.

"Have you called Tucker?" Mel asks carefully.

Her question confuses me. "No."

"Sloane—"

"He's on the ice," I tell her, gripping the bed rail, staring at the jagged lines tracking each baby's vitals.

Mel recoils. "Sloane. Come on."

I shake my head. "He's in the middle of a professional hockey game, Mel. He can't get here even if he wanted to. I need to get used to this, being the dependable parent. Being present."

Mel opens her mouth, then closes it. Then says, "Sloane, he's not playing anyway. He's benched."

I whip my head toward her. "What do you mean benched?" The worry fades away for a moment, replaced by icy dread.

"He didn't tell you?" Her eyes dance in the bright lights, and I try to focus on her face, on what she's saying. "He spaced out or something, and a teammate got hit on Tucker's watch. I'm working on his case with the player's association…to get more emergency family leave."

I swallow down bile as I realize Tucker has been lying to me.

Keeping me in the dark while he somehow thinks he's protecting me.

A doctor comes in and snaps me back to the crisis at hand—not Dr. Patel, someone younger. She introduces herself as Dr. Kim, checks the monitors, examines me with careful hands.

"Your blood pressure is elevated," she says. "Combined with the bleeding and cramping, we're concerned about preeclampsia. We need to keep you here for observation."

"For how long?"

"At least overnight. Possibly longer, depending on how things progress." She makes notes on her tablet. "Is there someone we should call? The father?"

"No." The word comes out too fast, too sharp. "There's no one."

Dr. Kim and Mel exchange a look.

"Sloane," Mel says quietly. "Maybe we should—"

"No," I repeat. "I'm making my own damn decisions for once."

Mel falls silent. Dr. Kim finishes her notes and leaves, explaining that the staff will move me to a room upstairs.

I'm alone with Mel and the steady beep of monitors and the sound of my babies' heartbeats.

"I thought you guys were being open with each other." My friend crosses her arms and bites her lip.

"Yeah, well, I thought he was different than my ex."

"Tucker isn't Josh."

"Really? Lying. Secrets. What else isn't he telling me?" I put my hand on my belly. "I'm losing myself. And I can't—I can't do that to these babies. Can't be one of those women who disappears."

"Honey, you're not going anywhere."

"See? Even you can see that I'm stuck."

Mel doesn't have an answer for that. She sighs. "You should tell him."

"Why? So, he can rush back here and then I feel guilty for interrupting his comeback plans?"

"Or so he can be here for you when you're scared and in the hospital."

"I'm not scared." But my voice shakes when I say it.

Mel just looks at me.

"Anymore," I insist. "We're fine. The babies are fine. I want him on a list of people who cannot come in here."

"Sloane—" Mel starts.

"He's been lying to me. Just like Josh did. Making decisions about what I can handle, what I should know." A wave of pressure steals my breath. When I can speak again, my voice is steady. "I won't do this again. I won't build a life with someone who thinks I'm too fragile for the truth."

Not to mention, I have to get used to him being gone. Because this is exactly what I have to look forward to. Long stretches of time where it's just me... and dozens of his relatives with suggestions and casseroles.

———

Dr. Patel returns during evening rounds.

She's calm and professional as always, checking my chart, asking questions, examining the monitor readings. But when she sees Mel sitting beside my bed, her eyebrows rise.

"Where's Tucker?" she asks.

"Out of town. On a road trip."

"Does he know you're here?"

The question hangs in the air between us.

"He's not reachable," I say. The words come out flat, final. "And I'd like my chart to reflect that he's not welcome."

Dr. Patel and Mel exchange another one of those looks. The kind that says they think I'm making a colossal mistake but are too polite to say it out loud.

"I'm making my own damn decisions for once," I snap. "Isn't that what everyone wants? For me to be independent? To take control of my life?"

"That's not—" Mel tries.

Dr. Patel pauses, pinches her lips together, then finishes her notes. "Blood pressure is still high, Sloane. We'll keep monitoring you overnight. Try to rest. We'll talk more in the morning."

She leaves, and my best friend rolls after her. Judging me, probably. Thinking I'm making a mistake.

Maybe I am. But it's my mistake to make.

Alone in the hospital room, surrounded by beeping monitors and the steady rhythm of my babies' heartbeats, I finally let myself cry.

Not the scared crying from earlier. This is something deeper. Grief, maybe. For what I thought this would be. For what I wanted and can't have.

I wanted to be independent. Strong. Someone who doesn't need rescuing.

But lying here, hooked up to machines, my babies in danger because my body is failing them—I've never felt less independent in my life.

I put my hand on my belly, feeling the twins move. Strong, healthy movements that make me cry all over again.

"It's going to be okay," I whisper to them. "I'm going to figure this out. We're going to be okay."

But I don't believe it.

Because this—lying alone in a hospital bed, pushing away the person I love because I'm too scared to need him—this doesn't feel like okay.

This feels like I'm dying.

And I have no idea how to stop it.

Outside my door, I hear nurses talking, monitors beeping in other rooms, the sound of life continuing while mine falls apart.

The babies kick. I close my eyes and try to remember who Sloane Campbell is supposed to be.

But all I can think about is Tucker. His smile. His hands on my belly. The way he says my name, cooks me food, and bursts into my room to tell me something he learned.

Then I remember that happy guy? He's gone more than he's around, and I cannot let myself rely on his support.

This is what independence looks like, I think. This is what I wanted.

So why does it feel like I'm losing everything that matters?

CHAPTER 32

TUCKER

I'M BENCHED.

Not because I'm injured. Not because Coach is rotating lines. Because I'm playing like shit and everyone knows it.

"T-Stag, you're out," Coach Thompson barks during the second period. "Sit and think about whether you actually want to be here."

I skate to the bench without arguing. What am I supposed to say? I do want to be here, but my brain won't stop replaying Sloane's face the last time I saw her. The way she turned away from me, shut me out, made it clear she doesn't want me around.

The game continues without me. We're losing to Boston 3-1. My fault, mostly. I missed an assignment in the first period that led to a goal. Took a stupid penalty in the second that gave them a power play.

I'm a liability. Coach is right.

Around me, the bench is tense. Mayhem keeps shooting me concerned looks. Alder won't even make eye contact—he's too disappointed.

My phone is in my locker, but I can feel its absence like a phantom limb. Has Sloane texted? Called? Probably not. She's barely responded to anything I've sent in days.

I watch the clock tick down. Each second feels like proof that I'm failing at everything.

The buzzer sounds. End of the second period. We file into the locker room, and I head straight for my stall, sinking onto the bench.

My phone sits in my bag. I pull it out.

No messages from Sloane.

Three missed calls from a number I don't recognize.

Before I can check voicemail, my phone rings. The same unknown number.

I answer. "Hello?"

"Tucker? It's Mel."

My stomach drops. Sloane's friend wouldn't call me to shoot the shit. She would have had to work to get my number. "What's wrong?"

"Sloane's in the hospital." Her voice is careful, measured. "She had bleeding and cramping. They brought her in by ambulance."

The locker room disappears. The noise of my teammates fades to nothing.

"What hospital?"

"Magee Women's. Tucker, she—" Mel hesitates. "She knows you haven't been playing, and she's really hurt. She wouldn't let me call you. I waited as long as I could, but you need to know."

Hospital. Hurt. Sloane.

"Are the babies okay?"

"So far, yes. They're monitoring her. Preeclampsia, they think."

"I'm coming. I'm leaving right now."

"Tucker—"

I hang up. Stand. My hands are shaking.

Coach is across the locker room, talking to the assistant coaches. I walk over, my gear still on, skates still laced.

"Coach. I'm leaving."

He turns. "What?"

"Sloane's in the hospital. The mother of my children. I have to go."

His face hardens. "We're in the middle of a game."

"I know. I'm sorry. But I have to leave. Now."

"She's getting help at the hospital. Tucker, if you walk out of this arena, there will be consequences."

"I don't care." My voice is too loud. Other players are

watching now. "My family is in the hospital and I'm going to them. Fire me if you want."

Coach's jaw works. He looks like he wants to argue, to threaten, to make me stay.

Then a voice behind me: "Let him go."

I turn. Grentley is standing there, his expression unreadable.

"Grentley—" Coach starts.

"Mayhem can step up. Turner can take his spot." Grentley looks at me, and for the first time since this whole mess started, there's no hostility in his eyes. Just understanding. "Go."

I stare at him. Josh Grentley, who has every reason to want me to fail, just vouched for me.

"Thanks," I manage.

He nods once. "Don't fuck it up."

I'm already moving, stripping off my gear as I go. Jersey, pads, skates. I'm down to my base layer in seconds, grabbing my phone and wallet.

"Tucker!" Alder catches my arm. "What do you need?"

"A way back to Pittsburgh. Fast."

"I'll call Brian. He'll get you a plane."

I'm pulling on jeans, a sweatshirt, shoes. Everything is happening in fast motion while my brain feels like it's moving through mud.

Sloane's in the hospital. The babies might be in danger. And she told the doctors I'm not allowed in.

My phone rings. My agent.

"I'm leaving the game," I say before he can speak. "I don't give a fuck about fines or consequences or—"

"Tucker, breathe." His voice is calm. "I heard. Where do you need to be?"

"Pittsburgh. Magee Women's Hospital."

"Give me ten minutes."

I'm dressed now, bag in hand. Alder is on his phone, speaking quickly to someone. Other teammates are gathering around—Mayhem, Spinner, even guys I barely talk to.

"Go," Mayhem says. "We got this."

I nod, not trusting my voice.

Alder hangs up. "Dad's going to meet you at the hospital. Odin's already on his way to the airport to pick you up."

My family. Mobilizing in seconds, no questions asked.

"Thank you."

"Go." Alder pulls me into a quick hug.

———

Brian has me taking a helicopter to Logan Airport, and on any other day, I'd be freaking out about how fucking cool this is.

A private jet waits to take my vibrating, anxious carcass the rest of the way to Pittsburgh, and we're in the air before I can fully process what's happening.

Sloane's in the hospital. My babies might be in danger. I'm thirty thousand feet up and completely helpless.

I try calling her. It goes to voicemail.

I try texting.

> I'm on my way. Please be okay.

No response.

I call my mom.

"Tucker, we heard, baby," she says. "Your father and I are heading to the hospital now."

"Is she okay? Are the babies okay?"

"We don't know yet." Mom's voice is gentle. "She's going to be okay, honey."

"She won't let me see her."

Silence on the other end. Then: "What?"

"Mel said Sloane told the doctors I'd be 'out of the picture.' She didn't want me to know she was hospitalized."

"Tucker—"

"I fucked it up, Mom. I fucked everything up and now she won't even let me near her."

"You didn't fuck anything up. You're in a plane right now, leaving a game, risking your career to be with her. That's not fucking up."

"She doesn't want me there."

"But you'll be there anyway," Mom's voice is firm. "You'll sit outside her room if you have to. You'll wait as long as it takes. That's what love is, Tucker. Showing up even when it's hard."

After we hang up, I sit in the dark cabin, watching clouds pass below.

The flight attendant stops to relay a message from my Uncle Tim, who says the players' association is still not budging on their emergency family leave protocols. I should have been paying more attention to that struggle. Should have had Brian on the horn, following up, getting public.

I shouldn't have to be threatened with getting fired in front of the whole fucking team when there's a life-threatening baby emergency.

The league thinks it's me being soft.

Right now, I don't care.

Right now, all I care about is getting to Sloane.

I should have known something was wrong. Should have pushed harder when she pulled away. Should have stayed in Pittsburgh instead of going on this goddamn road trip.

I should have chosen her sooner.

———

Odin is waiting at the private aviation terminal when we land.

"How is she?" I ask as soon as I see him.

"I don't know, man. I just got the call from Dad twenty minutes ago." He grabs my bag. "Let's get you there."

The drive to the hospital in Odin's SUV takes fifteen minutes but feels like fifteen hours. My big brother doesn't try to make conversation, just drives fast and gets me there.

He pulls up to the main entrance. "You want me to come in?"

"Yeah." I don't want to be alone when I find out how bad this is. He doesn't say a word, but hops out and tosses his keys to the valet.

We walk through automatic doors into a bright, sterile lobby. The information desk is straight ahead—a tired-looking woman in scrubs behind a computer.

"I'm looking for Sloane Campbell," I say. "She was admitted earlier today."

The woman types. "Are you family?"

"I'm the father. Of her babies."

More typing. Her expression doesn't change. "I'm sorry, sir. She's on a restricted visitor list. I can't give you any information."

The words don't make sense at first. "What?"

"The patient has restricted her visitor list. You're not on it."

"Those are my babies. "

"I understand, but without the patient's permission—"

"Can you just tell me if she's okay? If the babies are okay?"

"I'm sorry. I can't release any information."

Beside me, Odin puts a hand on my shoulder. "Tucker—"

I step back from the desk before I say something I'll regret. Hospital security is already watching us.

She's in this hospital, possibly losing our babies, and she made sure I couldn't get to her.

My legs give out. I sink to the floor right there in the lobby, back against the wall, head in my hands.

This is it. This is what losing everything looks like.

Odin slides down beside me. We sit there on the hospital floor like a couple of idiots, and I can't bring myself to care.

"She's scared," Odin says quietly. "That's different from not wanting you."

"She literally put me on a list of people who can't see her."

"She's probably terrified. Fear makes people do stupid things."

"What am I supposed to do? I can't force my way in."

"No. But you can wait."

"For how long?"

"As long as it takes."

I lean my head back against the wall. Around us, the hospital moves on. People checking in, people leaving. Life and death happening while I sit on the floor.

"You're really okay with potentially losing your job over this?" Odin asks.

I close my eyes. "What kind of question is that? I'm okay with it. Because what's the point of having a career if I lose my family?"

He puts his arm around me, and I rest my head on his shoulder, wondering where everything went so wrong.

We sit in silence. Minutes pass. Then more minutes.

My phone rings and I bark out, "Yeah?" Without waiting to see who it is.

Uncle Tim's voice comes through, gruff and staticky like he's on the move. "Tucker, I know you and Mel Ortega got off to a rough start, but—"

"Uncle Tim, I really can't talk about parking right now."

He chuckles. Who can laugh right now? "Tucker, I was going to say … she's a force of nature. She just got the league to eat their own words."

I look at my brother and back at the floor. "What are you saying? Is this about me leaving the game tonight?"

Tim's voice is firm but light. "She and my firstborn just won your case with the players' association, kiddo. I'll call you tomorrow with more details, but just know that you do not have to worry about your career while you take care of your family right now."

"My family?"

"Yes," he soothes. "Your family. You're doing what matters."

"What I'm doing is sitting on a hospital floor because the mother of my children won't let me see her."

"You're showing up. You're being there even when it's hard. That matters too." Tim pauses. "I've been in your shoes, son. I'm here to talk when you're ready."

"Thanks."

———

More time passes, and my brother just sits by my side, a quiet, giant presence. Hospital staff walk by, some giving us curious looks. Security keeps an eye on us but doesn't make us leave.

The PA system announces that visiting hours are ending in thirty minutes.

"You planning to stay all night?" Odin asks.

"If that's what it takes."

"They'll kick you out eventually."

"Then I'll sit in the parking lot. I don't care. I'm not leaving."

The automatic door to the lobby opens. My dad steps through, spots us immediately, and crosses the space as people murmur his name.

"Boys."

We stand. Dad looks at me, taking in the situation without asking questions. Then he sits down on the floor, back against the wall.

Odin and I exchange a look, then join him.

The three of us sit on the hospital floor, silent, but their presence gives me a tiny bit of strength. I can figure this out. They'll help.

"Your mom wanted to come," Dad says. "I told her to wait. Too many of us might overwhelm Sloane."

"She won't see me anyway."

"She will. When she's ready."

"What if she's never ready?"

Dad doesn't answer that. We just sit.

CHAPTER 33
SLOANE

AFTER MEL LEAVES, I'M ALONE WITH THE BEEPS. I'M SO TIRED, DOWN to my bones, and someone took off my necklace. I reach for it, not finding it at my neck, and for some reason, it's that final injustice that sends me over the edge.

Sobs pour from my body. I'm moaning and clutching my stomach and just crying for all the things I should have cried about years ago.

I weep for my grandmother, who raised and sacrificed for me. I weep for my parents, my father gone, and my mother too mired in grief to parent me. And as I feel the babies swim inside me, I weep because I'm terrified that I am robbing their father of the chance to be different.

It's true, Tucker is hundreds of miles away. Unreachable.

But he left three dozen backup Stags to step in, and what did I do? I pushed them all away out of my own stubborn foolishness.

I can't be on bed rest without help.

All Tucker Stag has done since July is grow, while I've floundered and pushed him away. No wonder he felt like protecting me from his work struggles. We need to be honest with each other, or this whole thing goes up in flames.

The babies' heartbeats swirl and tick on the monitors, and it becomes a chorus, chanting CALL HIM. CALL HIM.

I don't have my phone, and I don't think anyone at this hospital will know how to reach him, but I need to do something.

I need to make a change. I reach for the red button on my bed rail and press for the nurse.

I cry some more while I wait for her to arrive, which probably explains her worried face as she rushes to my bedside. "Sloane, what can I do?"

She starts checking my vitals, and I shake my head. "This is probably inappropriate for me to ask."

The nurse, Shelby, pauses and meets my eye. "I promise you won't be the first person to ask, whatever it is."

I laugh, relief washing over me at this small return to levity. "I don't think I have my phone here. And I need to reach my room — I need to call the babies' father."

"Ah." Shelby smiles knowingly and pats my hand. "Actually, I think this one's an easy win for me. Hang on."

Two minutes later, my door opens again, and Tucker steps inside.

He looks terrified. His hair is a mess, like he's been running his hands through it. There are dark circles under his eyes.

He looks like he's been through hell.

Because of me.

"Hi," I whisper.

He closes the door behind him and just stands there, staring at me. At the monitors. At my belly under the thin hospital blanket. At the IV in my arm.

"Sloane." My name comes out broken. "Oh god, Sloane."

I want to apologize. Want to explain. Want to tell him I'm sorry for shutting him out, for not calling him, for putting him through this.

But all that comes out is: "I'm okay. The babies are okay."

He moves then, crossing the room in three long strides. Stops beside the bed, his hands hovering like he wants to touch me but doesn't know if he's allowed.

"Can I—" His voice breaks. "Can I touch you?"

I nod, not trusting my voice.

His hand finds mine. Large, warm, familiar. He sinks into the chair beside the bed, still holding my hand, and drops his head against our joined fingers.

"I thought I lost you," he says into my skin. "I thought—"

"I'm sorry." The words rush out. "Tucker, I'm so sorry. I shouldn't have—I was scared and I wasn't thinking clearly and—"

"Stop." He lifts his head, his blue eyes meeting mine. "Don't apologize for being scared."

"But I shut you out. I told them you were 'out of the picture' and I—"

"I know. Mel told me." He wipes his free hand over his face. "I've been treating you like you're this thing that's happening to me. Like you're pregnant with my babies and that's all that matters. I haven't been seeing you. Sloane. The woman who's trying to start fresh, figure out her life, and maintain her independence."

My throat tightens. "I—"

"I've been so focused on providing, on being there, on doing the right thing that I missed what you actually needed." His thumbs stroke across my knuckles. "I've been smothering you when I thought I was supporting you. Trying to solve things without you, and I know that's a sore spot for you."

The tears come then, hot and fast. "I'm so messed up, Tucker. I don't know how to let someone take care of me without losing myself. And you—" My voice breaks. "You're so good to me, and I'm terrified that if I let myself need you, I'll wake up one day and not know who Sloane is anymore."

"Hey." He stands, carefully moving to sit on the edge of the bed. "Look at me."

I meet his eyes, those impossibly blue eyes that have been haunting me for weeks.

"We can come back from this. We can tell each other things, and be honest, and trust that we have each other's back." His hand moves to cup my face, thumb wiping away tears. "You're so strong, baby." He leans closer. "Fucking fierce."

I let out a wet laugh. "Fierce?"

"Yeah." He's smiling now, that crooked smile that makes my

heart stutter. "You're fierce." His expression softens. "I love that about you."

The words hang in the air between us.

"What?" I whisper.

"I love you." He says it simply, like it's the easiest thing in the world. "I love your resilience. I love your fire. I love how hard you work to be independent, even when accepting help would be simpler. I love watching you fight for your degree, for your future, for yourself." He brushes hair back from my face. "I love you, Sloane. Not the situation. Not the babies, though I love them too. You. The woman who won't let anyone—including me—tell her who she should be."

My chest feels too tight. "Tucker—"

"It doesn't scare me," he continues. "Your independence, your strength, the way you push back when I try to take over—none of it scares me. It makes me want to be better. Want to be worthy of you."

"I love you too." The words tumble out before I can stop them. "I love how you think about what I need before I know I need it. I love that you see me trying to be independent and you don't try to fix it, you just... make sandwiches and buy the right kind of prenatal vitamins and leave books around the apartment that you think I'd like." I'm crying again. "I love your thoughtfulness, and it scares me because I've never had someone care like this. Care about me, not just what I can give them or who they want me to be."

"Sloane—"

"I love you," I say again, stronger this time. "Not your apartment or your money or your ability to provide for us. I love you. Tucker Stag. The man who fights on the ice to protect his teammates. The man who left a game to be here, even though I told the hospital to keep you out." My voice breaks. "I love you and I'm terrified of losing myself, but I'm more terrified of losing you."

He leans in then, his forehead resting against mine. "You're not going to lose yourself. And you're not going to lose me."

"How do you know?"

"Because we're going to figure it out together." He pulls back enough to meet my eyes. "Not my way. Our way. You tell me what you need, and I'll support that. Really support it, not just say the words while secretly trying to make you dependent on me."

"I need to be Sloane," I whisper. "Not Tucker's girlfriend or the mother of your babies. Just... Sloane."

"I know. And I'm going to remember that this time. I promise." He kisses my forehead, gentle and sweet. "You're Sloane, who happens to be pregnant. Not pregnant, Sloane. There's a difference."

"There is."

"And Sloane, who happens to be pregnant, is fucking incredible." He grins. "Even when she puts me on a hospital restricted visitor list."

I laugh, the sound watery but real. "I'm sorry about that."

"Don't be. You were scared and trying to protect yourself." He shifts carefully, mindful of the monitors and IV. "But Sunshine? Next time you're scared? Call me anyway. Let me be scared with you."

"What if I can't?"

"Then I'll wait until you're ready." His voice is matter-of-fact. "That's what I did tonight. Sat there with Odin and my dad until you asked for me."

"You sat on the floor?"

"For hours." He shrugs. "Would have sat there all night if that's what it took."

Fresh tears spill over. "Tucker—"

"I'm all in, Sloane. Completely, terrifyingly all in. I'll wait as long as you need. I'll give you space when you ask for it. I'll be here when you're ready to let me in." He takes both my hands in his. "I'm not going anywhere. Even when you try to push me away."

"I don't want to push you away anymore."

"Good. Because I'm pretty stubborn about staying where I'm wanted."

"Even when I'm a mess?"

"Especially when you're a mess." He kisses my knuckles. "That's when you need me most. Even if you won't admit it."

I stare at him—this man who left a game, risked his career, sat on a hospital floor for two hours, all for me. For us.

"I need you," I say quietly. "I don't know how to do this without disappearing, but I need you. Is that okay?"

"It's more than okay." He stands, toeing off his sneakers. "Scoot over."

"Tucker, there's not enough room—"

"There's plenty of room." He's already moving, carefully climbing onto the narrow hospital bed beside me. The monitors protest slightly as I shift, but he's gentle, mindful of the wires and IV.

He wedges between the bedrail and my belly, facing me. "This okay?"

I laugh and shake my head. "You are ridiculous. And massive."

He grins and wraps his arms around me, my head on his chest. I can hear his heartbeat, steady and strong, under my ear.

"We're going to figure this out," he murmurs into my hair. "You're going to finish your degree. You're going to have your own career, your own life. Maybe get ourselves some therapy."

I put my hand on my belly, feeling the twins move. "They're really okay?"

"We will make sure of it." His hand covers mine on my stomach. "They're fighters. Like their mom."

We lie there in silence, just breathing together. The monitors beep steadily. Hospital sounds filter through the door—nurses talking, other monitors, the occasional announcement over the PA system.

"I left the game," Tucker says after a while. "Coach said there would be consequences. I told him I didn't care."

"Tucker—"

"I meant it. I don't care if they fire me. I don't care if this ruins my career. You and these babies matter more than hockey."

"Hockey is your life."

"You're my life." He says it simply, certainly. "Hockey is just what I do. You're who I am now."

I tilt my head to look up at him. "That's too much pressure. I can't be your whole life."

"You're not my whole life. My family is my whole life. And you're part of that family now." He kisses my forehead. "You, these babies, my parents and brothers, my ridiculous extended family—that's what matters. Hockey is just... hockey."

"You love hockey."

"I love you more." He shifts slightly, getting more comfortable. "And honestly? If loving you means I have to find a different career? I'm okay with that."

"You shouldn't have to choose."

"I'm not choosing. I'm prioritizing. There's a difference." His hand strokes my arm, soothing. "Besides, apparently your buddy Mel has cracked the code and convinced the bigwigs that hockey players are human beings."

"She did what?" I draw my head back, not sure what he's talking about.

He emits a rumbling sound deep from his chest. "Uncle Tim said I can take emergency leave and not lose my job." He pauses. "But that's later. Right now, I'm just focused on you."

I close my eyes, letting myself relax against him. Finally, mercifully, the anxiety loosens its grip. The fear is still there—I'm still terrified of losing myself, still worried about dependence, still scared of becoming someone I'm not.

But Tucker's arms are around me. His heartbeat is steady under my ear. "Tucker?"

"Yeah?"

"Thank you for coming."

"Always." He kisses the top of my head. "I'll always come when you need me. Even when you don't know you need me yet."

I smile against his chest. "That's what scares me."

"I know. But we'll work on it." His voice is getting drowsy. "We'll figure out boundaries. Figure out what works. We'll probably screw it up a bunch of times."

"Probably."

"But we'll fix it. Together."

"Together," I repeat.

The word settles over us like a blanket. Together. Not him taking care of me. Not me doing it alone. Together.

My eyes are getting heavy. The exhaustion of the day—the fear, the pain, the emotional rollercoaster—is catching up with me.

"Sleep," Tucker murmurs. "I've got you."

"You can't stay in this bed all night. We'll all lose circulation in our limbs."

"A few more minutes."

"The nurses will kick you out." I try to wriggle, but there is no space.

"Let them try." I can hear the smile in his voice. "I'm pretty good at fighting."

I want to argue. Want to tell him to go home, get rest, take care of himself.

But instead, I let myself drift. Let myself be held. Let myself need him without losing myself.

And for the first time in a long time, I feel safe.

CHAPTER 34
TUCKER

Sloane's blood pressure is better, but Dr. Patel says she needs to stay on bed rest until the babies arrive. Like it or not, she is about to receive the full Stag family care committee.

I know we come on strong, and as soon as my parents convinced me to leave the hospital to get supplies, I gave them a stern talking-to about their enthusiasm.

Now I'm back to pick up my sunshine and our two internal daughters. Daughters! Who knew a Stag even had X chromosome sperm?

I poke my head into Sloane's room to make sure the coast is clear. She's perched on the edge of the bed, staring down at her belly with a gorgeous smile on her face.

"Hey, fam." I step in and walk to sit beside her. "You ready for this?"

She shakes her head. "No, but I have to be, right?"

"That's the word on the street." Mel and my cousin Pete have things arranged so that I'm only doing games and practices in Pittsburgh until the babies arrive. Which means I have about an hour and a half before I have to head back up to the hockey complex.

I place a hand on her thigh, giving it a squeeze, hoping that's reassuring and not titillating since Dr. Patel said sex is absolutely off the menu. "Which Stags do you find least annoying?"

She rolls her eyes. "They're not annoying, Tucker. They're just …"

I laugh. "We're a lot. It's okay. But I want to make sure you have people to wait on you."

We go through my long list of relatives as the patient care tech wheels Sloane out to the car. We talk about temperaments and cooking skills, and Sloane surprises me when she says, "Is your dad okay to hang out till you get home from practice?"

My grin feels like it's going to split my face bruises wide open. "Hell yeah, he is. Great choice, Sloane. Ty Stag is gonna love on you like crazy."

———

When I get home from practice, Dad has set up the loft for maximum efficiency. Sloane has a rolling cart with electronics, her school supplies, and very fancy Stanley cups full of electrolyte drinks.

My fridge is bursting with ready-to-eat meals from Aunt Alice in tiny portions for pregnancy cravings.

There is more lotion in my bedroom than in the skincare aisle at Sephora.

Dad kisses me on the cheek with a salute and slips out through the elevator when I drop my bag, so I crawl into bed beside my … well, I don't have a noun yet for Sloane.

She looks at me with amusement. "Good practice?"

I shrug. "Coach is irritated that he has to tweak his lineup. And Grentley is being nice to me, which feels like a trap."

She nods. "I'm back to online lectures. It's like early lockdown days."

"But better, because there will be babies," I offer, reaching out for the churning belly where I can see the babies' little limbs poking out.

We lie in comfortable silence. I can feel the babies moving under my hand on her belly. Strong, healthy movements that make my chest tight.

Sloane moans appreciatively at my touch. "You're always so warm."

"Yeah."

She places her hand over mine. "What are we going to name them?"

I smile. "I don't know. What do you want to name them?"

"Something strong. Something that means they can handle whatever life throws at them."

"Like their mother."

"And their father." She tilts her head to look at me. "I think you're the best man I've ever known. And I think I'm really lucky. And I think I'm still terrified but less terrified than I was yesterday."

"That's progress."

"Yeah." She yawns. "It is."

"Sleep. I'll be here when you wake up."

"Promise?"

"Promise."

She falls asleep within minutes, her breathing evening out, her body relaxing completely against mine. I stay awake, watching her, feeling the babies move, thinking about how close I came to losing this.

I won't make that mistake again.

———

I only leave the apartment for work. There's a small cluster of photographers outside my building and the arena, but that's nothing new, and I avoid them all. I don't need my face in the news right now. I have shit to take care of.

Sloane is acing her classes and planning to take the spring semester off. My uncle said everything was handled with my contract. Literally, my entire focus can be the hockey I'm able to play and my little family tucked away in my loft.

So I'm a little surprised to find my agent waiting outside the locker room when I show up for morning skate.

"We need to talk, T-Stag." Brian tips his head toward a meeting room down the hall. I arch a brow but follow him, as he never waits around for stuff like small talk or typical greetings.

He tosses a folder on the desk in the room. "Do you have any idea what's been happening?"

"I've been taking care of Sloane."

"Right. Which is why you haven't been on social media or watching the news or answering any calls." Brian turns a tablet to show me. "This is what's been happening."

I look at the screen. It's a news article. The headline reads: "Enforcer Walks Out Mid-Game for Family Emergency—Team Threatens His Job."

"What the hell?"

"Keep reading," Uncle Tim says.

I scroll. The article details everything—me leaving the Boston game, Coach's threats, Sloane in the hospital. There are quotes from anonymous teammates supporting me. References to the lack of family leave policies.

"Who leaked this?" I ask.

"Several people, apparently," Brian says. "Teammates, arena staff, hospital workers. The story went viral."

He swipes to show me more articles. Pictures. Reels. Videos. All of them supporting me, criticizing the team, calling out the league for punishing players who prioritize family.

"There's more," Brian says, "because of course your family is involved."

He flicks to videos of my brothers and cousins, all Brian's clients. My cousin Wyatt, who doesn't even play sports in this country, stares into the camera in one video and says, "I am a soccer player, always, but I'm a man, too. And real men show up for their family."

Alder, Gunnar, Wes… even my Uncle Hawk all made videos about the importance of being human. Of caring for family.

The videos have millions of views. Comments from other athletes, celebrities, regular people all echoing the same sentiment.

Brian swipes again.

More videos. More articles. More support.

"The entire world is Team Tucker," Brian says simply. "It's everywhere. Sports media, mainstream news, social media.

People are calling for boycotts of Fury games until the league implements family leave policies."

I stare at the tablet, not quite processing. "I didn't ask for this."

"I know," Brian says. "But it happened anyway. And Tucker? It's working."

"What do you mean?"

Brian grins and shakes his head. "Other guys are staying back with their sick partners and newborn babies. And I've got diaper companies calling me day and night, wanting your smug face on their packages. You're a freaking poster child, and not for shitty condoms."

My brain can't quite catch up. "What?"

Brian smiles. "You're rich as hell, you're a trend setter, and after the kids are born, you get two entire weeks of leave. That's really unprecedented, kid."

"Two weeks?" It's not much, but it's something. I haven't been home for two consecutive weeks in-season since I was four years old. I look at the tablet again, at all the support, all the attention. "Sloane is going to hate this."

Brian ruffles my hair. "The whole world is watching you choose this woman and your babies. You're a heartthrob, and she's a role model. She'll be okay."

Brian rushes away, shouting something about getting my signature later. And then it's just ... business as usual. I warm up, skate with the guys, and listen to Coach critique my form.

Grentley tips a nod at me like an eagle passing by. I shower, and I go home.

I find Sloane in bed, closing her laptop, looking tired but satisfied.

"How was class?" I ask.

"Good." She stretches carefully. "I think I can actually pull off finishing this semester."

"Of course you can." I sit on the edge of the bed. "You're brilliant."

"I don't know about brilliant, but I'm stubborn." She smiles. "It helps."

I kiss her and she lets me, and for a minute I forget about the rest of the world. But a sharp kick between our bodies reminds me of what I wanted to tell her. "So, have you been online lately?"

She snorts. "I'm stuck in bed full time. Yes, babe. I've been online."

I pull back, surprised. "You're not upset?"

She scoffs. "At my man being called a hero and an inspiration? No. I am not upset about that." She pulls up her phone to a video of a bunch of dudes in college jerseys saying they didn't think they could be dads AND hockey players. "It's really hot, Tucker."

"Mmm. Not too hot, though. We can't do hot right now."

She grins and tilts her head up to kiss me. It's soft, sweet, full of promise.

"I love you," she says when we break apart.

"I love you too." I settle her back against the pillows. "Now rest. Before I get hotter."

"You're very bossy when you're changing professional sports culture."

"Get used to it. I plan to be very present and very bossy for the foreseeable future."

She laughs. "I think I can handle that."

I stretch out beside her, pulling her carefully against me. My hand finds her belly, feeling the twins move.

"Hey, babies," I say quietly. "Your mom and I are figuring this out. You just keep growing, okay? We'll handle the rest."

Sloane's hand covers mine. "We should probably give them actual names at some point."

"Probably." I grin. "But for now, we can call them nuggets and beans."

"You're ridiculous."

"You love me anyway."

"I really do."

The reality of that, of Sloane safe in my arms, our babies growing strong, our future stretching out ahead of us—it feels so right. I never thought anything would top the experience of winning a championship. Of standing with my brothers and hoisting a trophy over my head. Now that seems irrelevant when all I want to do is cuddle my family.

I've always had a huge family, but this little circle of people, right here in this bed with silk and curls and fierce determination … this lights my fire. And I don't ever want to look away.

CHAPTER 35
SLOANE

I FEEL LIKE A BEACHED WHALE, NO MATTER HOW MANY TIMES TUCKER tells me I'm more like Noah's Ark. But the babies are healthy and almost grown enough to safely exit the womb.

It took some patience getting used to Tucker's family underfoot. Virtual therapy has helped a lot–Tucker's cousin Odin hooked us up with a couples counselor who seems like an oracle. I've learned that when Mr. Stag showers me with gifts or Aunt Alice brings an entire restaurant for us to taste, that this is them expressing their love for Tucker and for anyone Tucker loves.

This family just really is that tight.

I hear the elevator doors open, and Judge's voice calls out, "Sloane? It's me!"

"Hey!" I call back, adjusting the pillows behind me for the thousandth time today. There's no comfortable position when your body is full of active watermelons.

Tucker's mom appears in the doorway, smiling brightly and emanating a delightful aroma. "Chicken pho coming up! With lime and basil."

My eyes actually water. "You're a saint."

"I'm a judge who knows how to delegate takeout to my staff." She sets up the food on the overbed table. "How are you feeling today?"

"Huge. Uncomfortable. Grateful." I accept the container of

soup, breathing in the steam. "Your son has been... he's been amazing."

"He's happy." She settles into the chair Tucker usually occupies, the one with the permanent imprint of his body. "He's really coming into himself."

We eat in comfortable silence for a few minutes, slurping our soup. Judge has this way of being present without being overwhelming—something I'm learning runs in the family, once you get past the initial tsunami of Stag-thusiasm.

"I think about your work a lot," I say, rubbing my stomach. "Family court ... kids removed from their parents."

She nods. "Nearly thirty years on the bench now. It was once me on the other side, and I bring that experience with me to every case."

"Do you..." I pause, finding the words. "Do you ever feel like you're making a difference? Like the system actually works?"

Her expression grows serious. "The system is broken in a thousand ways. But yes, I think I make a difference. Not by fixing the system—that's beyond any one person—but by building support structures into my rulings. Making sure kids have what they need. Holding parents accountable while also giving them resources."

"That's what I want to do." The admission comes easily. "Not the legal side, but the policy side. Building those support structures so families don't fall through the cracks."

"You will." Judge's certainty is absolute. "Your research project —Tucker showed me the abstract. Sloane, that's exactly the kind of work that changes things. You're going to be incredible in this field."

Something in my chest loosens. "I spent so many years having adults tell me what I couldn't do. My mother, my ex-husband. They had opinions about my capacity, my choices, my future." I touch my grandmother's necklace—the sun pendant Tucker returned to me. "My grandmother Essie believed I could be anything I wanted. Even if she wasn't sure how to make it happen."

"And now?" she asks gently.

"Now I feel like I'm on the roundabout road toward a goal." I laugh a little, watery. "It's overwhelming and wonderful and terrifying."

Judge Juniper grins. "You're working so hard."

I set down my soup container. "I never had this before. People who just... show up. No conditions, no judgments. Just love."

She reaches over and squeezes my hand. "You're family now, Sloane. That means you're stuck with us."

"I'm starting to think that's not such a bad thing."

As she gathers her things, I can tell she wants to say something but is holding back. "What is it?" I bite my lip, still uncertain about how to think of her, what to call her. Tucker's parents have been so wonderful and I am working on relaxing into their informal way of being.

Judge looks at me, eyes watery, smiling. "I am just really glad you're here with us."

Something warm and pleasant blooms in my chest. "I'm glad, too...Juniper." I grin and she leans in for a hug, which I return to the best of my ability from my position lying down with an entire globe jutting from my middle.

After Juniper leaves, I lie in bed staring at the ceiling, thinking about family and futures. The babies are doing their afternoon gymnastics routine, little feet and elbows poking out at odd angles. I rest my hand on my belly, feeling them move.

"We need to give you actual names, huh?" I murmur. "Can't keep calling you 'the girls' forever."

Tucker and I have been circling around names for weeks, but nothing felt right. He suggests options, asks my opinion, and tries to find something meaningful. And then we can never decide.

More and more, I find myself wanting to do something special for him, to thank him for his patience with me, for the love he's teaching me to accept. As I digest the food his mother brought for lunch, I realize what I can do to stoke this fragile fire we've ignited together.

The names we give these girls should mean something, honor the full span of their heritage. An hour later, I've made my decision.

My heart pounds as I finally make a purchase with my own credit cards–a custom art project that should arrive this afternoon if I pay a steep enough rush fee. Which I happily do.

The afternoon drags after my shopping spree. I try to focus on reading for my last class, but my eyes keep drifting to the clock. The babies seem to sense my anticipation, kicking and rolling constantly.

"Your daddy's going to be excited," I tell them. "At least, I hope he will. If he doesn't, blame it on pregnancy hormones."

Finally, blessedly, I hear the elevator. Tucker's voice booms through the apartment: "WHERE ARE MY GIRLS?"

"Bedroom!" I call back, grinning despite my nerves. As if we'd be anywhere else.

He appears in the doorway, looking sexy in a T-shirt and sweats, hair damp from a shower. His face lights up when he sees me. "Hey, beautiful."

"Hey, yourself." I twirl a curl around my finger. "Did you bring up the packages from the lobby?"

"You know I did!" He holds up a finger, ducks out of the doorway, and returns holding a crate. "What's all this?"

"Open it." I pat the bed beside me. "Sit down first."

Tucker kicks off his shoes and settles next to me carefully, mindful of my massive belly. He examines the note on the crate. "This is from a frame shop."

"Open it," I repeat, my heart hammering.

He pries open the lid and pulls out two wooden frames. They're simple, elegant, and natural wood with white matting. And in the center of each, in beautiful calligraphy:

Shula Juniper Stag
Aurora Estelle Stag

Tucker goes completely still. His eyes move from one frame to the other, reading and rereading the names.

"Shula for fire, for passion," I say quietly. "Juniper for your mother, who's shown me what it means to be a strong woman and a loving parent. Aurora for new beginnings, for light. And Estelle—that was my grandmother's full name. Essie was short for Estelle."

Tucker's hands shake. My massive baby daddy sets the frames down carefully on the bedside table and covers his face with his hands.

"Tucker?" I touch his shoulder. "Are you okay? If you don't like the names, we can—"

"They're perfect." His voice cracks. He drops his hands, and I see tears streaming down his face. "Sloane, they're perfect. But you... you gave them my last name."

"Well, we're a family, aren't we?"

That does it. Tucker completely breaks down, pulling me as close as he can with my belly between us, sobbing into my shoulder. His whole body shakes with it—this huge, tough enforcer reduced to tears by two picture frames.

"I love you," he chokes out. "God, Sloane, I love you so much."

"I love you too." I stroke his hair, my own tears falling. "I'm all in, Tucker. With you, with your family—our family. With everything. I'm not going anywhere."

"You named our daughter after my mom."

"She's incredible. And Shula Juniper Stag sounds strong. Like she'll be able to handle anything." I rest my hand on my belly. "And Aurora Estelle Stag sounds wise. Like she'll know who she is."

Tucker pulls back to look at me, his face blotchy and wet. "You really want them to be Stags?"

"I want us to be a family. However, that looks. Whether we get married or not, whether—"

"We're getting married," Tucker interrupts firmly. "I mean, if you want to. When you're ready. I'm going to ask you properly, with a ring and everything, but Sloane—yes. We're getting married."

I laugh through my tears. "You're proposing by telling me you're going to propose?"

"I'm telling you I'm all in too." He cradles my face in his

hands. "You're it for me. You and Shula and Aurora. That's my family. That's everything."

"Even though I'm cranky and can't have sex because my blood pressure might spike?"

"Especially then." He kisses me softly. "Although I'm not going to lie, I'm really looking forward to when Dr. Patel clears us for activities again."

"Me too," I admit. "But for now, this is enough. You're enough."

We sit like that for a long moment, foreheads pressed together, hands intertwined over our daughters.

"Oh!" Tucker suddenly pulls away. "I almost forgot." He reaches for the mail he'd tossed on the bed. "This came too."

He hands me an invitation to a holiday celebration. I glance at the details. "You know we can't go to your family's ski house for Christmas. Well. I can't go."

Tucker grins. "I know you can't, and I'll be right here with you. Because my entire family—every last Stag—is going to the mountains for three entire days."

I meet his eyes. "So, it'll just be us for Christmas?"

He nods. "No chaos. No crowds. No hockey travel, thanks to Pete and Mel. Just me and my girl and our precarious fetuses."

I spurt out a laugh and reach for Tucker. He leans close and kisses me—deep and thorough and full of promise. "You're really okay with all of us? My huge family, the Sunday dinners, the constant opinions about everything?"

"I'm more than okay with it." I think about Juniper this afternoon, about Ty's visits, about the entire Stag support system that's been quietly surrounding me. "For the first time in my life, I understand what it means to have a family. Not just people related by blood, but people who show up. Who support me. Who love me without conditions."

"That's what you're giving Shula and Aurora," Tucker says softly. "They're going to grow up surrounded by that. Because of you."

"Because of us." I correct. "We're doing this together."

The babies choose that moment to do a particularly strong

series of kicks, making my whole belly shift. Tucker's hand immediately goes to the spot, his face lighting up.

"Hey there, Shula," he murmurs. "Hey, Aurora. Your mama just made me the happiest guy in the world. Again."

I watch him talk to our daughters, this man who swam up to me in a pool full of swagger and changed everything. Who fought for me even when I pushed him away. Who gave me space to be myself while making room for me in his life.

"Thank you," I say quietly.

Tucker looks up. "For what?"

"For seeing me. For not trying to change me, control me, or make me smaller. For making space for me to be Sloane while also being your partner and their mother."

"That's just loving you," Tucker says simply. "You don't have to shrink to fit. You just have to be you."

"I'm so glad I hit on you in that pool."

"Best decision you ever made." He grins and kisses my cheek. "Sunshine, the moment I saw you, I was calculating every possible way to spend more time with you." He kisses my belly, first one side, then the other. "Even if it meant infuriating my coach and risking my career."

"You really did that."

"I really did." He meets my eyes. "And I'd do it again. Every time. You three are worth everything."

Tucker settles beside me, carefully arranging us so I'm comfortable against his chest. His hand rests on my belly, right where our daughters are tumbling around. "Shula Juniper Stag and Aurora Estelle Stag. Our family."

"Our family," I repeat, and finally—finally—I let myself believe it.

Not just that I can be a mother, but that I can be a mother without losing myself. That I can accept help without becoming dependent. That I can love Tucker and his extensive family while still being Sloane Campbell, with her own dreams and goals. I think my checklist is just about complete, because this is about as serene a moment as I can imagine.

"I can't wait to meet them," Tucker murmurs.

"Me neither." I yawn, suddenly exhausted. "Although I could wait a couple more weeks. Let them finish cooking."

"Rest, Sunshine." He pulls the blanket up over both of us. "I've got you."

And as I drift off to sleep, surrounded by my partner and the steady beat of my daughters' hearts, I think: This is it. This is everything I never knew I wanted.

A family. A home. A future full of love.

THE BRASS QUARTET IS CRAMMED INTO THE ELEVATOR, THEIR instruments gleaming under the overhead lights. I paid them triple their usual rate to play a single song in my penthouse at ten in the morning on a Thursday. Worth every penny.

"You ready?" I ask the lead trumpet player, a woman in her sixties, who looked at me like I'd lost my mind when I explained what I wanted.

She nods, adjusting her mouthpiece. "On your signal."

I take a breath and push open the bedroom door.

Sloane is propped against a mountain of pillows, her laptop balanced on the overbed table Dad assembled for her. She's wearing one of my old Fury t-shirts and has her hair twisted into a messy bun. She's grouchy and uncomfortable these days—but she's beautiful. Always beautiful.

"Hey," she says without looking up from her screen. "Can you grab me more water? I think I'm dehydrated again."

"In a minute." I move to the side of the bed. "I need you to close the laptop."

"Tucker, I'm in the middle of transcribing this interview. Dr. Newman needs my analysis by—"

"Sloane."

Something in my voice makes her look up. She studies my face, suspicious. "What did you do?"

"Nothing bad." I gently lift the laptop from the table and set it on the dresser. "Trust me?"

"That's a loaded question."

"Fair." I pull the garment bag from behind my back. "But I'm asking anyway."

Her eyes widen as I unzip it, revealing the royal blue graduation gown with gold trim. The Pittsburgh University wildcat gleams on the sleeve.

"Tucker..." Her voice cracks. "What is this?"

"Your commencement." I lift the gown carefully from the hanger. "You worked too hard to miss it just because these girls decided they prefer you lying down."

Tears are already streaming down her face. "I can't go to commencement. Dr. Patel said—"

"I know what she said. Strict bed rest until the babies arrive." I sit on the edge of the bed, mindful of the monitors and gadgets checking on the girls. "So, I'm bringing commencement to you."

I help her sit forward, easing the gown over her shoulders. Her belly is enormous now, pressing against the fabric. Shula and Aurora have been measuring ahead of schedule since week twenty, and Dr. Patel thinks they could arrive with healthy lungs any day now.

"Arms through here," I murmur, guiding her hands into the sleeves. "There we go."

Sloane blows her nose. "How are you making commencement happen?"

I fasten the front closure, working around her belly. "You finished every requirement. Turned in your final project last week, even though you were conducting phone interviews from bed while simultaneously gestating two humans. You earned this degree, Sloane. You deserve to celebrate it."

"But—"

I press a finger gently to her lips. "No buts. Just let me do this, okay?"

She nods, and I retrieve the mortarboard from the garment bag. The tassel is gold, already positioned on the right side.

"Ready for the full experience?" I ask, twirling a finger at my waiting musicians.

"What do you—"

The opening notes of "Pomp and Circumstance" blast from the doorway.

Sloane's mouth falls open as the brass quartet begins to play, the ceremonial march filling our bedroom with all the pageantry she was supposed to experience in the arena with three thousand other graduates.

"Tucker Stag." She's laughing and crying at the same time. "You are so extra."

"Had to make it official." I place the cap carefully on her head, mindful of her bun. "Can't have a proper commencement without the music."

The quartet continues playing the march, and our other guests file into the procession as Sloane's mouth drops.

Mel wheels in first, dressed in business casual and grinning like she just won a case. Professors Newman and Khan follow, both wearing their academic regalia. Pete was supposed to be here too, but called this morning with some vague excuse about an emergency he couldn't get out of. The band finishes their song and rests their instruments on the floor, standing politely to the side of our makeshift ceremony.

"Ms. Campbell." Dr. Newman's stern expression softens into something almost tender. "I believe congratulations are in order."

Sloane is openly sobbing now. "You came."

"Of course, we came." Dr. Khan moves to the bedside, her own eyes suspiciously bright. "You've been one of my best students, despite some rather extraordinary circumstances."

"Your service learning project was exceptional," Dr. Newman adds. "The interviews with BIPOC prenatal care providers in the Pittsburgh region revealed systemic gaps that need to be addressed. Your analysis will inform policy recommendations for the health department."

"Really?" Sloane wipes at her face. "You're not just saying that?"

"I don't just say things." Dr. Newman's tone is dry, but kind. "Your work matters, Ms. Campbell. Which is why the dean approved your completion and conferred your degree."

I pull out my phone and prop it against the lamp, angling it so the camera captures Sloane. "Okay, everyone watching at home—you can unmute yourselves and applaud."

My phone screen fills with faces. Mom and Dad in the kitchen at their place. Alder in his apartment, Lena visible over his shoulder. Gunnar at what looks like Stag Law's office. Odin and various other Stag cousins all crammed into one frame.

"Did we miss it?" Mom asks urgently.

"It's all happening." I move behind Sloane's bed, one hand on her shoulder. "We're about to flip the tassel."

Dr. Khan steps forward with a dignity that makes this bedroom feel like a grand auditorium. "Sloane Campbell, having fulfilled all requirements for the degree, I am pleased to present you with a Bachelor of Science in Public Health from Pittsburgh University."

She hands over the diploma—actual parchment, embossed with a gold seal, completely official because I made about seventeen phone calls to get it handled in January, even though the semester technically ended in December.

Sloane takes it with shaking hands, staring at her name printed in formal script.

"Now the tassel," Dr. Newman says, and there's actual warmth in her voice. "Go on and turn it, Ms. Campbell. You've earned it."

Sloane reaches up and moves the tassel from right to left. The simple gesture feels monumental.

"Congratulations, graduate," I whisper, leaning down to kiss the top of her capped head.

The phone erupts with cheers. My family is whooping and clapping, and I can hear Mom actually crying. Stellan is recording everything on his own phone, probably for some Stag family archive.

Mel wheels closer and takes Sloane's hand. "I knew you could do it."

"I couldn't have without you." Sloane squeezes back. "Any of you."

"Speech!" Odin calls from the phone screen.

"No speech," I say firmly, but Sloane shakes her head.

"It's okay." She looks around the room—at Mel, at her professors, at Stellan, at the phone full of Stags. Then her eyes find mine. "I spent most of my life thinking I had to do everything alone. That asking for help was a weakness, that depending on people meant losing myself." Her voice steadies. "But this degree, these babies, this life I'm building—none of it would be possible without all of you. Without Tucker showing up every single day, even when I pushed him away. Without my professors extending deadlines and believing I could finish. Without Mel being the sister I never had." She pauses. "I'm graduating today because I finally learned that accepting help isn't giving up control. It's building a foundation strong enough to hold all of us."

I'm not crying. I'm absolutely not crying in front of everyone.

"I want to say thank you while I still can. Thank you for showing me what family means."

"Okay, now I'm crying," Mom announces from the phone.

"Me too," Lena admits.

"Group hug!" Odin yells, and several Stags pile into the frame, all of them laughing.

Dr. Newman clears her throat. "Well. This has been highly irregular, but also deeply moving." She adjusts her regalia. "Ms. Campbell, I expect great things from you in your career. You have a gift for seeing systemic problems others miss."

"And for asking questions that make people uncomfortable," Dr. Khan adds with a smile. "The field of public health needs more of that."

They say their goodbyes and slip out, and I start to usher everyone else toward the door. "Okay, graduate needs rest—"

"Tucker." Sloane's voice is strange. Tight.

I turn back. She's gripping the edge of the overbed table, her face suddenly pale.

"What's wrong?" I'm at her side instantly.

"I think..." She looks down. "I think my water just broke."

For a second, nobody moves. Then everything happens at once.

Mel is on her phone, calling Dr. Patel and grabbing the hospital bag we've had packed for weeks. The French horn player is clearing a path to the door. My phone screen is chaos as my family starts yelling advice and congratulations at once.

"Okay." I force myself to stay calm even though my heart is trying to punch through my chest. "Okay, we've practiced this. We know what to do."

"Tucker." Sloane grabs my hand, and she's smiling through the fear. "We're having our babies."

"We're having our babies," I repeat, and suddenly I'm grinning like an idiot. "Holy shit, Sloane. We're having our babies today."

"Best graduation present ever," she manages before the first contraction hits.

I help her out of the gown—carefully, because she insists she wants it for photos later. After all, Sloane Campbell doesn't do anything halfway. Then I'm easing her into the elevator, grabbing the hospital bag, giving rapid-fire instructions to Mel about locking up.

"We'll meet you there," Mel says, shooing people toward the door.

I grab her shoulder. "You hear from Pete?"

She shakes her head. "Not today. Your uncle said they're working on his legal paperwork."

I grunt. My oldest cousin came through for me big time when I was drowning in my own family crisis. Now Pete needs us, too, and I'm still facing my own responsibilities.

Mel pats my arm. "Go get your girls."

My phone is still on FaceTime, and the last thing I see before ending the call is my entire family cheering.

"Go get 'em, Tucky!" Alder yells.

"You've got this!" Mom calls.

Dad's voice cuts through the noise. "Be the father those girls deserve, son."

"I will," I promise, and I mean it with everything I am.

Then I'm driving Sloane toward the hospital, her hand gripping mine so tightly I'm losing circulation, and I've never been more terrified or more certain of anything in my life.

"I love you," I say as we wait for the gate to open to leave the building. "I need you to know that. I love you and Shula and Aurora more than anything."

Sloane looks up at me, her green eyes bright with tears and

joy and fear and hope. "I love you too. Even when you hire brass quartets and orchestrate elaborate bedroom ceremonies."

"Especially then," I correct.

The light turns green, and I drive Wyatt's SUV slowly and carefully with precious cargo on board. Just the two of us for these last few moments before we become four.

"Ready?" I ask.

She interlaces her fingers with mine and nods. "Let's go meet our daughters."

EPILOGUE

TUCKER

The locker room echoes with silence.

I lean back against the tile wall after my shower, soaking it all up. I'm the last one here after endless media interviews as the new face of family-focused professional athletes.

The playoff win tonight was brutal—overtime, three fights, and Grentley got absolutely lit up in the third period. I had to step in when one of their forwards went after him, which meant five minutes in the box and a hell of a lot of pent-up aggression that I couldn't fully release on the ice.

My knuckles are bruised. My shoulder aches where I took a hit into the boards. And I've never felt more alive.

Last season, I would've gone out with the guys after a game like this. Hit a bar, let some puck bunny buy me drinks, stumbled home at 3 a.m. smelling like regret and cheap perfume.

Now? I'm standing in an empty locker room at ten-thirty on a Saturday night, waiting.

Because Sloane texted something cryptic during the second intermission about our two-month-old babies going to an after-party with the Stag Family Daycare and Sloane bringing me something special.

I've been half-hard since I read it.

The locker room door creaks open, and my head snaps up. Sloane slips inside, wearing a long green coat and boots that click against the concrete floor. Her hair is in braids since that's easier to care for with the babies, and she's got that look on her face—the one that says she's nervous and excited and trying to play it cool.

"Hey," she says, stopping a few feet away. Her cheeks are flushed. From the cold near the ice or from what she's thinking, I can't tell.

"Hey, yourself." I push off the wall, acutely aware that I'm wearing nothing but a towel. "You know players' significant others aren't technically allowed in here, right?"

"You gonna report me?" She grins. "Or you want to see what I brought you?"

I close the distance between us in two strides. "Just seeing you is amazing."

"Mmm. Impressive." Her eyes drag down my chest, lingering on the droplets of water still clinging to my skin.

My hands find her waist, and I pull her against me, not caring that I'm getting her coat wet. "Where are Shula and Aurora?"

"With your mom and dad." She loops her arms around my neck. "Wearing their tiny noise-canceling headphones and being absolutely spoiled."

I laugh, picturing it. "And they're good? You're good leaving them?"

"Tucker." She cups my face. "I fed them before I left. They're asleep. I got cleared for *all* physical activity at my appointment today. We have maybe ninety minutes before I turn into a pumpkin and my breasts start leaking."

"Jesus Christ, Sloane." I groan, well beyond half hard now. "You can't just say shit like that."

"Why not?" Her smile turns wicked. "You're the one who kept telling me how much you loved my body while I was pregnant. How you couldn't wait to—"

I kiss her. Hard. Because if she keeps talking, I'm going to lose what little control I have left.

She melts into me, making this small sound in the back of her throat that I've been dreaming about for months. Her hands slide into my wet hair, and she kisses me back like she's starving, like she's been waiting just as long as I have.

"Shower," I manage against her mouth. "Now."

"Bossy."

"Sloane." I frame her face with both hands, forcing myself to slow down. "Are you for real ready for this? Because once we start—"

"I'm sure." Her green eyes are bright with desire and trust. "Dr. Patel said everything healed perfectly. I'm ready, Tucker. I've been ready."

That's all I need.

I strip her coat off, then her sweater, my hands shaking slightly as I work the clasp of her bra. She's different now—fuller, softer in places—and absolutely fucking perfect. I trace the faint stretch marks on her hips with my thumbs.

"I earned these," she whispers.

"I know." I kiss one. Then another. "You're incredible."

She tugs at my towel, and it drops. We're both naked in the middle of the Fury locker room, and I've never felt more exposed or more certain of anything in my life.

I flick the shower back on, and steam billows out from behind the partition. I guide her under the spray, bracing one hand against the tile wall while the hot water cascades over both of us.

"This is insane," she laughs, tilting her head back. "We're going to get caught."

"Building's empty." I run my hands down her sides, relearning every curve. "And even if someone walks in, I don't give a fuck."

"Spoken like a man who's been celibate for months."

"One hundred seventy-nine days." I catch her earlobe between my teeth. "I haven't touched you like this in so long."

She shivers. "I remember. You were so careful with me."

"Because you were carrying our daughters." I slide my hand between her thighs, feeling her heat. "But right now, I just want to be with my girl."

"Then be with me."

I lift her, pressing her back against the tile wall, and she wraps her legs around my waist. The position is familiar but also new—we're both different people than we were last summer. I'm a father now. She's a mother. We're partners, co-parents, lovers.

But in this moment, we're just Tucker and Sloane.

I enter her slowly, giving her time to adjust, and the sound she makes—relief and pleasure and perfect rightness—nearly undoes me.

"Okay?" I manage.

"More than okay." She rocks against me. "Move, Tucker. Please."

So I do. And it's frantic and loving and desperate all at once. Water streams over us, and she's clutching my shoulders, leaving marks I'll see tomorrow in the mirror and wear like badges of honor. I tell her how much I've missed this, missed her, how fucking perfect she feels.

I dip a hand between us, finding the hard pearl of her clit, and she comes apart in my arms, biting down on my shoulder to muffle her cries, and I follow seconds later with her name on my lips.

We stay like that for a long moment—hearts pounding, breathing hard, connected in every way that matters.

"I love you," I say into her wet hair.

"I love you too."

I set her down carefully, and we finish actually showering, trading soap and soft touches. She mentions how excited my dad was to fill his minivan with car seats again–two for our babies, one for Gunnar's, and a booster for Pete's daughter.

Sloane wraps a towel around herself. "Have you talked to him about ... everything? He hasn't been to Sunday dinners."

"No idea. He won't return my calls." I pull on my jeans, frowning. "It's not like him. Pete's always been solid, you know? The responsible one. But lately he's just... gone."

"Maybe he's overwhelmed by your big-ass family." She grins. Sloane is coming around to the Stag way of loving.

But Pete's emotional distance bothers me. He was there for me when I needed his help professionally. He didn't judge, didn't lecture—just showed up. I want to do the same for him, but I can't help someone who won't let me in.

Sloane must read the concern on my face because she crosses

to me, fully dressed now, and takes my hand. "He'll reach out when he's ready. That's what you did, remember? You came to me when you were ready to change."

She's right. I finish getting dressed and pull her close one more time.

"Marry me," I say.

She blinks. "What?"

"Marry me, Sloane." I brush her still-damp hair back from her face. "You're it for me. I want you to be my wife. I want Shula and Aurora to have married parents. I want—"

"Tucker." She presses her fingers to my lips. "I'll think about it."

"You'll... think about it?"

"Mmhmm." Her eyes dance with mischief. "Give me a week or two. Let me really consider whether I want to legally bind myself to a man who thinks it's okay to have shower sex in a locker room."

"Sloane—"

"Also, if we're doing this, you're going to have to ask me properly." She taps my chest. "Ring, bent knee, the works. I deserve a good proposal story to tell our daughters."

I stare at her. Then I start laughing. "You're serious."

"Completely. Also, I'm saying yes." She rises on her toes to kiss me. "Obviously, I'm saying yes. But you're going to have to work for it a little. I have standards now."

"You're killing me."

"I know." She grabs her coat. "Come on. We have thirty minutes left before my boobs explode."

We leave the locker room together, and I'm already planning the perfect proposal in my head. Something with the twins. Something that shows Sloane exactly how much she means to me.

As we walk through the empty arena corridors, her hand in mine, I think about how completely my life has transformed. Last summer, I was a reckless kid playing hockey and fucking around. Now I'm a father, a partner, a man with actual plans for the future.

And I wouldn't change a single thing.

Thank you so much for reading Tucker and Sloane's story! If you love the Stag family, you're in luck: each of them has a book, including Brian the agent. **Grab Lit for Him** *and escape with his cozy story.*

My newsletter subscribers get a spicy glimpse into Tucker and Sloane's happily ever after. **Sign up at LaineyDavis.com** *or scan the QR code below.*

AUTHOR'S NOTE

I have loved my readers' response to Ty Stag's sons in the Playing series. It's been so wonderful to create these heroes and figure out the women who would win their hearts. But I didn't get here alone!

I owe so much to my hockey authenticity reader, Val Sweeney, and to my critique partners, Elizabeth Perry, Ember Leigh, Liz Alden, and Melissa Wiesner. Becky with Bookcase Media provided an eagle eye as my editor. I had the great honor to receive feedback from Addie Woolridge and Amber Battaglia, who helped me approach my first biracial protagonist with care —I learned so much from them both and am grateful they shared their lived experiences.

If you're reading this with your eyeballs, I do hope you'll also check out the audiobook. Zoe Black and James Cassidy have taken this series and turned it into an incredible performance.

It's a true pleasure for me to partner with so many humans in bringing this story to you. Including my cover artist, Qamber Designs, and audio engineer Kyle Gaffney, Playing with Fire provided paid work for seven people.

Thank you for reading and helping to fund the team!

ALSO BY LAINEY DAVIS

Stag Brothers Series

Sweet Distraction (Tim and Alice)

Filled Potential (Ty and Juniper)

Fragile Illusion (Thatcher and Emma)

A Stag Family Christmas

Beautiful Game (Hawk and Lucy)

Stag Generations Books

Forging Passion (Wes and Cara prequel)

Forging Glory (Wes and Cara)

Forging Legacy (Wyatt and Fern)

Forging Chaos (Odin and Thora)

Playing for Keeps (Gunnar and Emerson)

Playing for Payback (Alder and Lena)

Playing with Fire (Tucker and Sloane)

Lit for Him (Brian and Noa)

Bridges and Bitters series

Fireball: An Enemies to Lovers Romance (Sam and AJ)

Liquid Courage: A Marriage in Crisis Romance (Chloe and Teddy)

Speed Rail: A Single Dad Romance (Piper and Cash)

Last Call: A Marriage of Convenience Romance (Esther and Koa)

Lesson Plans: An Education in Romance (Doug and Amy)

Planted and Plowed series

Against the Grain (Eila and Ben)

The Burgh and the Bees (Eden and Nate)

Yule Be Sorry (Eliza and Reed)

Sappy Go Lucky (Eva and Asher)

Since You've Bean Gone (Ethan and Lia) *part of the Farm 2 Forking
series